HUNDRED IN THE HAND

Joseph M. Marshall III

❧ LAKOTA WESTERNS ❧

UNDRED IN THE HAND

Fulcrum Publishing
Golden, Colorado

Library of Congress Cataloging-in-Publication Data

Marshall, Joseph, 1945-
  Hundred in the hand / Joseph M. Marshall III.
    p. cm. -- (Joseph Marshall's Lakota Westerns)
  ISBN 978-1-55591-653-4 (pbk. : alk. paper) 1. Indians of North
America--Fiction. 2. Lakota Indians--Fiction. I. Title.
  PS3563.A72215H86 2007
  813'.54--dc22

                                         2007019479

Printed in the United States of America by Thomson-Shore, Inc.
0 9 8 7 6 5 4 3 2 1

Editorial: Sam Scinta, Katie Raymond
Cover and interior design: Jack Lenzo
Cover image: *A Hundred in Hand.* Prismacolor pencil and India ink on antique ledger paper dated Nov. 19, 1937. © 2007 Donald F. Montileaux

Fulcrum Publishing
4690 Table Mountain Drive, Suite 100
Golden, Colorado 80403
800-992-2908 • 303-277-1623
www.fulcrumbooks.com

To honor the memory
of two Lakota warriors:

Corporal
Brent L. Lundstrom
1986–2006
Sixth Regiment
Second Marine Division
United States Marine Corps
Oglala Lakota

and

Private First Class
Sheldon R. Hawk Eagle
1982–2003
320th Field Artillery
101st Airborne Division
United States Army
Mniconju Lakota

IF WE CANNOT RELY ON THE HONOR OF
MEN, THEN WE GROW WEAK ...

CONTENTS

GLOSSARY

Translated Lakota names for current or historical Euro-American names for landmarks and places in south-central and north-central Wyoming and elsewhere.

Lakota	Euro-American
He Wiyakpa or He Ska (Shining Mountains or White Mountains)	Bighorn Mountains
Makablu Wakpa Canku (Powder River Road)	Bozeman Trail
Pte Wakpa (Buffalo Creek)	Piney Creek
He Egna Wicahcala (Old Man in the Mountains or Cloud Mountain)	Cloud Peak
Pankeska Wakpa (Shell River)	North Platte River
Canku Wakan Ske Kin (The Road Said to Be Holy or Holy Road)	Oregon Trail
Hehaka Wakpa (Elk River)	Yellowstone River
Mnisose or Mnisose Tanka (Great Muddy River)	Missouri River

LAKOTA CALENDAR

The annual calendar used by pre-reservation Lakota was based on the thirteen lunar months. The names for the months were based on characteristics or occurrences in nature consistent with the weather and time of the year. Names were not universal, however, in that different Lakota groups would often use a different name for the same month. Furthermore, the lunar months did not begin or end on the same days as the Gregorian calendar.

Wiotehike   late December to mid-January
(Moon of Hard Times)

Tioheyunka Wi   mid-January to mid-February
(Moon of Frost in the Lodge)

Cannapopa Wi   mid-February to mid-March
(Moon of Popping Trees)

Istawicayazan Wi   mid-March to mid-April
(Moon When Eyes Hurt)

Magagluhunnipi Wi   mid-April to mid-May
(Moon When Geese Return)

Ptehincala Sape Wi   mid-May to mid-June
(Moon When [Buffalo] Calves Are Red)

Wipazuke Waste Wi   mid-June to mid-July
(Moon When Berries Are Good)

HUNDRED IN THE HAND

Wicokannijin   mid-July to early August

(Moon When the Sun Stands in the Middle)

Wasutun Wi   early August to early September

(Moon When Things Ripen)

Canapegi Wi   early September to early October

(Moon When Leaves Turn Brown)

Canapekasna Wi   early October to early November

(Moon When Leaves Fall)

Waniyetu Wi   early November to early December

(Winter Moon)

Waniyetucokan Wi   early December to early January

(Middle of Winter Moon)

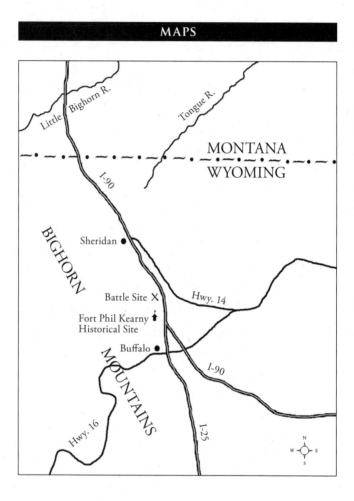

Little Bighorn R.

Tongue R.

MONTANA
WYOMING

I-90

BIGHORN

Sheridan ●

Battle Site ✕

Hwy. 14

Fort Phil Kearny ✝
Historical Site

Buffalo ●

MOUNTAINS

I-90

Hwy. 16

I-25

N
W ◇ E
S

Great Muddy R. (Missouri)

Knife R.

Elk R. (Yellowstone)

Powder R.

Rosebud R.

Tongue R.

Greasy
Grass R.

BLACK
HILLS

Bighorn R.

Powder R.

White Earth R.

Running Water R.

Sweetwater R.

SHINING MTNS
(BIGHORN MTNS)

Shell R.

Horse
Cr.

Blue
Water R.

Wolf R.

(N. Platte)

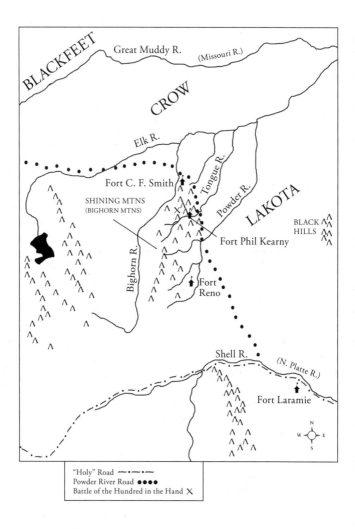

BLACKFEET

Great Muddy R.

(Missouri R.)

CROW

Elk R.

Fort C. F. Smith

SHINING MTNS
(BIGHORN MTNS)

Tongue R.

Powder R.

LAKOTA

BLACK
HILLS

Fort Phil Kearny

Bighorn R.

Fort
Reno

Shell R.

(N. Platte R.)

Fort Laramie

N
W   E
S

"Holy" Road —··—··—
Powder River Road ●●●●
Battle of the Hundred in the Hand X

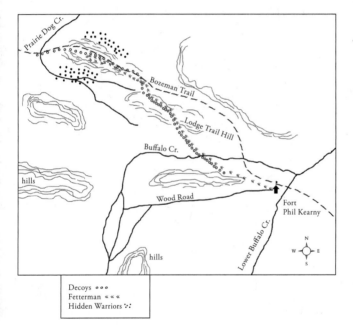

Decoys ○○○
Fetterman « « «
Hidden Warriors ∴

The Monument of Stone— Summer 1920

John Richard Cloud walked the final forty yards to the stone monument standing on the windswept ridge. Behind him came his two daughters, Katherine Fontonneau and Anne Hail, and his grandson, Justin Fontonneau. Not once did he glance west toward the jagged peaks of the Bighorn mountain range.

They had driven him the nearly three hundred miles from the Rosebud Sioux Indian Reservation in a borrowed car to the site of a battle that had occurred nearly fifty-four years ago. In early spring, the old man had suddenly begun insisting he wanted to see this place again, after he had seen pictures in an old newspaper about a monument that had been dedicated. Katherine convinced her father to wait until her son was discharged from the army so he could drive them.

Cloud stopped before the monument and noticed the plaque on the east face of it. His long gray braids hung down over his wool coat, and his deeply seamed face looked tired, attesting to the ups and downs of eighty-one years. He squinted, trying to read the words on the plaque, and then motioned to his grandson. "Grandson, can you read that for me?" he asked in a soft voice.

Justin stepped forward, looked at the plaque and

cleared his throat, and read:

> On this field on the twenty-first day of December, 1866, three commissioned officers and seventy-six privates of the 18th U.S. Infantry, and of the 2nd U.S. Cavalry, and four civilians, under the command of Captain Brevet Lieutenant Colonel William J. Fetterman were killed by an overwhelming force of Sioux, under the command of Red Cloud. There were no survivors.

Cloud's shoulders sagged. It was not at all what he had expected.

He was twenty-seven when he had fought here. His people, the Lakota, along with the Cheyenne and Arapaho, knew it as the Battle of the Hundred in the Hand.

"No survivors? What does that mean?"

"I think they mean the soldiers, Grandpa," Justin explained.

"We lost men here; many were wounded, and some died of their wounds days afterward. But many of us survived. Perhaps the whites have forgotten that."

"Maybe they have, Grandpa." Justin leaned closer to his grandfather. "Grandpa, was this a massacre, like a lot of people say it was?"

Cloud shook his head as he tried to look toward the narrow ridge north of the monument where he had been that day and where most of the fighting had occurred.

It had been so cold, so very cold, that blood from wounds thickened and froze almost at once. As a matter of fact, the bitter cold had probably saved his life. He might have bled to death otherwise. And the gunfire was continuous, because the soldiers did fight hard.

"No," he replied. "It was a hard fight. The toughest battle I can remember."

Justin nodded. That was saying something. His mother had told him that his grandfather had been in several battles, including the Little Bighorn, before the reservation days. In fact, that was why Justin himself had volunteered for the army in 1918: to honor his grandfather's legacy as a warrior. True, his battlefields were across the ocean and he had fought under the same banner as the soldiers who had fought and died here, but he had gained some insight into his grandfather's experiences.

Katherine stepped up with a jar of tea while Anne held up a bag of sandwiches she had brought along.

"We could find a nice spot to sit and have a bite to eat," Anne suggested.

Cloud nodded. "When was this thing put up, this pile of rocks?"

"In 1908, I think," Justin said.

After a derisive chuckle, Cloud turned and walked away, oblivious to the stiff breeze tugging at his braids.

Anne caught up with him. "Dad," she said, "I have never heard your side of the story of what happened here. Mom told me bits and pieces over the years. I think I would like to hear it from you. Can you do that for us?"

Cloud stopped and looked into his daughter's face.

Katherine followed and grabbed her father's arm. "I know it may not be easy, but it would be very meaningful if you would tell us here, where it happened."

Cloud nodded and then pointed north. "There were some rocks there," he said, "below the ridge. Lot of hard fighting there, I remember. We should go there, and sit, and I will tell you what I can still remember. But first, Grandson, see if you can find some sage. We have to burn some sage."

After a long walk, they found the rocks on the northwest slope of a ridge. Cloud braided the sage Justin had found and then lit a match to it. Because the sage was fresh, the smoke billowed white and swirled around slightly as the old man uttered a prayer. When he finished, he squinted and looked out across the land as the memories began to gather like clouds over the western horizon.

"The Battle of the Hundred in the Hand happened here," he began. "A man who had the power to see the future was asked if there would be a victory, so he rode out into the hills. He returned saying he had a few soldiers in his hands. He was sent out again and came back saying he had more soldiers. But that was not enough, so they sent him out again. Then he returned saying he had a hundred soldiers in his hands. So we knew there would be a victory.

"The night before the battle, Crazy Horse asked

me if I would join him as one of a few men who would try to lead the soldiers into a trap. There were nine of us that he asked, so there were ten including him.

"But the story of this battle began before it was fought here. And there was another battle, in a way, a quiet one. One that was fought by your mother and grandmother. No one died in that battle, but because she persevered, we are all here."

Anne and Katherine exchanged puzzled looks.

Justin leaned in closer. "You mean Grandma Agatha?"

Cloud smiled. "Yes. That was her name later. Just before we were married, she was given the name Sweetwater Woman."

Then Cloud glanced briefly toward the south. "There was a place many miles south of here," he said. "That is where the story begins."

CHAPTER ONE

Moon When Berries Are Good— June 1866

Five brown-skinned men hidden inside a tight grove of short oak trees stood holding their horses as they silently watched a column of seven riders slowly moving north along the dry, dusty trail that lay to the west of the grove. Five pairs of intense dark eyes noted every detail they could pick out at a distance of a long arrow's cast—about two hundred yards. Even from that distance, they could see that every one of the riders had a rifle. Weapons were the first things anyone looked for when whites were seen. It was never a question of whether they were armed, because it could always be counted on that they would be. How well they were armed was the more important concern.

Farther west, beyond the trail, hazy foothills sloped upward until a line of jagged ridges rose like shadowy giants—the Shining Mountains. Overhead, the glaring orb of the sun was just past the midway point in the cloudless sky, beating down on a hot day in the Moon When Things Ripen. The land was silent, as if it were expecting something to happen. Even the breeze floated cautiously over the sagebrush and sparse grass along the Powder River Road, as the Lakota called the old trail the riders were following. Whites named it the Bozeman Trail. For them, it was a road to riches, connecting the Oregon

Trail in southern Wyoming Territory to the Yellowstone River in Montana Territory and leading to dreams of abundant gold near the town of Virginia City. Therein was the problem: whites were drawn to gold like moths to a flame. Consequently, the Lakota in the Powder River country were more frequently seeing travelers on the trail.

The riders came to a lone cottonwood tree, stopped, and dismounted. The second in line was leading a string of five pack mules, each laden with a canvas-covered load. All the other riders were watchful, each keeping his rifle in hand even as they loosened saddle girths on their horses.

The five men hidden in the grove of oak neither moved nor spoke but kept steady hands on the horses to prevent an errant snort or inquisitive whinny. Only three of them carried a firearm, but all of them were armed with bows and arrows.

Cloud, the leader of the group, glanced sideways at the muzzle-loading rifle hanging in its elk-hide case from the neck rope of his bay gelding. Although he had nearly a dozen lead balls, he had powder for only five shots. Taken Alive had some powder and bullets too, as did Goings. But together they probably had no more than twenty shots. On the other hand, any one of the white men they were watching had more powder and shot than that. If there were to be a fight, it would not be even. White men always had more guns and bullets.

But Cloud had already decided that they would stay hidden and let the white men pass. If he and his companions were going to attack, it would be better to wait until the intruders were strung out along the trail and the terrain favored the attackers. He was about to whisper that thought to the others when he felt a tug on his arm.

Rabbit had stepped next to Cloud. He was an inquisitive young man, barely twenty, and the youngest of the group. He was inquisitive enough to have learned some of the white man's language when he had stayed with his uncle's family for two years near the town called Fort Laramie. Two days ago, they had found him alone along the Powder River. Cloud had insisted he join them, though not because he was an experienced fighting man. On the contrary, he was inexperienced, not yet a proven warrior. He sometimes did things without thinking, such as wandering off alone. The only thing he had in common with his companions was his brown skin and glistening black hair in two long braids. Like the others, he was shirtless because of the heat.

"Cousin," he whispered, "those men have things to trade in those bundles on the pack mules."

"What does that have to do with us?" asked Cloud.

"I could talk to them," offered Rabbit.

Cloud was taken aback. "No," he said, irritated. His intense brown eyes bored into the younger man's face.

Goings, Taken Alive, and Little Bird listened intently to the whispered conversation, all the while keeping an eye on the seven white men.

"They are not traders," Cloud went on. "They are probably going north to dig for gold in the mountains in the western part of Crow lands. That is why they are following that trail. Right now, there is nothing we can do. They have more guns, seven against three, and any one of them has more powder and bullets than all of us do. So we will stay out of sight and go back north to the Tongue River and tell the old men leaders what we have seen."

Rabbit bit his lip in disagreement but said nothing. Cloud was a physically powerful man and more than a competent fighter. Goings and the other men said nothing, but Rabbit knew they agreed with Cloud. The young man nodded to hide his embarrassment and turned away.

Goings edged closer to Cloud. The two had been the best of friends since Goings had married into Cloud's uncle's family. "I think you are right," he said. "Those whites are gold seekers. They probably have tools and supplies in those packs."

Cloud nodded. "A lot can happen between here and the Elk River. They do not know the country. There are places farther north that are right for ambush. We can go east and then north toward home. After that, with more men, we can plan an ambush."

Goings and the others nodded. Cloud was experienced in fighting whites. This past spring, Cloud had ridden with Crazy Horse and Hump and Spotted Tail, the renowned Sicangu Lakota fighting man, as well as Red Cloud, when they had rescued a group of Loafers—

Lakota people who, foolishly, had wanted to live near the whites—as they were being taken away to a prison by soldiers from Fort Laramie. There had been a swift, well-coordinated, mounted attack, and the rescuers had driven off and killed a number of the soldiers and captured many Long Knife horses as well.

Just as important, Cloud was a good man, not given to careless thinking, so they trusted his judgment.

"We will wait," he said. "They will rest and go ahead, and we will let them get far ahead before we move. Remember, keep your horses quiet."

Just as Cloud finished speaking, they heard a horse's soft snort and the quiet thud of hooves. Before they could react, they saw that Rabbit had already mounted and was loping northward along a deep, dry watercourse. Then, to their astonishment, he turned up a low bank and walked his horse toward the seven whites resting in the shade of the big old cottonwood.

"Lay your horses down!" hissed Cloud.

In a few heartbeats, the four men still in the oak grove cued their horses by kicking them lightly several times behind the right knee joints. Almost instantly, all the horses lay down on their right sides and their riders crouched low next to them. They would not be seen behind the grass and sagebrush, even from a short stone's throw away.

Rabbit, meanwhile, his right hand raised high, was slowly riding toward the white men.

Cloud peeked over the sagebrush. Rabbit was

already halfway to the old cottonwood. Three of the whites were down on one knee, aiming their rifles at the young Lakota.

Cloud inhaled and exhaled sharply and turned toward Goings and Taken Alive. "Get your guns ready," he said. "We might have to help that foolish boy!"

Grabbing their rifles, they hurriedly fitted percussion caps to the hammers. After that, there was nothing to do but wait. A thought struck Cloud like a splash of cold water: Rabbit might let it slip that they were in the grove! If he did—

Boom!

The rifle's blast was muffled by the distance. To a man, they rose up cautiously above the top of the sagebrush in time to see Rabbit twist and fall from his horse. Other shots blasted the silence. Rabbit's buckskin mare became a runaway and was galloping north like a devil was on her tail.

Cloud handed his rifle to Little Bird, and then his bag of bullets and powder horn, and pointed. "You go there!"

He looked at Taken Alive and Goings and pointed north. "You spread out that way! Shoot at the whites, and then ride north beyond the reach of their guns. If we get separated, we can meet at the cave above Little Wolf Creek!"

"What are you going to do?" asked Goings.

"Go after Rabbit!"

Cloud tugged at his horse's rein and then jumped on as the bay gelding scrambled to his feet. With two powerful lunges, the horse was out of the oak grove and galloping toward Rabbit, who was rolling around in the dust well within the range of the whites' rifles. There was no time to assess the risk or feel any anger toward Rabbit; Cloud was guided by pure instinct. The other three men were only a moment or two behind, bursting from the grove to take up their firing positions.

Cloud hoped that the white men could not hit a moving target. He heard rifles boom after the bullets whistled far overhead, but he kept his attention on the wounded boy, who staggered a few steps after rising then fell again behind a large clump of sagebrush. The boy did not have the sense to stay down and tried to rise again. From either side of the grove, Goings, Taken Alive, and Little Bird opened fire, trying to divert the whites' attention away from Cloud and Rabbit.

He heard the screams over the pounding of his horse's hooves, leading Cloud to guess that Rabbit had not been hit in the stomach or chest. As he started to slow the horse, he saw large splotches of blood spattered over the dirt and the surrounding sagebrush as if it had been tossed out of a bucket. Cloud slid the bay to a stop and was off in one smooth motion, hanging on with grim determination to the long rein. Rabbit was kneeling, bent over, clutching his arms across his abdomen, wailing in pain. Blood spurted rhythmically from the boy's elbow into the dust.

"Come on!" shouted Cloud as another bullet whined over their heads.

The bay jumped about nervously but stood his ground. Cloud heard his companions firing sporadically; he knew it took them a long time to reload the muzzle-loaders.

Rabbit did not respond, even when he turned his face to look up at Cloud. It was contorted, and he gagged and retched. There was no choice but to manhandle the delirious Rabbit. Cloud grabbed him by the belt and pulled, yanking the boy to his feet, then carried him to the jumpy bay. A round erupted in the dust nearby. One of the whites was finding the range. With a loud grunt, Cloud hefted Rabbit onto the horse and swung up behind him, reaching around to grab a handful of mane. He yanked the horse around and drummed his heels into its flanks. The bay needed no urging to race away to the safety of the dry watercourse. In Cloud's peripheral view, he saw the others mount and gallop north. The whites were still firing, but falling far short. Only then did Cloud feel his heart pounding, as though someone had shoved a drum into his chest.

He stopped after a long gallop along the floor of the dry creek to rest the horses. The others were waiting behind a bend. Goings rode to a rise to have a look and returned in no particular hurry. "No one is following," he reported.

"He is very pale," observed Taken Alive, pointing to Rabbit and then indicating the blood running down the horse's shoulder. "He is losing much blood."

Rabbit was bent over, moaning from deep within his chest. Cloud suddenly felt the boy's body sag.

"Look!" Little Bird's hand shook as he pointed at Rabbit. "Look at his arm!"

Cloud slid from the horse and lowered the body of Rabbit to the grass. The others dismounted and pushed forward to see what Little Bird was talking about. As Cloud turned Rabbit over onto his back, the right arm at the elbow squirted blood and the forearm and hand flopped at an unnatural angle.

None of the men spoke for several long moments. They could only stare. A sharp splinter of bone was visible at the elbow, and the rest of Rabbit's arm was hanging by stringy shreds of skin and muscle.

Cloud took several deep breaths. "Water!" he said. "Give me some water and something to wrap it with."

No one moved.

"Did you hear me?" he asked sharply. "Water and something to wrap his arm! Hurry!"

Goings shook his head and reached for the water flask tied to his horse. Taken Alive turned and reached into the small rawhide case hanging on his horse and pulled out a roll of brain-tanned hide. Little Bird turned away and gagged.

"What will you do?" asked Goings.

Cloud shrugged. He took the water flask and lifted the nearly severed arm and poured water over it. Blood pushed out weakly. Reaching for his knife, Cloud clenched his lips tightly and poised the blade above the remaining shreds of torn muscle and skin.

"No!" pleaded Taken Alive. "Leave it!"

After another deep breath, Cloud put away his knife and began to wrap the two ends of the severed limb with the tanned hide. Blood began to seep through immediately. "We have to get him back to High Eagle as fast as we can," he said.

Everyone nodded. High Eagle was a skilled medicine man. He was Rabbit's only chance. But they were two days from home. One, if they rode through the night.

"We can take turns carrying him," suggested Taken Alive. "That way, it will be easier for the horses."

Cloud looked at Rabbit's face. The boy was very pale. *How could one round bullet do so much damage?* he wondered.

"What was he trying to do, approaching those whites the way he did?" asked Goings.

"If he lives, we can ask him," replied Cloud. "In the meantime, we have to get going."

Goings turned a smoldering stare in the direction of the whites.

"No," said Cloud quietly. "Killing one or more of them will not save this boy. Besides, the only way to deal with them is to have more guns and bullets than they do."

Goings nodded and gestured toward the wounded boy. "My horse is stout and has a lot of endurance. I will carry him for a while."

With Rabbit slumped over in front of Goings, they rode out and stayed along the dry watercourse because it offered shelter. Little Bird rode to a plateau to have a look and came back to report that he could see no one following them.

Cloud looked down at his hands, which were splotched with blood, Rabbit's blood. When they stopped for water at Little Wolf Creek, he intended to wash them. In his mind, he could still hear the boy screaming in pain.

Taken Alive guided his horse next to Cloud. "My friend," he said, "that was a very brave thing you did, rescuing your cousin. Sometimes the foolishness of others is cause for bravery."

Cloud shook his head. "Maybe," he replied after a moment. "I know for sure that foolishness might be the death of my cousin. Look what it has done to him already."

"I do not think even High Eagle can fix that arm," commented Taken Alive.

They rode on in silence, glancing occasionally to the west. In the hazy distance, the jagged horizon of the Shining Mountains seemed to claw at the sky. Cloud looked down at the blood on his horse's withers, already turning dark as it dried in the heat of the afternoon. Then he felt a cold anger rising in him. *Who*, he wondered, *created white men?*

CHAPTER TWO

Four Graves for a Dead Arm

Several people in the encampment near the Tongue River were already up and about when Cloud and the others splashed across the river at dawn. Worn to the bone, they reached home the second day after Rabbit's encounter with the white men. They had pushed the horses to the limits of their endurance, and even Cloud's stout bay was stumbling after a day and a half of only brief rests. News of the scouts' return spread quickly, especially after someone spotted Rabbit's blanket-wrapped body slumped in front of Goings. Cloud immediately sent Taken Alive to the lodge of High Eagle, the medicine man. After the limp and unconscious Rabbit was unloaded at the sunshade where High Eagle usually treated the sick and injured, he asked Yellow Wolf and another young man to look after the exhausted horses. The shade was situated a stone's throw from the outer row of lodges, a long lean-to covered with willow branches along the cold creek that emptied into the Tongue from the north. Goings had hurried to the lodge of Rabbit's parents to take them the news. They rushed to the creek-side shade before the medicine man arrived.

White Hill Woman, Rabbit's mother, began weeping at the sight of her deathly pale son. Her husband, Big Voice, stared grimly and quietly assured his wife that the boy was still breathing, but the sight of Rabbit's mangled and bloody right arm tied together with hide sent her into fresh bouts of sobbing.

High Eagle arrived. He was a slender man in his fifties with graying hair and dark liquid eyes that could quickly focus into an unrelenting stare. His skin was dark brown from the summer sun, and a few of last summer's Sun Dance scars on his chest were visible under the robe hanging loosely over his thin shoulders. From his left shoulder dangled an antelope-hide bag. A probing glance took in the scene and stopped on the wounded boy's bloody arm, which was lying at an odd angle.

"Sister," he said gently to the softly sobbing White Hill, "I have come, and I will try to help your son."

Wiping her tears, the woman, with her husband's assistance, moved off to one side. Rabbit was their only son and had been born to them when they thought they would never have children, when White Hill was in her late thirties, so they doted on him.

High Eagle motioned to the gathering small crowd to stay back, and he knelt at the boy's side. He bent down and laid an ear to Rabbit's mouth and did the same at a spot over his chest. Then he pinched the boy's side sharply, but there was no response. Nodding to himself, he removed his own robe and covered Rabbit.

"Niece," he called to a young woman nearby, "I wonder if you could boil a kettle of water for me?"

The young woman nodded and hurried away.

Next, he turned a questioning glance up at Cloud.

"Muzzleloader," Cloud said. "Several white men. A close shot. He has lost a lot of blood. Now and then through the night, he was mumbling. We took turns carrying him."

"A good sign—the mumbling, I mean," said High Eagle. "That means he is still on this side." He motioned for a young man standing at the edge of the small crowd and said, after he stepped forward, "Down by the creek is a thick patch of new grass in the shade of the small oak trees. Pick a big bundle for me."

The young man trotted away to perform his chore.

A tall, muscular man with flecks of gray in his hair and a steady gaze in his dark eyes slipped through the small crowd. He stopped and spoke to them. "Move back," he said gently. "Give our medicine man some room."

His name was Grey Bull, one of the older warriors, though not yet an elder. The people stepped back several paces.

Grey Bull gazed briefly at Cloud, Goings, Little Bird, and Taken Alive. "I will help my cousin," he said, indicating the medicine man. "You all look like you are asleep on your feet. Go home, go to bed. We can talk later."

Cloud nodded at Goings, Taken Alive, and Little Bird, who took the hint and trudged away, almost in slow motion.

Cloud called out to Goings, "Tell my wife I will be there in a while." Then he took a seat on the ground.

High Eagle might have further questions.

High Eagle was glad Rabbit was still breathing, though he was secretly surprised. The boy had been unconscious for more than two days. If he lived, he would likely have to face life without half of his right arm.

The young man returned with a large armload of grass, which High Eagle arranged under the injured arm. He gently probed the nearly severed ends of the arm and then turned to Big Voice and White Hill Woman. "My friends," he said quietly, "I will send for the two of you later."

Big Voice pulled at his wife's arm. Although she resisted slightly, she allowed him to lead her back to their lodge. Several women came forward to comfort her and walk with her.

After the couple was well away, the medicine man started loosening the bloody hide-wrapping from the upper stump. "What exactly happened?" he said to Cloud.

"We were watching seven whites going north on the Powder River Road. I decided to let them pass because every one of them had a rifle." He indicated Rabbit, pointing with his chin. "He rode out to meet them anyway. I think he wanted to trade with them. They fired and hit him. We managed to get him and get away. His horse is gone."

High Eagle pulled the last bit of hide away from the shattered arm. "A lost horse is the least of his troubles," he muttered.

He turned to Grey Bull and spoke in a low voice. "I have to cut away the skin and what is left of the flesh. I will need to boil some rawhide to make a covering for the stump. This all should be done while he is unconscious."

Next, he glanced at Cloud. "Go home and get some rest. There is nothing for you to do here. You have brought him home, and the rest is up to him."

———————

Sweetwater Woman had just finished making tea when Cloud arrived at their lodge on the west side of the encampment, her deep auburn hair a sharp contrast with her pale skin. He embraced his wife briefly and sank into the willow chair near the door.

His grandmother Willow emerged from the lodge with a container of meat stew. "Are you hungry?" she asked, sitting down near the fire.

Cloud shook his head and reached for the cup of tea his wife held out. "No," he said before he took a sip. "I think I will sleep after this tea."

"Your cousin Goings stopped," the old woman said. "He told us what happened." Her deeply lined face, framed by gray braids, showed a trace of worry. "I did not know that Rabbit went along with you."

"He did not," replied Cloud, staring pensively at the fire as his wife added wood to it. "He was alone near Wolf Creek. I made him come along. Maybe we should have let him go his own way."

"He is impetuous," replied the old woman. "Several

days ago, he was heard scolding his father. If you did not rescue him, he would be dead and his parents would be mourning."

"He still might die."

"But that would not be your fault," insisted Willow. "You cannot always bear the burdens of others and forget your own."

"Right now, I am so tired my legs are trembling," he said after he drained the last of the tea from his cup.

"I will prepare the bed," Sweetwater Woman said and entered the lodge.

The old woman poured the stew into a small metal pot and hung it from a tripod positioned above the flames. "A messenger came up from the white town near Horse Creek. More Long Knives, he said, came to the outpost, and some peace talkers. They want to talk, and Red Cloud is there."

Cloud shook his head. "More Long Knives because of the wagon people. The people on the Holy Road are afraid they will be attacked. So they send for the Long Knives. Something bad is bound to happen."

"The men you saw, were they Long Knives?"

"No. I think they were going north to dig for gold. They had mules laden with supplies."

"I was afraid of that. Gold brings more whites, and behind them come the Long Knives. I hope Red Cloud will tell them to stay away, all of them."

Cloud shrugged. "Do you think they will listen to him?"

"I do not know," the old woman replied sadly. "I do not know."

The young man Yellow Wolf arrived, carrying the coiled neck rope and a jaw rein as well as Cloud's lance, encased rifle, encased bow and quiver of arrows, and the small packs from his horse. He hung all the gear on the sturdy willow tripod to the right of the lodge door.

"Thank you," said Cloud. "There will be stew, if you are hungry, and tea. How are the horses?"

"Even your horse is standing with his head hanging down. We are rubbing them, and then we will let them rest. They will recover."

There were questions in the young man's eyes, but it was evident that Cloud was exhausted. The questions could wait. "I will help with the horses," Yellow Wolf said, standing to leave.

"Thank you," Cloud repeated. "We can talk later." Cloud watched the young man depart and then finished his tea.

Sweetwater Woman stepped out through the door. "He looks up to you," she said. She sat down and carefully scrutinized her husband from head to foot, looking for injuries he might not admit to having. He had done that before, and, given what Goings had told them, she would not have been surprised if he had done it again. But she could see nothing to worry about.

"He will be a good man. He already is," Cloud said.

"The bed is ready. We will tie the door shut behind you so you can sleep as long as you like."

He smiled into her deep brown eyes and struggled to his feet.

━━━━━━━━━━━━━━━━

At midday, Cloud was still asleep, but High Eagle and Grey Bull were alert and waiting for Rabbit to awaken. There had been indications he would return to consciousness, and the medicine man wanted to be ready. The stump at the end of the boy's upper right arm was encased in rawhide. High Eagle had carefully shaped it around the end when the hide was still wet, and now it was drying quickly and shrinking, tightening around the stump little by little.

The medicine man poured a thin concoction from a pan into a narrow buffalo-horn cup and placed it so it would be at hand. Grey Bull was seated on the other side of the wounded boy, ready to lend a hand.

At mid-morning, the crowd had drifted away, and High Eagle was glad. Shortly after that, he sent a man out of the camp with the other half of the arm. It was dead, so he wrapped it in a bundle and gave instructions for it to be buried deep.

Rabbit's legs suddenly twitched, and he moaned.

"Grab him!" said High Eagle.

Grey Bull took the boy by the shoulders and lifted him to a half-sitting position as the medicine man forced his mouth open and poured the liquid from the horn into it. Rabbit swallowed and coughed. Before he could react again, more of the liquid was poured in. High Eagle pinched the boy's nostrils, forcing him to swallow. The boy instinctively tried to push away the cup and High Eagle's hand but could do it with only his remaining hand. His right arm, only a stump now, waved up and down with an odd, unnatural arc. Both men grimly hung on until Rabbit stopped moving. High Eagle nodded to Grey Bull, who lowered the boy down to the robe.

They watched for a moment, waiting for any further outburst, but none came. "Yes, that should make him sleep longer," said High Eagle. "His color is coming back. I think he will survive."

"He probably will," agreed Grey Bull, "but how will he react to—to the loss of his arm?"

High Eagle shook his head. "Hard to say," he admitted. "He is young and has a good chance of it healing well. As far as anything else, I do not know. That is up to him and his family."

Grey Bull went to the lodge of White Hill Woman and Big Voice and told them the reassuring news. They hurried to the willow shade to sit with their son.

"I could not save his arm," the medicine man told them. "He will wake eventually, and it will be good if he can see the two of you when he does. Whatever happens, do not let him pull off the rawhide covering. And he needs to eat and drink."

"Can we take him home?" the woman asked.

High Eagle nodded. "If he does not wake by sundown, we can have some of the men carry him to your lodge."

"Thank you," said Big Voice, "for helping him."

The medicine man stood up, fatigue evident on his face. "I think he will heal. His state of mind is what we should worry about most."

Cloud awoke in late afternoon to news that Rabbit had probably survived his ordeal. Then Yellow Wolf came with an invitation from the old men of the council. They wanted to know about the white men on the Powder River Road and would meet after sundown. After a bowl of his grandmother's elk stew, Cloud went with Sweetwater Woman to bathe in a hidden bend in the creek. She waited on the bank with fresh clothes for him.

"Everybody is talking about what happened to Rabbit," she said. "His arm, I mean. Grandmother has never known that to happen."

Images of blood splattered on sagebrush and splintered bone protruding from the skin flashed through his memory as she spoke. "I will never forget all the—I will never forget what happened," he said.

Sweetwater saw the shadow move across his face. He had slept fitfully, she noticed. Something was bothering him, and she felt bad for talking about Rabbit's arm. "When you finish, I will braid your hair," she said, smiling, as he shivered in the cold water. "You have to look good for the old men."

She ducked as he splashed water at her.

Just after sundown, he went to the council lodge.

"They were going north, probably to dig for gold," he told them after he smoked the pipe and passed it on. He, Goings, Taken Alive, and Little Bird were in the council lodge with the old men. "Their mules were loaded with packs, big packs."

"Yes," agreed Bear Looks Behind. "There is more and more word down from the north. The Crow are seeing more of them, it is said, heading west toward the Beartooth Mountains. For several years now, the white people have been digging for gold near one of their towns."

"Last summer," said Black Shield, "we saw more of them going north on the Powder River Road than the summer before. Now this summer, there is more. Now we hear that peace talkers are at Fort Laramie. I am afraid they want something."

"Let us not forget the Long Knives that came up here last summer and attacked the Blue Clouds near here," said Good Road. "Then they put up a fort near Dry Creek on the Powder, and those Long Knives are still there. The good thing about them is they have not bothered us. But it bothers me that they are still there."

Grey Bull cleared his throat. "The wise thing is to assume that all white men have guns, Long Knives or not. The seven men my nephew and the others saw three days ago all have guns and plenty of powder and ball. They are probably still south of us. So the question is, what shall we do about that group?"

Bear Looks Behind glanced toward Cloud. "This young man probably has some thoughts about that."

Cloud nodded and inhaled nervously. "If any one white man or a group of them travels through our country uncontested, they will be encouraged. I would like to take all the men among us who have guns and go after them. We can wait until night and run off their animals. After that, we attack them."

Every old head in the council lodge nodded in silent assent. Bear Looks Behind tossed a pebble at Cloud's feet. "Make your plans. I think you will not lack for men to follow you."

"We will leave in the morning, early. If we find the whites, we will wait until night," Cloud told them.

And so it was. Late the next afternoon, they found the seven white men and followed them until they made camp south of a rocky outcropping along the Bozeman Trail north of Crazy Woman Creek, nearly a day's ride south of the Tongue River encampment. They had a bright fire and only one sentry.

Like shadowy ghosts, Taken Alive and Little Bird slipped down from the rocks in the darkness and sliced the picket lines where all the horses and mules were tied and then went back up into the rocks. From that vantage point, Taken Alive took out the sentry with a silent arrow. That was Cloud's signal to open fire.

At the sound of gunfire, the loose horses and mules scattered into the night. Before one of the white men thought to douse their campfire, several of them had been hit. Cloud and his fifteen-man patrol, ten with guns, waited in the darkness. They heard the cries of wounded men and whispered conversations. As dawn broke, they saw that the whites had built a barricade of saddles and other equipment around the cold ashes of their extinguished fire. Only four could be seen moving about.

Cloud had his men conceal themselves and positioned them surrounding the whites. At mid-morning, one of them, a big man in a wide-brimmed hat, left the barricade and climbed the rocks; he was probably looking for their horses and mules. Little Bird, camouflaged and hidden in a sagebrush thicket, wounded the climber with an arrow; it was a long shot. The man managed to scramble back to the barricade, the arrow buried deep in his lower right abdomen. As the day wore on, he was not seen to move.

Evening came, and then the night, a cool night for midsummer. Cloud and his men huddled inside their elk and buffalo robes, ate their dried meat, and listened intently. But no sound came from the white men's cold camp.

As another dawn broke, they were seen bundled under blankets and peering cautiously over their barricade.

Cloud signaled two of his men to fire at them, a reminder that the unseen enemy was still there.

That evening, after dusk, Cloud and his men slipped away silently, leaving the surviving white men hiding behind their barricades. The next morning, they found seven horses and five mules bunched together and grazing peacefully in a meadow. Days later, a scout saw heavy smoke and found the remains of a camp near Crazy Woman Creek. The white men had burned most of their supplies, and their footprints headed south. There were three sets of footprints; four poorly disguised graves had been left behind.

The scout came to Cloud's lodge one evening with the news. Sweetwater Woman watched her husband nod, but there was no joy in his eyes, perhaps because of the news about Rabbit.

Big Voice had stopped by just before the scout came. "He awoke the evening after High Eagle treated his wound," he said, "not long after they carried him to our place."

Big Voice's wife, White Hill, was a cousin to Cloud's mother.

"He did not seem surprised at what had happened to his arm, but he was angry, and he wept to himself quietly. We heard him in the night. He has not spoken to us since he awoke."

"Not at all?"

"No. Not a word. He eats and drinks because his

mother pleads with him, but only after we leave him alone. At night, he goes out to relieve himself. During the day, he stays under his sleeping robes, with his back to the door."

"How is his arm?" Cloud wondered.

"I think it is healing. I know there is some pain; I can tell."

"Have you talked to High Eagle?"

Big Voice nodded. "Yes, he wants to look at the injury. He is worried that it will fester. I have told my son, but he did not respond."

"What will you do?"

The anguish in the older man's eyes was hard to ignore. "I do not know, but his mother and I keep praying for his spirit to heal. If his spirit heals, his arm will also heal. I just wanted to thank you for saving his life. This is a difficult blessing, if you know what I mean. I believe his bodily wound will heal, but—"

"Yes, I think I understand. Perhaps I will go to see him in a day or two."

Cloud was silent for a long time after Big Voice had left. Eventually, he glanced toward the back of the room. Among his weapons, there was a six-shot revolver. He had always liked it. It was heavy, but it also felt solid and gave him a sense of confidence each time he carried it. *Maybe*, he hoped, *that sense of confidence could be as good as a missing arm.*

CHAPTER THREE

The Snake

On the second day of Cloud's siege against the seven white men along the Powder River Road, four days' ride to the southeast—two hundred miles—an old Lakota man saw trouble slide over the horizon, like a snake crawling over a log.

Old Deer Tail finished cutting the last of the willow stalks he had found along the narrow little creek. Sitting against a small oak tree, he stripped off the small branches and leaves and tied the bundle together with a cord. His task finished, he turned his full attention to the curious sight to the southeast. A strange thing had appeared earlier, first as nothing but a narrow dark swatch between the horizon and the sky. In a while, the swatch became a line and grew longer.

He had grown fond of roll-your-own smokes and traded for the packs of papers and little bags of tobacco whenever he could. It helped that he could speak the language of the Long Knives and other whites. Leaning against a stump, he fashioned a smoke as he contemplated the long dark line in the distance.

By the time he built a small fire and used the burning end of a twig to light his smoke, he knew what he was seeing: Long Knives, hundreds of them, in wagons and riding on horses, the most he had ever seen in one column. By the time Deer Tail finished his smoke, the column had stopped, and it looked as though they were going into camp. That puzzled him, because they were about two miles from the cluster of buildings at Fort Laramie.

He fashioned another smoke. He needed time to think about what to do. After lighting it, he buried the small fire, grabbed his cane, and labored to his feet. With the bundle of willow stalks over one shoulder, he trudged toward the column. He would ask them where they had come from.

A place called Fort Kearny, they told him, south of the Wolf River, to the east, and also south of the Sand Hill country. Twelve days of travel had brought them to Fort Laramie.

Deer Tail could be downright charming when he wanted to be. To the newly arrived soldiers, he was nothing more than an inquisitive and harmless old Indian dressed in wool trousers and a blue calico shirt. His gray hair hung in two thin braids. All in all, he did not fit the descriptions of "marauding and murderin' savages" from the stories they had been hearing.

As luck would have it, Deer Tail struck up a conversation with a thin, studious-looking soldier, older than most of them. Carrington, he said his name was, Henry Carrington. And he said he was in command.

"You go to Fort Laramie?" inquired Deer Tail.

"Briefly," replied the man named Carrington, "only for a short rest. Then we are headed for the Powder

River and the foothills of the Bighorn Mountains. Do you know that country?"

Old Deer Tail nodded affably. "Yes," replied Deer Tail, "I know that country."

He walked a ways from the dusty and tired soldiers, many of them unhitching mules from the wagons. The only puzzling thing was the women and children. Never had he known soldiers to travel with their women and children. Something about that bothered him, but he hid the feeling with a benign smile, occasionally waving in response to inquisitive glances cast in his direction. Then, unobtrusively, he turned and trudged back toward his own village.

Deer Tail had gone looking for willow stalks after his wife grumbled that she needed to repair two of the old chairs in their lodge. Several of the thin willow lattices had broken and needed to be replaced. He knew of a place where a few patches of willow were hidden. If not for the broken chairs, he would not have wandered this far from the encampment near Fort Laramie, and he would not have seen the new column of Long Knives come from the east.

Now, thanks to broken chairs and his wife's grumbling, he had news for Red Cloud.

Sweetwater Woman watched intently as her husband cleaned the big six-shot revolver. It was a weapon he used hardly at all. He had been home for several days and had not said one word about the raid against the whites.

"I found this last fall," he said by way of explanation, "when the Long Knives abandoned their wagons at the lower end of the Powder River after the ice storm killed their horses. They burned their supplies and walked east. Someone lost this, I think, or threw it away."

She looked worried. "Yes," she said, "I remember when you came home with it. Are you planning on leaving again, to watch the Powder River Road?"

"No," he replied immediately. "I am worried about my cousin Rabbit. His father said he has not spoken to him or his mother since he awoke several days ago. So I thought I would give this to him." He turned the empty cylinder and hefted the weapon, feeling its weight.

"It is hard to imagine what it must feel like," she said sadly, "losing part of your body, I mean."

"Having a good weapon is part of what makes a fighting man feel strong and worthwhile," he pointed out. "All Rabbit had was a bow, but it was tied on his horse, and who knows where it is. It was not with the horses and mules we found after—after Taken Alive and Little Bird cut them loose from those white men. Anyway, he cannot use a bow now."

"I do not think of Rabbit as a fighting man, even before this happened to him," she admitted.

"Perhaps, but I think he needs to feel like a man first. Then we will see what happens."

Cloud found White Hill Woman and Big Voice sitting with High Eagle under the sunshade. It was past midday, and the encampment seemed unusually busy this afternoon. Cloud said as much, and High Eagle reminded him that the horse herd was being moved to new grazing from south of the encampment to the northwest.

The encampment of slightly more than forty lodges was situated in a thin grove of oak and cottonwood trees northwest of the Tongue River. It was one of several villages in the area, most of them farther downstream in the wide valley the river followed. Here, Black Shield and Bear Looks Behind were the head men. There were nearly thirty able-bodied fighting men, though some were away hunting or scouting. Overall, in all the villages in the Powder River country, there were probably four hundred fighting men.

High Eagle glanced at the holstered pistol on the leather belt draped over Cloud's shoulder but said nothing.

"Uncle," Cloud said to Big Voice, "with your permission, I have something to give to my cousin."

Big Voice nodded and smiled in appreciation. "It would be good if you could talk to him," he said. "He is awake. His mother left him some food, but he waits for us to leave and then eats. Just go in."

Cloud arrived at the lodge and scratched at the door, pausing for a moment before he entered. He heard a soft rustling and saw Rabbit quickly lay down and pull the robe over his head, his back toward the door.

"Cousin," Cloud said nervously, "I brought you—ah, I brought you this six-shot pistol. I do not like to see a man without a weapon. There is a bag of powder as well, and several round bullets."

Beneath the covers, Rabbit's eyes darted about.

"My uncle and aunt tell me you are—you are recovering. But I wanted to know for myself how you are."

There was no reply, as Cloud had expected. He was squatting on the balls of his feet, ready to turn and leave, uncertain as to what to say or do. He decided to try once more.

"I was never that good with this weapon," he said, placing it on the floor next to the cold fire pit. "But I can show you how to load it. I would be glad to go with you if you want to practice shooting it, whenever you like."

There was movement beneath the robe. Rabbit lifted his head ever so slightly and softly cleared his throat. Cloud waited.

"I, ah—I never liked shooting a rifle," he whispered. "The six-shooter might be good, I think."

"Yes, I think so. It is a good weapon."

Rabbit slowly pulled himself to a sitting position, though slightly turned away from Cloud. He was careful not to let the robe slide from his right shoulder. His hair was loose and disheveled, and Cloud could not see his face.

"Anytime you want, we can go and shoot this gun." Cloud pushed it toward the boy.

Rabbit nodded.

"Think about it and let me know."

Rabbit nodded again. "Thank you. Ah—thank you."

Cloud stood and turned toward the door.

"You know, there is something strange," the boy said suddenly. "Sometimes I think I can feel my fingers, the fingers on the hand that is no longer there. What do you suppose that means, Cousin?"

Cloud stared at the floor. "I cannot say. Maybe High Eagle has an answer. We can ask him, if you want."

The boy nodded slowly again. "Ah, my mother fixed some food, coffee and roasted elk. It is over there. Maybe you can eat with me?"

Cloud moved toward the bowl and plate by the fire pit and took a seat. "Yes," he said.

The boy turned to join Cloud and paused to run his fingers through his hair. Then he pulled the covering higher over his shoulder. His cheeks were hollow and there were dark circles under his eyes. In his eyes was a look of uncertainty.

"I heard my father telling my mother that you went after those white men," he said, staring at the pistol in its holster.

"Yes, we did. We ran off their horses and mules, and they went back toward the south. They—they left four graves behind."

"I do not remember how I got home. I remember

the gunshots that day."

"Maybe it is not important for you to remember. It seems to me that it is important that you are home."

Rabbit reached for the pistol and slid it out of its case. "It is heavy," he said.

"Yes," agreed Cloud, "but you are strong."

The boy aimed the pistol upward and the look of uncertainty in his eyes faded. An angry scowled flowed across his face, like a cloud blotting out the sun. Cloud would never forget that look.

As Cloud and Rabbit shared the roasted elk, a tired and dusty young man rode into the east end of the encampment, slid from his horse, and asked for directions to the lodge of Black Shield. He was taken there as afternoon shadows began stretching across the valley of the Tongue River. The elder was sitting on the east side of the lodge in the shade. He invited the young man to join him.

"Uncle," said the young Blunt Arrow, using the title of respect for an older man, "my father sent me to bring news about the Long Knives. Things have happened at Fort Laramie." He paused to drink from the dipper of water handed to him by the wife of Black Shield. "Thank you," he said.

"We knew things were happening there," said Black Shield. "I take it the news is not good."

Blunt Arrow nodded. "I have traveled for four days. The peace talkers and the head men among the Long Knives were asking to build outposts along what they call the Bozeman Road. Red Cloud and the other old men refused. But new Long Knives with wagons arrived, even before Red Cloud said no. He was so angry, he left the meeting. He walked out on the peace talkers."

Black Shield shook his head in astonishment. "They must have thought Red Cloud would not refuse. Or they thought to do what they wanted no matter what. Where is that column?"

"It started out the day before me, along the road next to the Shell River."

Black Shield let out a growl of anger. "Haun!"

"There are many wagons," added Blunt Arrow, "and over five hundred Long Knives."

That night, the old men sat in council, the news of the Long Knives coming roiling in like the taste of bile on the tongue.

"First, we must know where the Long Knives are," said Grey Bull. "My nephew," he paused to nod toward Cloud, "and I can scout to the south and locate them. We need to know how many of them there are and how they are armed."

Heads nodded in affirmation. Black Spotted Horse cleared his throat. His hair was snow white and lines crisscrossed his face like so many trails. "I remember the white man they call Bozeman," he said. "Three or four years ago, we watched him pounding stakes into the ground and laughed. We stopped laughing after we realized he was marking a trail for other whites to follow. That was after we heard of the gold diggings up north, west of Crow lands. That is how it started. It worries me because of what all those wagons did to the land along the Shell River Road. They left it bare and stinking with their dead animals. They left graves of their dead. They spoiled the land so badly the buffalo do not go there anymore. I do not want that to happen to us up here!"

Growls of affirmation flowed through the gathering of old men, like warnings from cornered wolves.

"The young man Blunt Arrow went down the valley," Black Shield told them, "to carry the news to the other villages. My friend and I," he said, pointing to Bear Looks Behind, "will send a messenger to the other councils. We should talk, all of us old men and the leaders of the fighting men, so that we can agree on how to solve this problem."

"In the meantime," said Bear Looks Behind, "Grey Bull and Cloud can take some young men and go south to scout. We need to know exactly how many Long Knives there are and what they are doing. This much I know. They intend to stay and build outposts. We cannot allow that."

Grey Bull glanced toward Cloud. "We can leave at dawn," he said.

"Do not fight them," instructed Black Shield. "We are sending you as our eyes and ears. To defeat an enemy, it is necessary to know as much about him as we can. This is one kind of enemy, unfortunately, that is like the shape-shifter: he is hard to know."

Grey Bull came to talk with Cloud later in the evening. Willow gave him the chair at the back of the room next to Cloud, a place reserved for special guests. Sweetwater Woman brought him tea and broiled fish on a stick.

"Thank you," he said to the women. "Where did you get the fish?"

"Some boys caught several," explained Sweetwater. "They were testing their fish traps."

"I guess the traps work," chuckled Grey Bull. He made short work of the fish and wiped his mouth. "Grandmother," he said to the old woman, "I suppose you have heard that we are going on a scout to the south."

The old woman nodded. "I heard," she replied.

"Yes, your grandson and I and a few young men. We have to see what the Long Knives are doing. They are coming."

Willow leaned back in her latticed chair. "When I was a girl, there was a story about them traveling up the Great Muddy River in a large boat made of wood. It is said that the boat had white wings. The story came from the Sicangu, who lived along the river. In those days, there were so few of them—the whites, I mean. Now they keep coming from somewhere."

"At the Council of Long Meadows fifteen years ago," recalled Grey Bull, "their peace talkers told us they only needed room for their wagon wheels, leading us to think they would only pass through our country. But they are staying, and that is the trouble."

Sweetwater Woman had taken a seat next to Cloud. As Grey Bull spoke, she reached for her husband's hand. She kept her eyes down and listened. Suddenly, she felt the older man's gaze on her face.

"Niece," he said gently, "you know my words are not meant to hurt you."

Sweetwater felt her face grow warm. She nodded.

"My grandson's wife became a Lakota when she was but a child," said Willow. "She will always be a Lakota."

"That is true," Grey Bull said. "That is true." After a moment, he spoke again. "I came to tell you that we are not going south to fight the Long Knives. We are only to scout. I do not know how long we will be gone, but we will be back."

"Yes," replied the old woman. "We are glad to know that, and we will pack plenty of food so you will not have to hunt."

Grey Bull finished his tea and took his leave.

The old woman pounded dried meat and finished making *wasna* (pemmican), a mixture of dried, pounded chokecherry and dried meat. In this case, it was buffalo meat. It was a hearty, substantial meal always carried on long patrols by fighting men and on long hunts by hunters.

Suddenly, there was a soft scratch on the outside of the door.

"Come in," called out Cloud.

They waited, but no one entered. The scratching came again.

They were all puzzled. Cloud arose and went to the door, lifting a reassuring hand to his wife and grand-mother. He thought he knew who was at their door.

He was right. Outside, his face hidden by the robe pulled completely over his head, stood Rabbit.

"Cousin," said Cloud, "it is good to see you up and around."

The boy let the robe slide down to his shoulders. His hair had been braided, and he looked rested, and he wore a shirt made of tanned deerskins. He nodded in greeting. "I heard that you are going on a scout." He spoke in a near whisper.

"Yes. Long Knives are coming up the Powder River Road. The old men want us to watch them."

"Who is going with you?" Rabbit asked cau-tiously.

"Grey Bull and I are taking Goings, Taken Alive, Little Bird, and Yellow Wolf."

The boy nodded and looked toward two young men passing nearby in the dark. "I would like to go too," he said.

Cloud was not surprised. "Are you strong enough to ride?" he wondered.

"If I am not, I will turn back," said Rabbit.

"This—this is not a revenge raid."

"My father said there is time for that, if I choose.

44

He also said I could learn much from you. I will not be a burden if you let me go with you."

"How is your arm? Is it healing?"

Rabbit nodded. "High Eagle came to see it. He said for me to keep it clean. In a while, he will remove the rawhide. I think—I think it is healing. There is some pain, but only a little."

"Be here with your horse before dawn," Cloud said. "If Grey Bull has no objection, you can go with us."

"Thank you. I will be here."

Cloud listened to the boy's footfalls fading into the night and ducked back through the doorway. From the back of the room, he took his weapons and sat down and began to inspect his arrows. In a few moments, he looked up at his grandmother.

"Watch him closely," she advised, seeming to read his mind. "There is more that was wounded than his arm. When the spirit is badly wounded, even a grown man can lose his way."

CHAPTER FOUR

Buffalo Creek

An annoying breeze grew into a steady wind on the second day, turning sand into stinging pellets. But the dust from the wind provided cover for the scouts, though they also had to contend with the hot sun and an occasional scorpion as they watched the activity around the squat buildings north of the fork of the Powder River, a place the Long Knives called Fort Reno, two hard days' ride south from the Tongue River.

Cloud positioned the men so that each one had a different view of the outpost. Only two had a field glass, but everyone had keen eyesight. Every evening after dark, the scouts regrouped on a plateau well northeast of the outpost to report to each other. But outside of the alarming fact that there were more than six hundred of them, the Long Knives did little more than behave like a colony of ants. They seemed to be working on the buildings of the outpost, and although they did post sentinels all around, no mounted patrols were sent out. Only once was there a near encounter.

A horse pulled loose from one of the picket lines and loped away, and two soldiers ran after it. The animal was more concerned with food than freedom, however. Unfortunately, it found a patch of grass a mere stone's toss from Little Bird's hiding place, unaware that he had instigated the age-old struggle between life and death.

Little Bird watched the horse from beneath a pile of driftwood on the bank of a dry watercourse and saw the soldiers approaching. He strung his bow and drew two arrows from his quiver for two fast, silent shots, if necessary. At this range, he decided that a throat or heart shot would be the best. That would stun and disable the soldiers immediately. After that, he could finish them with a knife or, better yet, his war club.

But the two soldiers were concerned with nothing more than catching the errant horse. Neither of them was armed. Grabbing the horse's lead rope, they led him back toward the outpost, never to know they were briefly in the sights of a Lakota bowman who could shoot the eye out of a jackrabbit at forty paces.

Watching from a distance at separate locations, both Cloud and Grey Bull breathed sighs of relief.

Cloud kept Rabbit with him. No one had protested outright that the boy was along on the scout, but none of them was pleased. There were no dark stares, and no one ignored Rabbit, but the unspoken uncertainty was palpable. To his credit, the boy kept his place, performing his share of chores to keep up the camp. By the third day, most of the unspoken anxieties over Rabbit's presence had dissipated somewhat, mostly because he did not complain or make excuses because of his arm. Cloud was relieved, because they needed to pay attention to the harsh reality of several hundred Long Knives invading Lakota territory.

On the evening of the third day, as the shadows of dusk darkened into night, the six scouts and Rabbit gathered on a plateau east of the Long Knife outpost. The wind had diminished a little. They checked on their horses and took them to water at a narrow stream hidden among some boulders. Back on the plateau, they ate and rested without building a fire. The air was still warm and a fire was not needed, though it would grow chilly before sunrise. There would be a moon later.

Rabbit, as usual, sat apart. He knew the others were being polite to him as a favor to Cloud. But it was no more than he expected. What they might think of him was not as important as what he could learn from them. To a man, they were all self-assured and confident, skilled and experienced fighting men. He envied them, and he wanted to be like them. At the moment, he did not want them to know that he was gritting his teeth against the pain in his arm.

"This morning, about eighteen of them rode away to the south," reported Grey Bull. "I think they were ones already here; their clothing was different. My guess is they are going to Fort Laramie."

"From what Blunt Arrow told Black Shield," said Cloud, "the Long Knives are doing what they said. They came here to this post, but I wonder if they will stay, because there is not enough shelter here for all of them, unless they stay in those little tents. Sooner or later, they will eat all of the cattle they have with them and they will have to hunt."

"They have tools," observed Little Bird. "Maybe they will build houses, and pens for their animals."

"For that, they will need to go to the foothills to cut down trees," pointed out Grey Bull. "That is nearly a day of travel with wagons, a long way to haul trees."

"In two days, I will send Yellow Wolf back to report to the old men," decided Cloud.

The young man nodded at the sound of his name, pleased to be picked for an important task.

"We still have food and water, so the rest of us can remain for several days after that." He looked to Yellow Wolf again. "But if you bring back food, we can stay longer. I think we should do that until it is clear what the Long Knives intend to do."

"I will bring food," said Yellow Wolf.

Early the next morning, the Long Knives changed everybody's plans. The outpost was loud with activity. Mules were hitched, and wagons were loaded. Not long after sunrise, the column formed and started north. Mounted soldiers rode on either side of the line of wagons as they rolled in a slow and ponderous procession, but relentless as well.

Watching with a glass from the rim of the plateau, Cloud saw that about forty men were left at the outpost. Clearly, the column was headed elsewhere, probably to establish a new outpost, which had been Grey Bull's guess. *He was probably right*, Cloud thought, *because there were no other outposts along the Powder River Road. The question was, where?*

They stayed well east of the northbound column, easily matching its pace because it was moving slowly. Knowing the Long Knives would follow the road, the Bozeman Trail to them, the scouts kept to the east side of any hills and used dry creek beds and gullies as they traveled to avoid being spotted. They were careful not to raise any telltale dust.

As the sun began to drop behind the jagged mountain ridges to the west, the Long Knives stopped and made camp along a stream flowing out of the foothills. Goings found a suitable spot for the scouts along the same stream but much farther to the east, in a grove of young cottonwood trees. A sharp rise nearby provided an unobstructed view of the Long Knife camp. The scouts again made a cold camp without a fire.

"The road they are following crosses the Tongue River, about two days' travel, even as slow as they are moving," pointed out Grey Bull. "If I were them, I would pick that area for an outpost. There is water, plenty of trees for the kinds of houses they build, good grazing for their animals, and it is on what they call the Bozeman Road."

"True," said Cloud, "but I wonder if that is not too far from the outpost called Reno. But that does not matter. They intend to stay, and any place they build an outpost is not what our people want to see."

He motioned to Yellow Wolf. "The old men will want to know what is happening. Can you leave before dawn?"

The young man nodded.

"Good! Tell them what we have seen, that the Long Knives are bringing their tools and their women and children."

Grey Bull nodded thoughtfully. "And tell them to send word to all the other villages. Our fighting men need to be ready."

Cloud looked toward Grey Bull. "I have a thought," he said. "If my cousin is willing, I would like him to go with me to get in close to the Long Knives' camp and listen. We might hear something."

Rabbit had hardly spoken all day. His arm was throbbing and the stump was itching fiercely inside the rawhide covering. Out of the corner of his eye, he saw Grey Bull glance in his direction, but in the growing darkness, it was hard to see what was on the older man's face. *Doubt*, Rabbit guessed.

He nodded. "I can do that," he said.

"Yes," said Cloud, "I thought you would say that. We should leave soon and get close before they are bedded down and quiet. While they are still busy and making noise, we can get in close. But there is one thing, Cousin: we will not take any guns. I will take my bow and a knife."

Cloud did not have to see the look of confusion and then disappointment cross the boy's face, but he could feel it.

Rabbit nodded silently and unbuckled the wide

black belt from around his waist and laid it next to his small bag of food.

"Nephew," said Grey Bull to the boy, "stay close to your cousin. There is no better scout among us. He will teach you things."

Rabbit nodded again.

In a moment, Cloud was ready. As they left the camp, he handed his war lance to Rabbit. "It is good for close-in fighting," he said.

The boy took it and followed Cloud into the night.

After several moments, Little Bird rolled out his elk-hide robe and lay down. "I do not know what to think of him," he admitted.

"You mean Rabbit?" Goings wanted to know.

"Yes."

"I heard him moaning in the night," said Grey Bull. "I think his arm is causing a lot of pain."

"He has no one to blame but himself," said Little Bird.

"True," replied Grey Bull. "I am sure he thinks about that, probably every time his arm hurts, or when he sees nothing below his elbow."

Goings sighed and glanced at Yellow Wolf. Little Bird stared up at the myriad stars.

"It may be hard for us to look at him, at where his arm was. I know it is for me," admitted Grey Bull. "But he is the one who has to live with part of him missing. And what good does it do now to blame him? You think if we blame him enough times, his arm will grow back?"

"Uncle," said Little Bird, "what shall we do then?"

Grey Bull sighed deeply. "If he acts like a man and he treats you like a man, then do the same for him. That is what I think."

Several gullies away, Cloud and Rabbit were crouched behind a thick clump of sagebrush. Several campfires were glowing in the darkness. All the animals and the people were inside the large circular pen formed by the wagons. It was an effective deterrent, Cloud had to admit.

"If I were them, I would put sentries out in the dark," he whispered to Rabbit. "After it got dark, so anyone watching would not see where they are."

"You think they did that?" asked Rabbit.

"Hard to say, but we should make no noise at all just in case. Are you ready?"

Rabbit nodded and took a deep breath. The man who had wounded him was nowhere in that circle of wagons; likely as not, the man who shattered his arm with one bullet was dead. Nevertheless, fear mixed with a burning need to get even, and it seemed to fill his throat. He had a plan, nothing specific yet. Or perhaps it was nothing more than intent. He was glad Cloud had asked him to do this thing, because he had much to learn, and he wanted to learn quickly. After that, he would strike out on his own. But tonight, he would do whatever his cousin asked him to do so he could gain the experience. "Yes, I am ready," he replied.

Cloud tore off a branch from the sagebrush, stripped off the leaves, and rolled them between his palms. The sharp, pungent scent was hard to ignore. He handed the twist to Rabbit. "Rub it on all over. It will cover your scent."

When they finished, they walked deliberately at first, placing their feet carefully, and so made no noise. When they could clearly see the outlines of people occasionally crossing in front of the fires, they began to crawl, once again carefully placing hands and knees, and sometimes tossing aside brush or twigs that would make noise. They also had to be wary of snakes and scorpions, not to mention cacti. Rabbit found the short war lance to be invaluable in locating cacti. For the time being, he forgot the throbbing in his arm.

At about fifty paces from the wagons, Cloud saw a faint outline to the right of them: a man sitting next to a bush. He touched Rabbit's shoulder and pointed. After a moment, they moved again, two silent shadows below the sentry's sight line. About twenty more paces past the sentry, they could hear voices clearly. There, thirty paces from the eastern edge of the circle of wagons, they stayed utterly motionless among the sage, soap weeds, and rocks as Rabbit listened intently.

There were too many conversations, too many people, he realized. No way to know exactly where the Long Knife leaders were. Frequently, there was laughter and dogs barking, horses nickering and stamping hooves.

As the night wore on, activity diminished and conversation faded. One by one, campfires were doused.

Then he heard footsteps approaching, and he touched Cloud's arm. He was hearing them as well. Someone was moving slowly through the sparse undergrowth, obviously in the manner of a man not familiar with the terrain. The footsteps were headed toward them.

Cloud reached back and drew his fighting knife from its sheath. Touching Rabbit's shoulder, he laid the handle of the knife in his hand and grabbed the lance. Rabbit understood and relinquished the lance at the same moment he took the knife. His heart began to pound.

Ahead in the darkness, clothing scratched against the stalks of sagebrush. Then an inquisitive whisper: "Hey, Doerner, you out there?"

No answer.

"Damn it, Doerner! It be dark out here! Where are you?" The whisper was louder, almost frantic.

Behind Cloud and Rabbit, someone stirred in the brush.

A sleepy voice responded. "Here! Is that you, Jenkins?"

"Yes!" The footsteps turned toward the voice, passing by Cloud and Rabbit by no more than the length of Cloud's lance. "I come to relieve you."

A rustling as someone stood. "Good! I am ready for a bed."

Rabbit leaned over and whispered into Cloud's

ear, "New sentry."

Cloud nodded and whispered back, "The other might come through here. Be ready."

Rabbit felt his throat tighten and nodded. Then he nearly jumped as he heard another voice behind them and to the left.

"Jenkins! Doerner! I can hear you! Quiet!" Then more footsteps.

"Aye," someone said.

Cloud and Rabbit lay ready, but the footfalls on either side of them did not come near. Rabbit allowed himself a sigh of utter relief. He felt a tap on his shoulder.

"We are between them." Cloud's whisper was almost hard to hear. "We will wait a while and then go back the way we came."

Rabbit nodded, suddenly realizing that either his arm had stopped hurting or he had completely forgotten about the pain.

———————————

As the end of the star cluster known as the Seven Sisters was dipping toward the faint light in the east, Cloud and Rabbit walked back into the camp along the creek. Grey Bull was awake. In the dim light, he could see bits of brush and debris on their clothing, as well as dirt.

"I was beginning to worry," he said.

"No reason to worry," Cloud said. He brushed

himself off and crumpled to the ground and unrolled his elk robe.

Rabbit lay down with his back to the circle of sleeping men. His arm no longer throbbed, though the end of the stump itched to distraction. He had not expected the night to turn out the way it did. Although he was tired, he was exhilarated too.

"I thought maybe you went in close enough to snip some horse's mane," teased Grey Bull.

"That would have been too easy," countered Cloud.

"What did happen?"

"We slipped past their sentries," replied Cloud, "close enough to hear voices, but there was nothing—"

Rabbit sat up. "They have a word for us, a name: *savage*. The whites at Fort Laramie use it too. But mostly, they are afraid of the land. It is wild to them. I heard a man say that."

Grey Bull and Cloud glanced at each other. "Strange," the older man muttered. "If they are afraid of it, why do they come here?"

"It does not matter," said Cloud, "because they are not like us and do not belong here in our country. Out there in the darkness, I thought about how many of them there are. For many summers now, since I was a boy, thousands of them go through on the Shell River Road. Thousands of them! Now they will do that on the Powder River Road through here! That is what I thought about."

Fort Laramie was along the Shell River Road—the Oregon Trail, most whites called it. Rabbit had seen many of the countless wagons drawn by mules or oxen that would stop there all summer long. They were all passing through, men with faces burned red by the sun and pale women in bonnets shading haunted eyes, and the children, some with red or yellow hair. He had often wondered how there could be so many whites.

"There seems to be an endless supply of them, like mosquitoes," his father had said, "and only a few of us human beings. The difference is, mosquitoes only want our blood; the whites want everything. I am afraid it is past the time to swat them away."

Rabbit thought about telling them what his father had said but decided against it. To them, from now on, he was just the one-armed boy. He lay back down and pulled the robe over the stump of his arm.

Grey Bull tossed a pebble at one of the sleeping forms. Yellow Wolf threw aside his robe and sat up immediately. "Are you ready to travel?" he heard the man ask.

"Yes!" Yellow Wolf began to gather his things.

"Wait! Wait," said Cloud, chuckling. "Remember, tell the old men the Long Knives are planning to build an outpost. We do not know where. Tell them, also, that we think it is time to do something. Run off their horses, cause some confusion. I think the old men will agree that it must not be easy for the Long Knives. They have come this far from Horse Creek without any trouble."

Rabbit was listening. He had a plan, or at least the beginnings of one. His father and the other older men would think he was crazy if he told them. Cloud would stop him if he knew. Truth was, he could not tell anyone, because what he was thinking did not make sense. It would be best, he knew, to tell no one of his plan. Besides, no one else was missing part of an arm, so they would not understand.

Grey Bull nodded grimly. "Yes," he said, "I think you are right."

"Where will you be tonight?" asked Yellow Wolf.

"Wherever the Long Knives make camp, but I do not think they will make it as far as the Tongue."

Yellow Wolf finished tying up his bundle. "After dark, I will not be able to find you," he said, "so I will wait until tomorrow morning to come back with food."

"We will watch for you. When you get home, go to our families, if you would. Tell them we are safe and anxious to be home."

———————————

By early afternoon, Cloud had a feeling that the Long Knives would camp for the night along Buffalo Creek. He was right. Knowing the column would stay on the trail, the scouts had ridden fast after Cloud and Rabbit had had a bit of sleep. At midday, they crossed over the road and took a position on a high knob on the south rim of a broad valley.

In the valley below them to the north was Buffalo Creek. From the knob, they had an unobstructed view of the trail as far north as a pass called Lodge Trail Ridge. Just below the knob, they picketed the horses out of sight in a grassy bowl to let them graze while they rested and waited.

A few Long Knives reached Buffalo Creek in the middle of the afternoon and turned west. They went as far as a wide meadow and stopped in a thin grove of trees along the stream.

Grey Bull looked through his glass, saw one of the soldiers looking at the surrounding landscape through his glass, and grunted. "At least they know enough to pick a good spot for a camp."

After watering their horses, the soldiers retraced their route back toward the column.

By late afternoon, the column arrived. An uneasy feeling settled in the small of Cloud's back as he watched the wagons rolling into the meadow. He knew the area around Buffalo Creek well and felt it was one of the most beautiful places along the eastern slopes of the Shining Mountains. As a matter of fact, several Northern Cheyenne families had pitched their lodges in the meadow not long ago, before joining one of the Lakota villages farther north along the Tongue River.

All the scouts squatted in the tall grass on the knob, staring down into the valley, fixated on the seemingly endless line of wagons. As far away as they were from the meadow, the people were nothing more than dark, upright, undefined forms. The few children they could see were smaller and even less defined. For several long moments, no one spoke.

"I have a bad feeling," said Goings. "Every one of the Long Knives has a rifle and a six-shooter. That is more than—more than one thousand guns. We do not have that many fighting men among us, maybe three hundred, and not all of us have a gun—of any kind."

"I have eleven bullets for my rifle," said Grey Bull, "but not enough powder for eleven shots."

Cloud glanced to his left at Rabbit. In spite of the heat, he had a coyote hide draped over his left shoulder, hanging well below the stump of his right arm.

"But there is more to fighting than what you have in your hands when you go into battle," continued Grey Bull. He pointed down into the valley. "I think they feel strong because of their guns. Without them, what kind of fighters are they, really? I am a man. I believe I am a better man than any one of them, perhaps any five or ten of them. If we fight them man to man, we would defeat them, I know. But that is not their way, so we have to make sure they cannot use their strengths against us, and we have to know their weaknesses."

"They are afraid of the land," Rabbit said quietly.

"That is a weakness," said Grey Bull. "We must use it. My guess is that they are most vulnerable at night."

"Then we use it," said Cloud. "We take away their strength, which is numbers. If they come after us in large numbers, then we pick the place to fight. We take advantage any time there are only a few of them. We get them into a running fight because we are true horse warriors. They are not."

Grey Bull nodded. "And all of our fighting men have to understand those things," he said.

He looked at the three younger men. "This is a different kind of enemy. To them, war is for killing, as much and as many as they can. Woman Killer—the one named Harney—did that to Little Thunder on the Blue Water eleven years ago. They did that to the Cheyenne and Blue Clouds at Sand Creek two years ago. We cannot let them do that here. We will not."

They stared grimly down at the dark forms scattering along Buffalo Creek. Wagons, horses, and mules were not unknown to them, but the dark, faceless figures were. Who those faceless figures were did not matter; what they were and what they had done and could do again did matter.

"Are they not happy in their own country?" asked Little Bird.

"Do they have a country?" wondered Goings.

Rabbit spoke softly. "My father says they are not a happy people, so they are always looking for something. He says they will not know it even when they find it."

They stayed on the hill and watched white canvas tents pop up on the meadow south of the creek, and the horses and mules were unhitched, watered, and turned out to graze. The animals were guarded by only a few soldiers.

Cloud turned to Grey Bull with a twinkle in his eye. "I have an idea," he said.

CHAPTER FIVE

Tent Town

Three days later, Cloud and Grey Bull sat with Crazy Horse on a ridge northwest of the intruders' sprawling tent town. On the Buffalo Creek meadow below, the white tents were arranged in straight rows. The sight was an eyesore as far as the observers were concerned. Just as annoying was the antlike activity among and around them.

A few paces from them, Goings, Taken Alive, Little Bird, and Little Hawk, Crazy Horse's younger brother, sat in the grass. A warm breeze prowled the hills and gullies and ruffled the manes and tails of nine horses standing patiently in the gully just below the ridge. With them were the two horse holders, Yellow Wolf and Rabbit.

Like Cloud, Crazy Horse was in favor of immediate and hard-hitting action against the Long Knives. They were both surprised to hear some of the older leaders advise the warriors to wait for Red Cloud to arrive from one of the lower encampments on the Tongue River.

Black Shield had a different opinion. "Doing nothing is the same as giving the Long Knives permission to stay on Buffalo Creek," he had said to Cloud.

Cloud liked Crazy Horse. There was an innate shyness about the younger man that precluded any pretense, even though he had a formidable reputation as a fighting man and was envied by many older warriors. Last year, he had been chosen as a Shirt Wearer, to the surprise of many people, though not because he lacked the character necessary to be one. Over the years, that position had become more of a political selection, as young men from influential families were most often picked. It was a way for the old men to curry favor. They seemed to have forgotten that Shirt Wearers of old were humble men who truly cared about the welfare of the people and placed it above their own needs.

Like everyone else, Crazy Horse was burned brown by the sun, but his brown hair seemed lighter in the summer. When he was a small boy, his mother had named him Light Hair, and Cloud remembered that some boys teased him because of his lighter-than-usual skin. No one was teasing him now. As a battlefield leader he had a strong and loyal following, and many felt that as a Shirt Wearer he was a throwback to what they were in the old days.

Crazy Horse put away his glass and nodded slowly. "You are right. I think they are planning on staying there."

Grey Bull's eyes flashed as he jabbed the air angrily. "They have been there three days, and we have done nothing!"

Cloud pointed to the large herd of mules and horses grazing in the meadow south of the creek. "For the past two days, they gathered them up around sundown and put them inside a rope fence for the night."

Crazy Horse plucked a blade of grass and chewed

on it briefly, staring thoughtfully at the distant herd. "Maybe the Long Knives are not as watchful because nothing has happened." He glanced toward the young men waiting nearby. "But we will need more men, if I understand your thinking."

Cloud agreed. "Yes, maybe twenty."

Grey Bull pointed to two dark specks on the high point south of the meadow. "We were there three days ago. I had a feeling they would put sentries there, because they can see the whole valley to the north and east with their long glass. Below us, there is a hill, and two sentries are there, too. They can see anyone moving in, but I think there is a way to fool them. We have some Long Knife horses, a few bays and sorrels like theirs," he said. "Perhaps we can use a few, four or so, to get in close to their herd. Some of you can dress in white-man clothes and slowly move in around sundown, walking with the Long Knife horses."

Crazy Horse smiled. "Yes. Good thinking, Uncle. Then we drive away as many of theirs as we can. Some of the men can help drive the herd, and some with guns can slow down any pursuers."

Cloud motioned toward their horses in the gully. "Yellow Wolf can ride anything. I was thinking," he said to Crazy Horse, "that you, him, and your brother and me can sneak into the herd, starting just before sundown, when the shadows are long."

"A good plan," said Crazy Horse. "I think it will work."

Grey Bull chuckled. "It will work, I know it. I will be one of those hiding and waiting and hoping that some of the Long Knives chase you."

Cloud glanced up at the sun hovering just above the western ridges. "Tonight, we can explain our plan. If we start early in the morning, we can be in place by early afternoon. The less we move, the less chance of anyone spotting us, or, especially, our horses."

Crazy Horse nodded. "Yes."

He motioned toward his younger brother. "We can meet you at the creek next to your camp at sunup. I will bring six men besides the two of us."

On the way home, northward to the villages along the Tongue, all nine riders stayed inside the tree line until they came to Goose Creek. As they stopped to water the horses, Cloud approached Rabbit. As usual, the boy was apart from everyone else.

"Do you want to be a part of the raid tomorrow?" Cloud asked.

The boy's eyes widened. He nodded slowly.

"Good. We will take as many as we can, and we will need to drive them fast east and then north through the valleys. I have a fast little mare you can ride."

"Thank you."

"She is broke to the gun as well. I trained her myself. But there is one thing I want you to do: have High Eagle look at your arm tonight."

"Yes, I will."

"Good. I will bring the horse to your lodge this evening. You can tie her there overnight."

———————————————

High Back Bone, a Mniconju Lakota, known better as Hump, was the same kind of man as his friend Grey Bull. They were veteran fighting men with nothing but disdain for white people, especially soldiers. At the moment, he was holding his anger in check, only because he was a guest at the lodge of Black Shield. Hump respected the older man and he was not angry with him, only at the news he had just heard.

"We have often faced the Long Knives when there were more of them, and they are always better armed," he said, knowing he was not stating anything new to Black Shield. "And when did talking to them ever do us any good? It sounds to me like someone wants the glory for getting rid of them single-handedly."

Black Shield smiled. It was a smile that told the younger man that he had correctly assessed the situation.

"We cannot wait," said Hump. "Cloud followed the Long Knives from the outpost on the lower Powder. He and his young men were ready to do something two days ago. Crazy Horse feels the same. They went to watch the Long Knives today. Who will stop them if they decide to do anything?"

"You know as well as I do, no one is foolish

enough to get in their way. A few might grumble among themselves."

Hump stood. There was an air of strength and competence about him. He was a physically powerful man still in the prime of life. "I will help them. I have a feeling there will be something tomorrow."

"That will be good," said Black Shield. "Those Long Knives should not think we are afraid of them."

———————————

Sweetwater Woman put a slice of roasted elk, a cup of tea, and a toy bow at her husband's elbow as he finished counting the bullets for his rifle, then she waited demurely on her chair. Light poured in through the open door, even though the sun had just gone down. The enticing aroma of the meat got his attention, and he glanced down at the wooden dish. A slight frown wrinkled his brow when he noticed the tiny bow. He lifted a glance toward his wife. A flush on her cheeks made his stomach flutter.

"There—there must be a very small being around here to use—to use that little bow," he stammered.

"There will be," she whispered, and nervously cleared her throat.

He felt his own face grow warm, and he quickly put aside the bag of bullets. "Ah," he said, staring at the toy bow, "does this mean that—ah, that—?"

A hand went to her chest as she nodded, her eyes

misting a little.

Cloud scrambled from his seat and was at her side, a smile spreading across his face. "When?"

"Grandmother Willow thinks during the Middle of Winter Moon," she replied softly.

No words came to mind, so all he could do was take her tiny, pale hands in his.

"Grandmother is so happy," Sweetwater told him. "She was there when you were born and cannot wait to help your son come into the world."

He could only nod. After a moment, he finally spoke. "I will be—I will try to be a good father." He cringed inwardly. It was weak and did not measure up to the happiness obvious on her face.

"You are like your father, Grandmother told me. She said he was a very good father."

"I know this for sure," he said. "Our child will be—is blessed to have you as his mother." He could think of no further words to match the emotions rising in him, and all he could think to do was to hold his wife. Her soft breath against his neck was strangely reassuring. After several long moments, he reluctantly moved away.

Cloud went out to find his grandmother. She was by the fire, stirring a pot of simmering chokecherries. She had lost her only son and a daughter-in-law to sickness of the bowels, the cholera. Yet there was a quiet strength in her frail being that he envied.

"Grandmother," he said gently, taking a seat nearby

as Sweetwater emerged from the lodge, "I am happy to know you will be there to bring our child into the world."

"My life has been good," she said. "I watched my son grow into a good man, and then you as well. Now I will hold your son in my arms. To be grandmother to the child of my grandson is a sacred thing. But you have a more important task: it is your responsibility to leave him a good trail to follow."

There was a different sense he could not label or describe about Sweetwater's presence as he lay next to her that night. His grandmother's words echoed in his head as he drifted off to sleep. They were still on his mind in the cool air of the new dawn as he tied the weapons on the neck rope of the sturdy chestnut gelding. Sweetwater Woman came with a bag of food and flasks of water. Her face seemed to glow, even in the gray light, causing a pang of anxiety in Cloud. For the first time in his years as a warrior, he felt a tinge of uncertainty. He was not uncertain about his abilities as a fighting man, however, but about something larger—his mortality.

His mother and grandmother had both reminded him now and then of the necessity of the warrior in the Lakota way of life. "Better to lay a warrior naked in death," they had said to him, "than to be wrapped up well with a heart of water inside."

The same words had been spoken by generations of mothers and grandmothers to sons and grandsons so that the nation would remain strong. And the nation was strong, but often it was a strength born of the grief of widows and fatherless children.

Cloud finished his task and took the food and water from his wife. "We will be home after dark," he said, "with a large herd of horses and mules, if we are lucky." As soon as he had spoken the words, the objective for the day did not seem as important as it had the day before.

Before he could say anything more, Rabbit, Yellow Wolf, and the others arrived, leading their horses. Grey Bull had managed to gather articles of white-man's clothing, which he had stuffed in a bag.

Cloud drew his wife close and held her. If anything happened to him, he would remember the softness of her cheek against his face. *Why had that thought passed through my mind?* he wondered.

———————

He was still thinking about Sweetwater Woman as he waited in a thicket east of Buffalo Creek and the Long Knife tent town. The sun was just above the western ridges. Some distance south of him, he could catch glimpses of Yellow Wolf, but only because he knew where to look for him. Crazy Horse and Little Hawk might as well have been trees for all he could see of them. It was all good. The moment the sun slipped behind the ridges, the four of them would slip toward the herd of mules and horses in the wide meadow to the west.

Cloud scrutinized the tall sorrel gelding he had brought with him. He was from Grey Bull's herd, an older and quiet horse. Grey Bull had put the headstall with the iron bit on him because the horse responded better to it. As far as Cloud was concerned, the iron bits were hard on a horse's mouth. He knew nothing of how whites trained their horses, but there were gentler ways to control a horse than iron bits. They were harsh and unnecessary. He looked down at the faded red shirt and dark gray wool trousers he had put on; at least they were comfortable. He felt sorry for the horse. As his gaze lingered on the trousers, he thought of his wife.

She was only two years old, or so most thought, when she had been found wandering alone in a desolate area north of the Sweetwater River. The Sweetwater was south of Elk Mountain and along the road the wagons used—the Oregon Trail. Two Lakota scouts watching the wagons noticed something moving along an old game trail. They had thought it was a fawn, especially after they heard what they thought was the bleating that fawns make. When they closed in, they were utterly astonished to find a little white child so very far from the line of wagons that had already passed. The child was happy to see them, but they were not about to take her back to the wagon people, so they did the only thing they could: they brought her home with them.

After the scouts told their story, the people began calling her Fawn. When she had her woman's ceremony years later, she was given the name Sweetwater Woman. As far as her adoptive parents were concerned, she had been born to them near the Sweetwater River.

Cloud allowed thoughts of his wife to linger and wondered what their child would look like. A sense of caution suddenly crept in, unexpectedly, and with an effort he returned his attention to the task at hand. He had always been cautious any time there was danger, but it was without thought. It was part of his nature as a fighting man. Now the thought was there like a pebble in his moccasin, seemingly of its own accord. After a deep breath, he looked south and picked out Yellow Wolf hidden in a plum thicket. To the west, half of the sun was behind a ridge. It was time to move toward the herd of Long Knife horses and mules. He stood and patted the horse's neck.

Two gullies to the south, Crazy Horse watched the sun slipping behind the ridge. The land east of the foothills suddenly fell into deep shadow. It was time to move.

He wore a gray wool shirt that chafed his skin and blue trousers that once belonged to a soldier. A big bay was his choice of a mount, one that he had found running loose after the revenge raid on Julesburg almost two years past. That had been after the Long Knives had attacked the Blue Clouds and Cheyenne at Sand Creek.

The clothes felt strange, but the horse was a good one. He tucked his long braids behind the collar of his shirt and led the horse up the slight incline out of the gully. The horse's ears perked forward as he caught the scent of the herd in the distance.

Farther to the south, Yellow Wolf and Little Hawk watched the sun go down and emerged from hiding. Little Hawk had been in among some rocks, and Yellow Wolf was in a plum thicket to the north of him. Both were dressed in white-man's clothing, following Grey Bull's advice. Yellow Wolf had a blue roan mare and Little Hawk a sorrel with no white markings.

None of the four—Cloud, Crazy Horse, Yellow Wolf, or Little Hawk—carried a firearm. Their task was to infiltrate the Long Knife herd and drive the horses and mules east, away from the tent town. Staying hidden were Grey Bull, Taken Alive, Goings, and twelve more men, including Rabbit, and they were all armed. Some of them would help drive the herd, and the rest would be the rear guard, to discourage any pursuit.

Rabbit was nervous, but not because of the impending raid. He was looking at three white men who were apparently not part of the Long Knife town. Rabbit had taken a position in an area suggested by Grey Bull. After looking around most of the morning, he had found a crevice between two boulders just high enough to hide him and his horse. Through the afternoon, he had improved his shelter by filling the ends of the openings between the boulders with cut branches. As a result, the boulders looked from a distance like they were choked with shrubs.

Near sunset, the three white men had stopped in

the gully below Rabbit's hiding place and proceeded to make camp. Rabbit could only guess that they had been coming up the Bozeman Road. He had to keep the mare quiet. There was no doubt he could escape if the white men were to spot him, but that would probably spoil the raid. The only thing he could do was wait and watch the sun go down as the whites built a small fire and picketed their horses. Then a plan began to form in his mind. It would only remain to be seen if he had the nerve to carry it through.

West of Rabbit's hiding place and unaware of his predicament, Cloud, Crazy Horse, Yellow Wolf, and Little Hawk, separated widely by trees, hills, and gullies, walked their horses slowly toward the Long Knife herd. Somewhere in the same trees, hills, and gullies, about a dozen Lakota fighting men waited anxiously as the shadows lengthened. But none were more anxious than Rabbit.

CHAPTER SIX

Two Hundred Mules

Although he knew he had to keep an eye on the white men, Rabbit had to resist the urge to duck out of sight. One of them might become curious and look among the boulders that sat only a few paces above their camp. Rabbit knew that Cloud, Crazy Horse, Little Hawk, and Yellow Wolf were slowly working their way toward the Long Knife herd. There was nothing to do but wait for the sound of galloping hooves. That could be soon or sometime in the middle of the night, knowing how patient and relentless Cloud and Crazy Horse both were. To make it worse, the mare was restless, and Rabbit guessed it was due to the cramped space between the boulders.

Shadows on the eastern slopes deepened quickly after the sun dropped behind the ridges. Cloud led his horse across an open area but kept a stand of trees between the herd and himself and his horse. Better to move in as close as possible without being seen, they had all decided. Among the trees ahead, he saw soldiers leading and driving animals north toward the line of wagons. If anyone did happen to spot him, he would simply keep moving forward as though he was looking for something. It would be a gamble, but one that he and the others would have to take because they had no firearms, only knives and war clubs. So far, he estimated he was about a hundred paces from the herd. He knew the others had not been spotted, because the Long Knives had not raised an alarm.

Crazy Horse was directly east of the end of the line of wagons, also about a hundred paces from the herd. Although he knew Cloud was south of him, he had no way of knowing how far or how close.

The plan was that he and Crazy Horse would sneak into the herd with their horses, then the man who was in position first would give a signal, the muted cry of a screech owl. Next, they would cause enough of a commotion to frighten the mules and horses into breaking out of the rope corral before the soldiers could respond. Once the animals were moving, Yellow Wolf and Little Hawk would enter the herd on their horses and help lead them east, or try to. But first, the guards had to be bypassed somehow—or eliminated. Earlier, he and Crazy Horse had decided it would be better to eliminate any guards who might be in the way. The only question was how.

Keeping within the intent of their plan, he and Cloud could decide to make a move if the opportunity arose. When or how that would happen would be a judgment call for either of them. He stood on the left side of the horse and watched the soldiers moving the mules and wagon horses into the temporary rope corral. Grabbing the reins, he walked several paces. Ahead, he saw two aspens side by side, a good place to wait unobtrusively. He led the horse toward them.

Little Hawk led his horse across a dry creek and stopped behind a tall shrub. He wore a blue calico shirt much too large for his slender torso. He had asked his mother to plait his long hair into one braid. Not having a rifle or six-shooter was not to his liking, but he accepted that condition. But he did bring the biggest knife he owned, and a stone-headed war club. Like his older brother, he worried about the impending challenge but rose to meet it once things were set in motion. And like his brother, he was slender and his skin was lighter than usual. In battle, he was every bit as daring. Unlike his brother, he was outgoing and gregarious and laughed easily. But his eyes could turn dark with intensity in a heartbeat. At the moment, he was intense and focused. He decided to wait behind the shrub until something happened. As he settled in, he picked out routes he might follow once Cloud and Crazy Horse began driving the herd. Waiting was not easy, but it bothered him more that several hundred Long Knives in the area had rifles and he did not.

Yellow Wolf had stopped moving as well. He knew he could move closer but decided against it. There was nothing to do now but wait. Stroking his horse's neck, he peered between the trees. The Long Knives had so many horses.

Three hundred paces farther east, Grey Bull had placed six of the young men along a route he could only guess Cloud and Crazy Horse would take. Hump did the same with the other seven. But when they saw the horses moving, all of them could move quickly to block any pursuers behind them. Grey Bull was worried about Rabbit but decided that the boy would probably do well. Besides, there was nothing to be done now.

Rabbit listened intently to the men around the campfire he could not see, though its glow was growing brighter. After a while, he could discern the three voices and was relieved that they seemed inclined to stay near the fire. The aroma of coffee wafted through the evening air. The whites were talking about a town farther north called Virginia City, a place associated with gold.

Rabbit shifted his attention toward the west, but it was impossible to see anything, and there were no sounds that indicated anything was happening. In the deepening dusk, coyotes were barking all around, sounding much closer than they were. Overhead, he heard the strange grunt of a nighthawk diving after insects.

Although there were occasional pauses in the whites' conversation, they talked almost continuously. They kept their voices low, however. Rabbit wondered if they knew they were near the Long Knives' camp. A clink of metal and the fire hissed, followed by an angry curse. Rabbit stroked the horse's nose reassuringly as footsteps came toward the end of the boulder. Then he heard the man relieving himself on the dry ground. In a moment, footsteps returned to the camp.

Anxiety and nervousness, more or less, made him forget the throbbing in his injured arm. High Eagle had soaked and removed the rawhide covering. The skin had started to heal over the stump but still itched fiercely after the covering was gone. He had to keep it clean, the medicine man told him, to keep it from festering. His mother had shortened the sleeves of a light doeskin shirt and had cut long fringes into the ends. As a result, at first glance, the stump was not so obvious. His biggest obstacle was learning to use his left hand. Even loading the gun was still a chore, but he was determined to overcome the clumsiness.

Rabbit reached down slowly and touched the handle of the six-shooter tucked into a narrow sash around his waist. It was entirely possible that something would stop the raid, or that something would go wrong. No matter what might happen, he was faced with two choices: he could stay hidden and do nothing or he could follow through with the plan he had in mind. The six-shooter suddenly seemed to push against his abdomen. It felt cold.

Dusk slid into evening, then night brought on shadowy hues. Dozens and dozens of fires glittered inside the line of wagons placed end to end as a protective wall. Cloud had moved to a clump of young aspen trees. Ahead of him were the rope fence and a soldier standing guard, a soldier armed with a rifle attached to a strap hanging from one shoulder. Cloud wondered how quickly that soldier could bring his rifle up to fire it. One shot in the quiet night air would spoil everything. Where there was one sentry, others were sure to be posted. The question was where, but he guessed they would be spread out along the rope fence. The soldier suddenly turned and yelled at a horse that approached. Cloud realized that the soldiers were there as much to keep the animals inside the flimsy rope fence as to guard against intruders.

He watched the soldier, who was about forty paces away. The sentry was looking into the herd and seemingly not concerned with possible intruders. Cloud studied the area between him and the soldier: tall grass and sagebrush, and fairly level. He spotted a thick and tall cluster of sagebrush halfway to the rope fence and knew what he would do.

For a moment, he stroked the horse's neck and then slowly led him toward the sagebrush cluster, staying on the left side of the horse. Reaching the cluster, he wrapped one long rein around a thick stalk, as if the horse had become entangled. Then he picked out a low spot in a patch of thick grass a few paces behind the horse. He knelt, mimicked a horse's throaty neigh, and ducked down.

The soldier turned, said something, and stared at the horse. In a moment, he approached and did not seem inclined to be cautious. Cloud ducked farther down and silently moved behind a thin bush.

"Hey, fella," the man said, "how did you get through the rope? Got yourself tangled, I see."

The soldier's rifle was still hooked to a strap that hung from one shoulder. He stooped and then knelt to untangle the rein. Cloud slid his heavy stone-headed war club from his belt and silently wove his way through the sagebrush and grass.

He paused behind the soldier only for an instant, to gauge the distance, and then swung. There was a hollow *thunk* as the club head connected with the man's skull just above the right ear, and the soldier slumped forward and fell. Cloud stepped to the startled horse to calm him. Beside them, the soldier's legs twitched and then he was still.

Kneeling, Cloud removed the rifle and bullet pouch. A quick search turned up nothing else of use. He considered taking the coat, but the man was small and it would not fit. He slid the wide black strap over his shoulder in the manner the soldier had worn it. Taking the horse's rein, he walked to the spot where the dead man had been standing and took up a position. Anyone still able to discern him in the rapidly fading light would see a sentry at his post with a loose horse. He was familiar with the rifle and how it worked, so if another soldier approached too closely, he could deal with it.

The next obstacle was the rope fence. It was attached to tripods of thin poles every twenty or thirty paces. The one next to him was surprisingly sturdy when he pulled on it. He decided to cut the ropes and leave a length to tie it off tightly. Farther up the fence, it would still remain tight, he hoped.

He finished the task and stood for a moment to listen. Everything seemed normal, or at least quiet. Voices drifted through the deepening night. He left the horse tied to a thick bush and walked down the fence line, cutting the ropes at the next two tripods, and waited. Off in the shadowy distance, he could make out the form of a man and had to assume it was another soldier. Turning, he silently made his way back to his horse. Wherever Crazy Horse was, it was time for Cloud to move into the herd.

The man Cloud thought might be a soldier watched his shadowy form fade into the distant darkness. Crazy Horse carefully dropped the hammer of the rifle he had taken off the soldier at his feet. The shadow had moved in a way that hinted he was probably not a soldier, but he could not be sure, so he had the rifle ready just in case. He knelt and grabbed the bullet pouch and pressed a finger to the side of the man's neck. The man was dead. Crazy Horse wiped the soldier's blood off his knife blade in the dirt and silently moved up to the rope fence. He was a long stone's throw east of Cloud, though neither of them knew that. Touching the ropes, he felt slack in the line and decided to slice them. *Once the lead horses pushed against it*, he thought, *the fence would easily collapse.* Now it was time to move into the herd. He walked back to the aspen trees and retrieved his horse.

At about the same time, Cloud was leading his

horse slowly into the herd. He could see the long ears of mules perking up inquisitively, but the presence of his horse dispelled any nervousness. Once inside the outer edge of the herd, he worked his way toward the western end. The pungent smell of horse urine was in the air. When he reached the western edge, he would stop and wait and mingle with the herd, giving Crazy Horse time to do the same. Even if he could not see him, Cloud decided that he would somehow startle the animals and push them east past the wagons. Even if he were not in position, there was no doubt Crazy Horse would do his part.

Beyond the wagons, nearly a hundred paces north, he saw the flickering glow of fires and heard voices drift into the air, engaged in conversations he could not comprehend. Somewhere, perhaps a stone's throw away, someone coughed. A sentry, he was certain. He let the horse graze but stayed next to him. Coyotes were barking and howling in the darkness all around, a chorus he knew well. Farther north of the wagons and the tent town was Buffalo Creek, angling southeast before it bent northeast. They would have to cross it with their captured herd and stay to the north of it. Cloud doubted the soldiers could mount an effective pursuit. Even if they did, Grey Bull and Hump and their young men would be waiting.

The rifle was heavy, the strap it was attached to pulling down on his right shoulder. He would have to hold the weapon in order to swing up on the horse, in order to control it. He wondered how the soldiers managed the weight and unwieldiness. Moments passed. His instincts told him it was time.

Cloud cupped a hand over his mouth and softly cleared his throat and attempted the warble of the screech owl. He nearly laughed at how pitiful it sounded. Clearing his throat again as quietly as he could, he tried again. The second attempt was better. Taking a deep breath, he let out a wavering call, satisfied that it was almost like the trembling voice of the tiny owl, and waited.

In a moment, he heard an answer somewhere in the darkness to the east. It had to be Crazy Horse, or a screech owl anxious for a mate. He decided it was Crazy Horse, because it was a short call, not the usual long, almost endless warble a real owl would make. Collecting the reins, he patted the horse's neck and swung up onto its back. The sudden motion caught the attention of a few mules and horses nearby.

Cloud secured his seat, took the rifle with his left hand and leaned the butt of the weapon on his thigh, gathered the reins with his right, and kicked the horse. Hissing softly, he was glad to see the animals closest to him respond and move away. He urged his mount into a slow lope toward the wagons, and when he heard the herd moving away, he spun and headed south. Switching the reins to his left hand, he yanked the war club from his belt and slapped a horse lagging just ahead of him. The resounding *whack* might as well have been a cannon shot. All the mules in front of him bolted. Nearby, he heard a shout and recognized Crazy Horse's voice. So far, so good.

Crazy Horse was mounted as soon as he heard and answered the screech owl call. He let out a low growl, imitating a bear, to startle the mules. The sound of milling mules turned into a steady, low staccato of running hooves. He heard Cloud's shout somewhere behind him and added his war cry to the growing din.

In the span of several heartbeats, panic gripped the herd. Those on the west end pushed their companions ahead. Somewhere at the western edge, Cloud and Crazy Horse maneuvered their horses to stay with the flowing mass. The first frightened and inquisitive shouts from sentries were drowned in the growing rumble of hooves that had now reached a gallop. The chase was on.

The rope fence stretched and snapped, no match for the powerful surge of bodies, sending a few of the tripod supports spinning up into the air as if propelled by a giant's sling. A steady rumble grew immediately into a low thunder as the herd galloped east.

Yellow Wolf heard the thunder and felt it on the soles of his feet and swiftly mounted his runner, the fastest horse he had ever owned. His intention was to move in near the point of the herd and lead them, or at least influence the frightened animals as much as he could into following. Little Hawk would do the same, wherever he was. At the moment, Yellow Wolf's first task was to match the speed of the herd while avoiding obstacles in the dark, such as low branches and sudden holes.

Fortunately, waiting in the darkness had acclimated Little Hawk's vision, and he also paced the herd before he tried to find where the leaders were. The undulating, shadowy flow of the herd was like a black flood, and just as dangerous. If he fell or his horse faltered, they would both be trampled.

Grey Bull also heard the thunder from the ground. His horse whinnied inquisitively. He pushed both pistols securely into his belt and swung onto the anxious bay. The approaching thunder was to his north.

"Get ready!" he shouted into the night, knowing the young men would hear.

Hump was already mounted and behind a thicket. The growing thunder was to the south of his position. There was nothing to do but wait. He hoped the young men would wait as they were told and attack only if there was any kind of pursuit from the soldiers.

Rabbit knew something was happening. The mare tensed and perked her ears and looked off toward the west. Then he heard the noise, and so did the white men in the little hollow below the boulders. His heart started pounding slightly.

"What is that?" he heard one of them say.

"Somethin' off to the west!" came the reply.

"You s'pose it be buffalo, maybe a stampede? Sounds like that!"

"Whatever it be, gents, I think we best get out of here!"

Rabbit heard boots scuffling and something being dragged over the ground. As though in a daydream, he put his thoughts into motion, driven by the sudden anger that rose like a bad taste and brushed aside any fear.

He yanked out the six-shooter and cocked it then kicked out the shrubs he had shoved in the front opening between the boulders. The motion startled the white men. Rabbit saw white faces in the firelight, wide eyes looking up at him. Without further thought, he pointed the six-shooter at the nearest man and pulled the trigger.

The blast overwhelmed the distant thunder for a moment, and the man doubled over as if kicked by a horse and fell back. Rabbit cocked the hammer and pointed the weapon a second time. The two remaining white men were frozen in place as the second shot blasted the night and the second man spun and fell. Rabbit felt the jolt of the recoil up his arm and cocked the six-shooter again. He jumped down the slight slope, surprised that the third man could only stare at him, his bearded face agape in fear. The gun boomed again. This time, Rabbit saw blood spurt from the third man's neck even as he fell back. Then all he heard was the nervous stomping of the mare still inside the boulder crevice.

The boy looked at the three bodies on the ground around the fire. At the first shot, the dead men's horses had bolted into the darkness. He was breathing hard and suddenly realized the acrid smell was from the six-shooter. It felt hot in his hand. They were dead, he knew it, all of them, and he had killed them. Involuntarily, he glanced down at the stump of his arm. Then he heard the rumble of thunder.

Slashing through the night, the herd thundered east, dodging trees, shrubs, and boulders in the dark. Many stumbled when the ground fell away suddenly into a gully or draw or dry watercourse. Somewhere in the midst, bells attached to some of the mules clanked a strange accompaniment to the thunderous song of flowing power and motion. Grey Bull had to hold tight to his horse as the herd flashed past him and was swiftly gone. He thought he saw a rider or two at the outer edge and heard a faint shout amidst the rumble.

As the rolling thunder of hooves moved past, he turned his attention toward the distant glow of fires from the tent town. Then he heard the hollow thuds of a few hooves that were either stragglers from the herd or soldiers riding in pursuit. A strident shout told him it was not stragglers just as gunfire erupted to the north of him and he saw muzzle flashes from different places in the dark. He guessed it was Hump and his young men shooting at the oncoming soldiers. Before he could join the fray, it was over. The pursuers stopped, an unfamiliar voice shouted, and Grey Bull heard hoofbeats retreating toward the tent town.

In a few moments, he heard the approaching footfalls of a walking horse as Hump materialized out of the night.

"I guess they are smarter than I thought," he joked. "They chose not to pursue too far."

Grey Bull grinned as other riders appeared in the dark to join them. "But I think we should wait here, just in case they decide to be stupid and come back this way."

"That was a big herd," someone said.

"You should hope they do not scatter too far. It will be your task to look for them tomorrow," said Hump half teasingly.

Grey Bull tucked one of his six-shooters back into his belt. "Maybe this will show anyone who is timid that these Long Knives are nothing to be afraid of," he said.

"Just as long as it convinces enough of them," replied Hump.

Farther east, Rabbit waited for several long moments after the last of the herd had passed by. It was dark because several horses had raced past the boulders and trampled the fire—and the bodies of the white men. He thought to search for their weapons but guessed they would be trampled as well. Throughout the stampede, he had stayed in the relative safety of the boulders but had to work hard to keep the little mare calm.

He led the mare out of the crevice and down into the now-trampled hollow. She snorted at the scent of dead bodies and shied away slightly. The herd was now a faint rumble farther to the east, and there had been no further gunshots from the west, where Hump and Grey Bull and the others had been. With an effort, he swung onto the horse from the right side. He decided to follow after the herd and away from the tents because he had only three shots left in his six-shooter.

Rabbit urged the mare into a fast walk, wondering at the sudden hollowness in the pit of his stomach.

CHAPTER SEVEN

Log Walls

Cloud looked up into the bright autumn sky, toward a persistent chirping, and spotted a group of split-tails swarming a lone raven, driving the bigger bird farther away from their nests among the rocks on one of the peaks in the Shining Mountains. He smiled as the big black bird twisted and turned to get away from the smaller, quicker swallows. It finally yielded and dove for the protection of the tree line along the mountain slope.

Cloud heard a soft chuckle nearby and realized that his wife had also been watching the fight in the sky. He pointed to the top of the ridge above them.

"We are nearly there," he told her.

Cool air clung to the slopes on this autumn day, and he wore a shirt of tanned deer hide, along with elk-hide leggings, breechclout, and moccasins. Sweetwater wore one of her finer deer-hide dresses, adorned with two rows of elk teeth around the shoulders. As befitted a modest married woman, she wore calf-high leggings above the moccasins, covered with fine quillwork, on her small feet. Across the withers of her horse, she had draped a finely tanned elk robe, in case the mountain air turned chilly.

She nodded and smiled, shifting a little to find a more comfortable position atop her horse to accommodate her expanding abdomen.

Near the crest, Cloud stopped and pulled out the binoculars he had found last year during the Battle of Platte River Bridge, below Elk Mountain along the Shell River. He would always remember that day because High Back Wolf, the noted Cheyenne warrior, had been killed charging the Long Knives alone. Cloud let the memory slip from his mind and turned his attention to the valley floor to the southeast, looking along the road used by the woodcutters from the fort along Buffalo Creek. Now, nearly three months since the two hundred mules and horses were taken, the Lakota were very familiar with the Long Knives' routine of sending out wagons and outriders to cut wood in the pine-covered foothills. But today, there were no soldiers or woodcutters to be seen. Returning the binoculars to their case, Cloud slid from his horse to help Sweetwater dismount. He folded her robe and placed it atop a low boulder, where she took a seat.

It was nearly the middle of the afternoon. They had started in the early morning from their village half a day's ride to the north, nestled in one of the wide gullies that opened onto the Tongue River valley. In another month, the people would move farther down the Tongue into the deeper gullies for better protection against the coming winter winds. They would divide into two encampments for the winter. Before the move, Cloud wanted to observe the fort from the western slopes of the Shining Mountains, while they were still only a half day's ride away from it. He and Crazy Horse had agreed to meet and talk as well.

Sweetwater had insisted on accompanying him, and he saw no reason to deny her. Following old hunting trails he guessed were unknown to the Long Knives and hunters from the fort, they came to the foothills north of Goose Creek. After that, they stayed inside the tree line until they found the ridge he wanted to climb.

Cloud swept the closest slopes with a swift, penetrating gaze before tying the horses to the trunk of a young aspen, satisfied that there was no imminent threat. But he also knew that the Long Knives, or any of the whites from the fort, for that matter, never came this high on the slopes. It was too far from the safety of the log walls. He untied the elk-hide case with the rifle inside from the neck rope of his horse and placed it in the crook of his right arm. The encased bow, and a quiver filled with iron-tipped arrows, he left hanging from the horse's neck rope. At his left hip was a large iron-bladed knife with its elk-horn handle in a porcupine-quill sheath.

Sweetwater watched her husband. He was what every Lakota man was bred to be: a hunter and a fighting man. His face, burned a deeper brown by the sun, gave him an aura of strength, which was by no means an illusion. He was a good man and had, at first, endured some criticism for taking her as his wife. But he had paid no attention to the whisperings of the gossipers, because his grandmother Willow had warned him that would happen.

Cloud reached for his wife's hand as he sat next to her, leaning the encased rifle against his right leg. He pointed to a spot down in the hazy reaches of the valley to the southeast. There, sunlight flashed momentarily on the surface of Buffalo Creek. On the opposite side of the valley, farther than any arrow or bullet could reach, were the undulating ridges of several high, grassy hills. Just beyond them was an old buffalo jump on a low bluff above Buffalo Creek. The Lakota had called it that because of the buffalo bones scattered about in the creek bottom. Hunters who had lived in the area many generations before them had chased buffalo off the low bluff and then butchered them in the gully below. Far beyond that, to the east, were the great, grassy prairies stretching endlessly, it seemed, until they reached the Great Muddy River, the eastern edge of Lakota territory.

Only twice in his life, the first time around the age of seventeen with his father, had Cloud traveled to the Great Muddy to visit with his Sicangu Lakota relatives. Then when his father died, two years ago, Cloud had taken his body back to the prairies of his birth, as he had wished.

On those prairies, herds of buffalo still shook the land when they ran, though they were not as numerous as they once were. That was a consequence of the intrusion of the white people. Aside from the Long Knives, there was disturbing new information about another kind of white man. They had powerful rifles that could shoot from one hilltop to another, and they killed buffalo. Hide Men, the Lakota called them, because they took only the hides and left the carcasses to rot. They were said to be able to kill one or two hundred buffalo in one day, a waste beyond imagination. That was only one of many reasons the Lakota wanted to drive the white men out.

The western border of Lakota territory was the Shining Mountains, and they were the last best hunting grounds. Deer and elk were plentiful in the region, but especially in the mountains and foothills, as were bighorn sheep.

It was just east of these mountains that a white man called Bozeman had laid out a trail heading north from the Shell River, eventually cutting across the Powder and Tongue rivers, then bending northwest from the Shining Mountains, past the Crow and on into the territory of the Blackfeet people. The Bozeman Trail was new to the whites but long known to the Lakota as the Powder River Road. But, of course, the whites called it a name that suited them. It was the road that took them to the gold in the mountains west of the Elk River. But that did not matter as much as the fact that it cut through the heart of Lakota lands. The town of log walls along Buffalo Creek was built to help and protect the gold seekers.

Rabbit had somehow learned that the pine-walled little town was called Fort Philip Kearny. No matter the name, it was like a thorn embedded firmly into a palm, and as hard to pull out. Lakota fighting men had already died from clashes with the Long Knives and with other whites traveling up the Powder River Road. But in spite of the loss of two hundred mules and some horses when Cloud and Crazy Horse had led the raid in the Moon When the Sun Stands in the Middle, nearly three months ago, the Long Knives had stayed. No matter the amount of harassment the Lakota had heaped on them since then, they could not drive them out. The problem was twofold, as Crazy Horse and Cloud and other warrior leaders saw it: the Lakota and their Cheyenne allies did not have enough guns and ammunition, and the Long Knives would not come out of their fort to fight a prolonged battle.

In the afternoon shadows of the broad valley below them, they could see the dark spot that was the stronghold of the Long Knives. It had been there since the Moon When the Sun Stands in the Middle. They had come in wagons piled high with their tools and belongings and built it, even while their leaders were pretending to ask for permission to build forts in Lakota territory. Now here they were, because gold was important to the whites. Perhaps it was one of their gods, old Bear Looks Behind had said.

Cloud looked thoughtfully at his wife, wondering if she could remember enough of her previous life as a white child to explain why gold was so important. He decided not to ask. For all intents and purposes, only her skin was white now.

Sweetwater had forgotten the language she had spoken as a child before the two Lakota scouts had found her wandering alone near the Sweetwater River. Now she was just as concerned as any Lakota over this continuing, annoying intrusion into their lands and into their lives. In her light-brown eyes were worry and confusion, especially after she picked out the lines of the fort's walls.

"Nothing to worry about," Cloud assured her. "We are too far away."

Cloud looked solemnly at the ground for a moment before he spoke again, his voice hoarse. "Killing is—it is not something I enjoy, but I will kill Long Knives if it is the only way to drive them out of our country."

The young woman grabbed her husband's arm. "Grandmother Willow thinks they are strange, as humans go. I wonder if I was strange, too, before I came to live with our people."

Cloud liked the sensation of her touch, and always had. He stole a glance. She had grown into a beautiful woman. Bright reddish brown hair hung in two proper married-woman's braids, with errant strands circling an oval face with a straight, slender, turned-up nose. Her full mouth turned easily into a smile. Her laugh was like the soft murmurs from the rock-filled Buffalo Creek.

"You were not strange," he recalled, "but you did have gangly legs, like a newborn colt, when you were a young girl. But you were never strange."

She returned his smile, squinting slightly in the bright sun, then lowered her head to his shoulder. They sat that way for many long moments.

The moment ended with the deep, distant *boom* of a cannon—a wagon gun.

The blast came from the fort. Cloud waited for the telltale tearing sound that would have told him the big round shell was coming in their direction. But there was nothing. Besides, the fort was much too far for even a wagon gun to reach them. Still, the soldiers did like to fire it now and then, perhaps to reassure themselves that they had some kind of power.

Cloud turned a mocking eye away from the distant fort, down to his wife's tiny feet, and removed a burr from the side of her left moccasin. Then he took out the binoculars to see if any soldiers would emerge from the fort.

"I heard that Red Cloud sent word to the Long Knives at Fort Laramie," he said to Sweetwater. "He tells them, 'We are standing on the mountains looking down at the soldiers, waiting for them to leave.' He says he will keep sending that message until they do leave, or we drive them out. He wants them to leave Buffalo Creek, and the fort on the Powder River to the south, and the one to the north. As if words will do any good," he added.

Sweetwater shuddered slightly. "I feel confused sometimes," she said. "This is a good time and a bad time at the same time. Bad because of the Long Knives and their people." She paused to look around at the pine-covered slopes. "And good because we live in the most beautiful place on Earth." Looking down, she placed a hand over her abdomen. "I hope our child will be born here. There can be no better place to come into this world."

"Yes," Cloud agreed. "These Shining Mountains

are like the Black Hills. The Black Hills are the center of our world, and these mountains are at the end of our world. I will fight to keep them."

Sweetwater looked into her husband's eyes and saw the grim determination and knew the level of his commitment as a fighting man, the warrior. She pushed the worst possibility out of her mind. Several Lakota men had been killed or wounded already. She did not want him to die. She wanted to grow old with him in this beautiful place.

"Is it true," she asked, "that your cousin Goings wants to go elk hunting to the south?"

He smiled, his eyes sparkling, and nodded. "Yes," he replied. "His first wife has run out of hides to tan. When that happens, he fears for his own hide. So he needs to go hunting. But Taken Alive says we should take our families along, like hunters sometimes did in the old days. I told them both it was a good idea. So maybe in a day or two, we will go. I hear the elk are thick as ants below The Old Man in the Clouds. We will go there, I think."

"What about whites?"

"The Long Knives mostly stay in the fort, and those who come up the Powder River Road have a tendency not to wander too far from it," Cloud said, a chill in his voice. "They are too afraid of anything they do not know, and they shoot before they think. The noise of their guns will tell us where they are."

Sweetwater Woman was reassured. Cloud was a skillful hunter. His family ate and dressed well. But the twenty-three eagle feathers he had earned in battle attested to his ability as a fighting man. Goings and Taken Alive were the same. The hunters and their families would be safe.

She glanced to the west and saw afternoon clouds just over the horizon, like a group of warriors peeking over a hill. She pointed to the binoculars and he handed them to her. Lifting them to her eyes, she searched through the shadowy valley until she picked out the fort. From this distance, even with the glass, it was hard to see anything in detail. But she could make out the upright pine-log walls.

There was one very tall pole inside, much taller than any lodge pole she had ever seen. From it hung the Long Knives' large cloth banner, though she did not know what it meant. Perhaps it was the story of their intrusion into Lakota lands, and into the lands of other people as well. Grandmother Willow had told her that they were like the giant who ate everything and everyone because his hunger was so great. He ate even those who had befriended him. Eventually, he ate everyone and everything, and so he died of loneliness.

She could see a little movement inside the fort, men and horses mostly. Knowing that the Long Knives had brought women and children along, she wondered if she looked like them. But that did not matter. She had lost touch with that part of herself long ago. The feelings in her heart were Lakota, as were her thoughts and words and dreams.

Cloud surveyed the valley floor. Nothing was

moving along the creek beds and groves of pine, oak, and willows. Far to the north, along Lodge Trail Ridge, he could see tiny dark specks on its crest. Lakota scouts, watching and waiting, and hoping for soldiers to leave the protective walls of the fort.

A movement below them caught his eye, prompting him to touch Sweetwater's arm in a warning gesture, even as he pulled the heavy rifle out of its case. He heard her slight intake of breath, but then she was still.

A man on a horse moved into view between two short pine trees. Cloud recognized him immediately, even at the distance of an arrow's cast, and put away his weapon. In a while, the man appeared again, much closer this time. They could hear a horse's hooves digging into the gravelly slopes as it climbed upward between young pine trees, following the same path they had used. Soon the horse and its rider were just below Cloud and Sweetwater Woman's horses. The man reined in his brown-and-white mare and raised a hand in greeting.

Sweetwater glanced in anticipation at her husband. She knew the man walking up to join them after he had dismounted and tied his horse to a tree.

It was Crazy Horse. He was known as a daring and resourceful fighting man, and also for his contempt for white people. She had seen him in the encampment a few times but stayed away because she was not certain of what he would do if he saw her. There was no way to avoid him now.

He was dressed in a plain shirt as well as leggings and a breechclout. His hair hung in two very long dark-brown braids. Although just past his twenty-fourth year, he was still slender as a boy, and his appearance did not match his reputation as a warrior.

But it was not his reputation that intrigued Sweetwater Woman. It was his fair skin and dark-brown hair. Lakota were brown skinned and their hair was black. She wondered if she had something in common with him but let the thought go as soon as it had come. According to Grandmother Willow, Crazy Horse's parents were both Lakota. On his father's side, he was Oglala Lakota, and his mother had been a Mniconju Lakota. His eyes were dark brown and burned with the same determination she saw in her husband's eyes.

Cloud stood to greet his friend. In a moment, both men leaned on their rifles, staring down into the valley at the fort that was like a bothersome boil on a beautiful face.

"They stay in their houses today," observed Crazy Horse.

"Yes," replied Cloud. "Perhaps it is their seventh day, the day the Cheyenne say they pray to their gods."

Crazy Horse smiled wryly. "They are hard to understand, at least for me. It would seem that they would be happy in their own towns, far back to the east. Why do they come here, I wonder, when they are afraid of anything outside their town?"

Cloud glanced at his wife before he replied. "As the old ones have told us, the whites have always been difficult to understand, and what they do makes them easy to despise."

A shadow came into the eyes of Crazy Horse. "True, I will never forget the mutilated bodies of women and children Woman Killer Harney left at the Blue Water eleven years ago. But there is something else that bothers me just as much," he said. "The first time I saw them was along the Shell River, when I was ten. Hump took me there to watch the wagons going west. They were hard to count, there were so many of them. Every summer now since then, those wagons have come, full of them. I am afraid there are more of them than there are of us."

It was well known that young Crazy Horse, as a fourteen year-old boy, had been the first to find what was left of Little Thunder's camp on the Blue Water on the southwest edge of Sicangu Lakota lands. A Long Knife general by the name of Harney had burned and pillaged the camp to avenge the killing of other Long Knives a year before.

In a moment, the man's face softened and he acknowledged Sweetwater Woman with a brief glance.

"Sister," he said, "I hope you know that my words were not meant for you."

Sweetwater nodded.

"I am glad to hear that you are bringing another Lakota into the world," Crazy Horse added. "We need more true human beings."

She felt her face grow hot and she reached for her husband's hand.

Cloud squeezed his wife's tiny, pale hand and clung to it.

"My friend," he said to the younger man, "we appreciate what you said. Like you, I am thankful to be Lakota. We must do what it takes to defend ourselves."

Crazy Horse nodded slowly. "True," he said. "There must always be Lakota in this world. The land would be lonely without us."

The two men stared grimly down into the haze at the dark blot on the land that was the Long Knives' fort. Together and separately, they had led raid after raid against the Long Knives as well as against travelers on the trail itself. But like a turtle stupidly impervious to the threat of a badger, the whites had plodded on. Lakota warriors did not lack for determination and courage. Lack of firearms and adequate ammunition for those they did have was a nagging problem, more so than many were willing to admit. Relying on their abilities as guerrilla fighters, they had been able to inflict casualties and create problems, but not enough to drive out the intruders.

Crazy Horse gestured toward the fort. "We cannot stop," he said. "We have to keep after them. We ride better, we are better fighters, and we know the land. Those are our strengths. They have more guns and bullets; without those things, they would not have any kind of strength. Their strengths are our weaknesses, and our strengths their weaknesses. That is how it is, and we have to turn it into advantage for us. Otherwise, we will not drive them out."

"I want my child to come into a Lakota world," Cloud replied, "and I want him to live strong and happy in a Lakota world. We all want that for our families and our sons and daughters. You are right. We have to keep after them. We cannot let the travelers on the trail sleep peacefully at night. We have to make sure they are afraid we might be behind every tree. They must not know peace when they walk on our lands."

Crazy Horse grabbed a handful of soil. "My father says we will all return to the earth one day. But he wants his bones to lie in soil sanctified by our trails, our footprints. So do I, when my time comes. I do not want this land spoiled by their arrogance."

As if in defiance, another *boom* from the fort broke the stillness of the autumn afternoon.

Crazy Horse unsheathed his rifle and aimed it toward the dark town of log walls. "I may not have many bullets," he said, "but my will to keep this land free of them will only die when I do."

CHAPTER EIGHT

A Nerve-Racking Journey

Clouds always seem to cover the peak that was higher than any other, invoking images of an old man with snow-white hair. For that, Cloud Mountain was also called The Old Man in the Clouds. There, they hunted for eight days.

Goings, Taken Alive, Grey Bull, and their families numbered nearly twenty men, women, and children, including Sweetwater Woman and Cloud. Two of the young men, Yellow Wolf and Little Bird, were unmarried.

The elk were moving down from summer grazing on the high mountain slopes and the hunters killed six, along with four deer. It was a good time. Evenings were spent telling stories around the fires, with the enticing aroma of roasting meat mingling with the laughter of children. The troubles brought by the whites along the Powder River Road seemed to be far away in distance and time.

In the mornings, ghostly wisps of late autumn mists filled the high mountain valleys. During one afternoon, the first thin lines of geese flew over, moving south to their wintering grounds to places many in the group had never seen.

"They are going to lands I will never see," Cloud admitted sadly to Sweetwater as they watched a seemingly endless flock pass overhead in great arrowhead-shaped lines.

They hunted with bows, as their fathers and grandfathers had done for generations untold. Although hunting was somewhat easier with firearms, those weapons were loud. Caution was just as important as food for staying alive. There was no way to know if a white man or two might be in the mountains, waiting to put any Lakota in their gun sights.

On the eighth evening, Cloud returned to camp with a deer hanging over a packhorse. He had stalked it for nearly half a day, finally crawling into sumac shrubs within sixty paces of the young buck. After he had shot an arrow into its chest, he tracked it until nearly sundown and found it dead in a thicket.

Close to camp, the sound of muffled voices and soft laughter chased away the aches of a long day. Just beyond the reach of the orange glow of the fires, a shadow moved through the trees in the dusky light, a shadow with a familiar outline.

Yellow Wolf, taking his turn as sentinel, moved with the silence and stealth of his namesake. The slender warrior flashed a smile of welcome as Cloud waved and continued toward the camp.

The women came forward to help Cloud unload the gutted carcass and hoist it to hang from a bare pole. After picketing his horses on long leads to let them graze, he joined Sweetwater near the fire.

The talk was of going home. They had traveled light, without lodge coverings or poles, and built temporary brush shelters instead—small dome-shaped frames of willow or gooseberry stalks covered over with hides or brush. Six of them stood around the main fire pit. It was a small, neat camp in a secluded meadow.

Behind the circle of shelters but inside the firelight were thirty picketed horses tied to stakes driven into the ground. Two dogs happily dozed near the fire, stuffed with meat scraps. One of them was half coyote and was alert even when she seemed to be asleep. She was a better sentinel than any human could ever be.

Tired from yet another day of carefree play, the children were settling down for the night. Adults sat in family groups in front of their shelters. An evening meal of roasted elk had just been finished. Flames in the center fire pit were low over the bed of red-orange coals, bending and dancing with every breeze that wandered through and mingling with the feeling of contentment hanging in the cool evening air.

Two days of travel had brought them to Cloud Mountain, but it would take three or four days to return to their village on the Tongue River because they would be laden with meat and hides. The Powder River Road would have to be crossed again. They had seen no wagons on their way to Cloud Mountain, but one of the young men scouting ahead had noticed a dust cloud beyond the southern horizon. That would mean wagons or Long Knives or both.

"When we are out of the mountains, we can

strike east, cross the road, and go northeast beyond the foothills," suggested Taken Alive. "As long as we stay away from the road, we will not see any whites, and any on the road will not see us."

Goings agreed, glancing cautiously at the younger of his two wives, who was Cheyenne. Walks in the Night had lost all of her family at a place called Sand Creek, far south of the Shell River in Arapaho country, when Long Knives had attacked her people's village two winters ago. Since then, horrible nightmares woke her frequently during the night. Sometimes they haunted her during the day as well. Now, even the mere sight of a white man, especially a soldier in blue, caused her to tremble and sob uncontrollably.

At Sand Creek, the Long Knives killed anything that moved. Walks in the Night survived because she had crawled into an abandoned beaver lodge and hid. After the Long Knives left, she walked north alone until Cheyenne and Lakota warriors found her a month later, almost dead from starvation and cold. From the beaver lodge, she had seen what the attackers did. First, there was the killing. Then women were scalped in the genitals, breasts were sliced off, and heads, hands, and feet were severed. It was no wonder, many thought, that Walks in the Night always had a frightened look in her eyes. If for her sake alone, Goings wanted to avoid whites.

"By now, our village has moved farther down the Tongue," said Goings. "If we travel east of the Powder

River Road and head straight north, it will be easier to find it."

"Yes," agreed Cloud. "And as long as we stay away from the road, we can avoid encountering any whites by chance."

Taken Alive and Goings murmured in assent.

Grey Bull, tall and dignified, was the oldest man in the group. Dark and knowing eyes, flecks of gray in his long braids, and a deep voice always caught everyone's attention. He motioned toward the racks of drying meat behind the shelters and toward Cloud's gutted deer carcass.

"We have done well," he pointed out. "We have plenty to take back, especially for the people who have no one to hunt for them. We have to be cautious going home, because all that meat will slow us down. My nephew," he said, nodding toward Goings, "is right. We should cross the road quickly. Our two young men can scout to the south to see if travelers may be coming up the trail. If it is safe, we move swiftly." He paused to gaze gently at the children, some of whom were already sleeping. "There are too many precious things here for us to be careless."

Murmurs of agreement came quickly. After a momentary silence, the conversation turned to other things. The low voices and soft laughter of men and women floated up through the tall pines, rising into the cool night air of the Shining Mountains. Somewhere in the deep forest, a bear paused as he heard the strange voices and then turned away from the distant fire glowing in the trees.

On a high ridge to the west, a wolf sent a resonant song into the night, a message that flowed from ridge to ridge. He was telling his relatives that the two-leggeds were still in the mountains.

"We will leave with the sunrise," said Grey Bull.

———————

The next afternoon, two tired and dusty men reined their horses to a stop on the crest of the highest point for miles. They dismounted to loosen saddle girths and allow the horses to rest for a few minutes. There was no shade on the treeless stretch of prairie to offer respite from the relentless sun.

The younger man turned his attention toward a thin column of dust far off to the northeast. He had spotted it earlier. But there were too many rolling hills in between, hiding whatever or whoever was making the dust. *Because it was near the Bozeman Trail, it had to be Indians*, he thought.

Max Hornsby cradled his Kentucky percussion rifle in the crook of his left arm, pulled out his telescope, and looked toward the dust again, deducing that a single rider or even two would not raise such a cloud.

"You suppose it could be a war party?" he asked his companion.

Angus Petersen squinted toward the east for a moment before tipping his broad-brimmed hat back on his balding head. "Nah," he said. "Dust's moving away from us. War party would be shadowing us. Their menfolk, the bucks, behave dif'rently when they's out by themselves. Likely this is a group with squaws and kids—if'n it's Indians at all."

"What tribe?" Hornsby removed his own hat to cool off the top of his head. He envied Petersen the knowledge born of two trips along the Bozeman.

The Bloody Bozeman, a trader at Fort Laramie laughingly told Hornsby, trying to instill fear in a newcomer in hopes of cashing in on it. Travelers heading up the Bozeman were afraid of Indian raids and bought extra bags of black powder and more lead balls and sometimes guns they didn't need. Hornsby replenished the shot and ball supply for his rifle without admitting to himself that the trader's tactic had worked on him.

"Sioux, more'n likely," Petersen replied. "Could be Cheyenne, too. They's in with the Sioux. Crow sometimes come down this far south, but not likely. Them Sioux like to chase after Crow more'n they do us."

Hornsby looked back to the west toward the line of seven large freight wagons, each pulled by teams of plodding oxen and raising their own dust. At a mile's distance, all he could see were dark shapes. Ten armed outriders and seven bullwhackers were nothing but black specks.

"Aren't we a little far from the wagons?" he wondered.

Petersen looked at his horse's front hoof before he

replied. "Could be. But we can see for 'nother mile or so, all 'round us. Somethin' comes, we can get back in a hurry."

Hornsby nodded and looked farther west toward the dark, hazy ridges of the Bighorn Mountains. Clouds sat on one tall summit. The Adirondacks, west of his boyhood home, were foothills in comparison.

The suddenness with which these rolling prairies ended and the abruptness of the jagged Bighorns reaching for the sky bothered the young blacksmith. It fit with everything else in this wild country: sudden heat, sudden cold, sudden death.

Two days ago, one of the bullwhackers had shot himself while toying with his Colt revolver and had died gurgling and coughing as blood bubbled out of the hole in his chest. The train's captain had the man buried practically where he had died. And the wagons rolled on, the captain with a new gun in his belt. Suddenly, there was one less bullwhacker.

Yet there was also something intriguing here. He had never seen such land full of sagebrush and cacti, dry creeks, swollen rivers, and endless rolling prairies. Furthermore, there was the ever-present sense that something was about to happen, and no one knew what until it did. Like the bullwhacker's accident with his own gun. And the dust cloud hanging in the distance. *Was there sudden death there, too*, Hornsby wondered, *this time in the form of a dark-skinned savage?*

Hornsby looked toward the wagons again. They

seemed not to have moved at all. Like the dust cloud that now seemed to be beckoning.

"Petersen," he said, looking ahead to the next high point to the north, "do you suppose a fellow can get a good look at whatever's making that dust from up there?"

The older man glanced in the direction of Hornsby's point and shrugged. "Could be, could be. Somethin' 'bout that dust got you in a knot, has it?"

Hornsby stroked his beard and narrowed his eyes until their gray color turned dark. "Yeah, guess so."

"Go 'head." Petersen shrugged again. It was as demonstrative as he ever was. "Go 'head and ride up to that next hill. Hell, life's a gamble. See what you can see. You be bettin' your life. Go 'head if you can cover that bet."

Hornsby turned to his horse, a gray, and began tightening the cinch.

Petersen eyed him suspiciously. "You really goin'?"

Hornsby grinned and mounted, pausing only to make sure his powder horn and bullet case were both within easy reach. "Yeah, guess so."

He kicked the horse and reined him around as he heard a torrent of low grumbling and cursing. In a minute, Petersen had caught up.

The next high point revealed nothing worth the effort, only another hill to the northeast. Hornsby could not resist. After a steady trot, they reached it and were now a good mile and a half east of the wagons. Petersen's mood, meanwhile, grew pricklier as the distance from the wagons increased.

"Boy!" he finally said. "This here's 'bout far 'nough!"

Hornsby stopped his horse, yielding reluctantly to the judgment of the more experienced traveler, and stretched out his telescope. It was a sailor's glass, one his father used on the schooner he had captained on the route from Passamaquoddy to Fort Sumter. He found the dust cloud and followed it down, suddenly realizing that he and Petersen had closed in on it more than he thought.

He saw people on horses, and a few of the horses were harnessed with drag poles, all standing against a high bank in an old creek bed. Hornsby tensed, rising up in the stirrups. One of the riders was different.

"Sweet Jesus, Petersen! Indians! And they got a white woman with 'em!"

Angus Petersen leaned over and spat angrily into the dust, on the verge of grabbing the reins to Hornsby's mount. "Damn easterners," he mumbled, forgetting for the moment that he was from Tinbrook, South Carolina. But Hornsby ignored him.

Framed in the circle of the glass, a woman mounted on a small bay turned to face west and confirmed Hornsby's first glimpse. She *was* white! A sudden shadow blotted her from view.

Confused, Hornsby lowered the glass and stared at two distant dark forms that seemed to be moving. A chill up his back came with an unexpected realization.

Two mounted Indians with horses in a flat-out gallop were charging toward him and Petersen! Hornsby sat and stared at the approaching horsemen.

A yell shook him out of his indecision. Petersen leaned over and grabbed the reins to Hornsby's horse and jerked the gray's head around. "Get 'em going, damn you! I knew no good would come of this!"

Hornsby kicked his horse mercilessly, but it was an eternity before the gray stretched out into a gallop. The faint, rapid thuds he heard were hoofbeats behind him, and they were getting louder!

Petersen moved into the lead, leaning low over his horse's neck with the reins in his left hand and a rifle in his right.

Hornsby could see the dark line of wagons to the west. After what he guessed was a two-hundred-yard gallop, they didn't look any closer. Risking a glance over his left shoulder, he did not see Petersen's horse swerve to avoid a cluster of sagebrush.

The gray changed direction slightly to avoid the same bush, throwing Hornsby off balance. He instinctively reached for the saddle pommel with his left hand as he felt himself falling to the right. His other hand grabbed for the horse's mane, and the Kentucky rifle slipped from his fingers. He didn't hear it hit the ground. A few seconds later, with a desperate shout, he lost his tenuous hold on the pommel.

Petersen heard a shout and turned in time to see

Max Hornsby bounce in the dirt and then roll. By the time he jerked his horse to a stop and turned, he was sixty yards past the fallen man.

The two approaching riders were at two hundred yards and closing in swiftly. Petersen measured the odds, hesitated a moment, and savagely kicked his horse.

Hornsby struggled to recover his breath as he saw Petersen riding toward him. His gray horse had angled to the right and was running away in a flat-out gallop. A notion to look for his rifle was quickly shattered by the sight of two approaching Indians. And they were a sight, awakening stark fear that he had not felt since childhood. Still, he could not help but gawk at the approaching riders. He had never seen anyone ride with such abandon! Torsos low over their horses, and no saddles that he could see! Dust billowed upward from the hooves of the Indian horses like a rolling flash flood. Disregarding the pain in his right knee, he scrambled to his feet and forced himself to stumble toward the approaching Petersen.

It seemed to take minutes for Hornsby to climb onto the horse behind Petersen as the relentless staccato of approaching hoofbeats grew louder.

———

Cloud raised his arm, motioning for a halt. He and Yellow Wolf slowed their warhorses and stopped to watch the two white men on one horse become smaller and smaller. A long arrow-cast ahead, dust spurted from the ground, followed by the distant, muffled boom of a rifle. Someone from the wagon train had wasted a bullet on a long, long shot.

By the time the two fleeing white men reached the line of wagons and joined the other small black specks, the two warhorses had found their second wind. But Cloud waited to see if anyone would ride out to challenge them. Although dark figures gathered in small clusters near one of the front wagons, no riders came toward them.

Another spurt of dust erupted from the ground, this time to the right and far short of the first shot. But it was just another wasted bullet. The dull, distant pop of the gunshot was a few heartbeats behind. Cloud and Yellow Wolf saw men galloping horses back and forth along the line of wagons. Soon some of the rear wagons were moved up. Cloud surmised they were preparing to defend themselves from attack. The horse without a rider had reached the wagons.

Cloud pointed. "They will not come after us. They think there are more of us and that we will attack. Good! Grey Bull can keep the others moving north. We will stay here and make the white men wonder what we are up to."

Cloud looked up at the sun. It was in the afternoon half of the sky, still well above the mountains. "When the sun is closer to the skyline of the mountains, we will leave," he told the younger man.

Yellow Wolf nodded and shifted to sit more

comfortably atop his bay gelding. A glint of light on the ground, almost like the sudden sparkle of sunlight on water, caught his eye. "Uncle, do you see that?" He pointed and rode toward it.

Yellow Wolf urged his horse forward and was soon smiling broadly, looking down near the front hoof of his horse. Dismounting, he reached toward the grass. In the next instant, he lifted a rifle over his head.

Cloud smiled as the younger man trotted back with his unexpected prize, leading his horse.

Stopping next to Cloud, he inspected the rifle closely and approvingly. It was not an old piece. He brushed off the dust and inspected the size of the muzzle. "The mouth looks like the same size as your rifle," he said, handing it up to Cloud.

"Yes, I think so, so it should use the same size bullets. Taken Alive has one like this," he said. "But either of us will be glad to show you how to use it." He gave the weapon back to Yellow Wolf.

The young man could not believe his good luck. "It is good of the white men to leave this here for me," he said, turning toward the line of wagons in the distance. "Thank you!" he shouted. "I will repay your kindness with your gift!"

Holding the weapon aloft, he let out a yell of victory.

Cloud smiled at the antics of the younger warrior. But there was one less weapon in the hands of white men.

Yellow Wolf swung back onto his horse, his face flush with happiness over his new weapon. One more Lakota had a powerful weapon.

They watched in amusement as the wagons in the distance finished forming into a circle.

"What are they doing?" asked Yellow Wolf.

"Watching and waiting. They probably think there are more of us in the gullies and hills. So they will sit there looking at us over their guns."

"Who are these people? Are they—are they really people?" Yellow Wolf wanted to know.

"I guess that is the question. I think that nobody knows, at least not any of our people. Some of us, like my cousin Rabbit, may have learned their language, but that means nothing. One of our men has become important to them, but even he does not know what they are really are."

Yellow Wolf glanced thoughtfully at Cloud. "Are you talking about Red Cloud?"

"Yes. I think he thinks he can understand what they are, but I am not so sure. I think they talk to him because he is the only one who listens to them." Cloud shrugged. "But that is only my opinion. No matter what Red Cloud thinks or says, those people will follow that road to find the gold. That is why the Long Knives built the town with log walls, to help those who seek gold. That means we will have to keep fighting them, the Long Knives and the gold seekers, because they do not care that this is our home."

Yellow Wolf thought for a moment. "I have a gun now and I will find bullets and powder. I will fight."

Cloud nodded. "When a rattlesnake crawls into your lodge the first time, you grab it and toss it out into the grass beyond the village. When it crawls into your lodge a second time, what do you do?"

The younger man rubbed the wooden stock of his new rifle. "Kill it," he replied.

Cloud stared toward the distant circle of wagons and nodded slowly.

———————

Captain Highsmith and Petersen found Hornsby reclined against a wagon wheel, nursing a sore shoulder. "Damn fortunate you lost only your rifle," scolded the captain. "Your horse came back."

Hornsby quickly deduced that Petersen had been quick to divest himself of any blame for the incident, especially after the captain's next remark.

"White woman or not, you got no call to put us in danger!"

Hornsby nodded. It was no use to protest and risk being ousted from the train. A white man alone in this desert wilderness was as good as dead, especially one poorly armed.

"I saw you had a six-shooter. If you still have it, best you prime it and prepare yourself. No telling what them heathens'll do!"

Hornsby nodded meekly and rose stiffly to his feet. The fall from his horse had jolted him more than he realized. "Yes, sir," he mumbled.

After the captain and Petersen left, he found his pistol in the saddlebag on his horse then lifted his glass toward the two horsemen on the distant rise. Anger rose like bile when he saw that both were carrying rifles, one of which looked like a Kentucky long rifle.

The two horsemen dismounted and sat on the ground but did not relinquish their position, forcing the nineteen men in the wagon train to keep their weapons ready as the sun went down and night came. Coyotes, wolves, and owls began their jabbering as darkness fell. On the captain's orders, half the company kept watch for half the night and the other half until the dawn finally broke. The two dark horsemen were gone.

The men with the wagons watched the sun climb into another cloudless sky.

Around mid-morning, the captain finally ordered the wagons to roll, but nineteen pairs of tired, wary eyes watched every gully, every bush, and every knoll where Indians were likely to hide.

The day fell into night once more, and the travelers stopped and made a cold, fireless camp. No one slept for more than an hour or two, fully expecting the night to erupt with gunfire or the piercing war cries of unseen savages. Morning brought a sense of relief, soon replaced with the relentless anticipation of hordes of dark-skinned riders swooping over the horizon. A merciless sun followed the cold night, and by the next sundown, they were rolling through the main gate of Fort Philip Kearny. It was the most nerve-racking journey any of them would ever make.

CHAPTER NINE

The Trader

Max Hornsby scoured the old Hawken muzzleloader with a sullen eye. Two weeks of helping the post blacksmith and a five-dollar gold piece from his hidden savings was the price for the old .50 caliber, but it did put him back among the ranks of the adequately armed. He did have his cap-and-ball six-shooter, but it had a very limited range and its accuracy was nothing to brag about.

In his considered opinion, being armed only with a pistol in this country was not much better than spitting. He preferred the heft and feel of a rifle, not to mention its far greater range and knockdown power. Besides, carrying a rifle gave a man the feeling of being armed.

Angus Petersen and the wagon train he was guiding had gone on toward the northern end of the Bighorns where a new outpost, Fort C. F. Smith, had been built. They had stopped at Fort Phil Kearny for two days, only long enough to recover their nerve and unload a few supplies. The train captain had requested and was granted an escort to C. F. Smith, so a squad from the Second Cavalry had accompanied them.

Hornsby had chosen to stay. Thanks to his trade as a blacksmith, he had been able to find a little work. More than that, he wanted a reason to stay. His story of seeing the white woman with a group of Indians found any number of sympathetic ears. But when it came to doing something about it, there were no takers.

Colonel Henry Carrington, the post commander, who looked more like a schoolteacher than an army officer, had listened politely. In the end, he had firmly denied Hornsby's request to send soldiers to rescue the woman.

Hornsby looked at his newly acquired old rifle and thought of the admonition from the colonel, the same one he had heard expressed in different ways from other people.

"My guess is, Mr. Hornsby, that by now that woman is well accustomed to her life with the Indians, no matter the circumstances which brought her to them. In any case, it is unthinkable for me to dispatch troops into a dangerous situation because of what you thought you saw in your field glass."

Sitting against the wall just outside the west gate on the northwest end of the fort, Hornsby snorted angrily. To the west were the mountain ridges, dark and forbidding. He could imagine dozens of savages lurking in the shadowy pine forests, waiting to kill. One of them was probably clutching his new Kentucky rifle.

In his mind's eye, he could still see the old mulatto, with graying hair and deep, dark, liquid eyes. The man had apparently been hired by Carrington to do some scouting because he knew about Indians and even had an Indian wife. Or so Hornsby was told.

"Hell," the man had said, "she has turned by now,

boy. If you seen what you say you did. She is one of 'em. Prob'ly had a few youngsters by some buck. I seen it happen. The only thing white about her now, boy, is her skin. No use to worry."

Knuckles whitened as he squeezed the stock of the Hawken. What did that old mulatto really know? He was probably kindly disposed toward Indians, what with his own Indian wife and all. If all he had heard about the man was true.

The stocky young blacksmith squinted up at the mid-afternoon sun. There had to be a way to find out something more about that white woman. Although there was general knowledge about Indian camps to the north along the Tongue River among the inhabitants of Fort Phil Kearny, no one could give Hornsby any details. He wanted to know the number of camps and their exact locations.

Those things he had to know, though he wasn't exactly sure why. Because the army was not about to do anything to rescue the woman; someone else had better consider her well-being.

The jingle of metal caught his ear, and he looked to the northwest. A small detachment of soldiers and a number of the civilian wood-train guards were escorting the wood train back from the pinery. The dark uniforms of the soldiers were clearly visible, even from a distance, as they rode in two lines behind the wagons. An officer off to the side stopped his horse to briefly glass the area behind them. Since the fort had been built, someone had told Hornsby, the Sioux had been constantly harassing the wood detail. Apparently satisfied that no one was behind them, the officer put away his glass and quickly put his mount into a trot.

The clunk of rolling wagons and the jingle of metal grew louder as the column approached the west gate of the fort. Few of the civilian guards or the soldiers looked at the man sitting near the gate as they rode through it, except for the officer. Hornsby stood as the officer stopped and dismounted. He felt himself being intensely scrutinized for a moment before the young lieutenant walked over to extend a gloved hand.

"I am Lieutenant William Bisbee," he said matter-of-factly, "and you are the gentleman who saw a white captive traveling with a band of Indians, I believe."

Hornsby allowed himself a cautious smile as he shook the man's hand. "That I did, Lieutenant. Not that anyone cared."

The lieutenant's eyes narrowed briefly before a slight smile curled the corners of his mouth. His moustache made him appear older. "White captives among Indians are an old story in these parts, sir. I did not catch your name."

"Beg your pardon. Max Hornsby. I came in with the Highsmith train some weeks back."

The lieutenant nodded, still sizing up Hornsby. "Saw you in the smithy's shop. Planning on staying with us?"

Hornsby nodded. "My trade is blacksmithing. Figured I could lend a hand, earn a few dollars and a place to bunk."

Bisbee noticed his mount gazing intently off to the northwest and quickly lifted his glass for a quick visual reconnaissance. "Tell me about the woman you saw," he said, the glass still to his eye.

Caught off guard, Hornsby cleared his throat. "Well," he said, "she definitely was a white woman. Young, I think, with reddish hair."

Still glassing, Bisbee replied, "I have not been here long, but I have seen one or two light-haired Indians. Word is that one of their warriors, fellow by the name of Crazy Horse, has brown hair."

Hornsby stood his ground. Reaching into an inside breast pocket, he pulled out his own glass. "Saw her through this," he told the lieutenant. "Look for yourself."

Lieutenant Bisbee lowered his own glass and looked at the polished-brass-covered telescope in Hornsby's hand. With a nod, he grabbed it and trained it on the same area he had been checking through his army-issue field glass.

"You have my apologies, sir," the officer said after a moment. "I have not seen one this good ever." Collapsing it, he returned it Hornsby. "However, even with that, I am sure you did not see into the mind and heart of that woman."

Perplexed, Hornsby shook his head. "Meaning?"

"White people have been coming onto the frontier for generations," Bisbee said, gazing coolly into the other man's eyes. "Many have died, but not all of them have been killed by Indians or their own ignorance. Some of them have cast their lot *with* Indians. I have heard stories, and I am sure you have as well. I cannot figure, for the life of me, why a self-respecting white man or woman would turn away from a civilized life to wander over this land and live in skin lodges. But some have made that choice.

"I can see that you are certain of what you saw. But can you tell me with equal certainty that the woman you saw was with those Indians against her will?"

Hornsby shuffled his feet uncomfortably and shrugged. "No, no, I cannot. But it bothers me. The thought of a white woman living, ah, cohabiting with one of them."

Lieutenant Bisbee gazed a moment longer at Hornsby before he turned toward his horse. "Bothers me, too," he said. "However, there is little I can do about it. You, on the other hand, are a free agent. You are not bound by orders or by the sad logic of an inexperienced com— Well, you get my drift, do you not?"

Hornsby nodded as the young officer mounted his horse and, with a wave and an enigmatic smile, rode into the fort.

Rabbit could have tossed a stone and hit any one of the men with the big wagons. Tossing a stone was not his intention, however, but he was that close. He had learned the art of invisibility.

He counted eleven men, all armed to the teeth. That was nothing new, nor were their five wagons with high, canvas-covered loads. They were taking supplies to both forts, the one on Buffalo Creek and the other farther north, beyond the Greasy Grass River. One man drove each of the four-mule teams pulling a wagon, and six were mounted guards. All were watchful and nervous, well aware that every soldier column or supply train had been attacked since the forts had been built. Some more than once before they reached their destination. This particular train had stopped to rest the teams. It was just past the middle of a cool autumn day.

Rabbit peered mockingly from beneath the scraggly branches of a long-dead cedar. To any casual observer, it was just a dead tree on a low knoll just above the trail. But Rabbit had seen possibilities. After days of digging, he hollowed out a space large enough for a man to sit or kneel in comfortably. He had left the larger of the dead roots as a frame and covered the opening with brush carefully woven together to look like nothing more than a pile of twigs. Once in the hole, Rabbit had an unobstructed view of the trail for a hundred or more paces in either direction.

This morning, he had spotted the approaching line of wagons. Out in the open, he would be outgunned, and his intention was not to trade shot for shot with them. His experience during the two-hundred-mule raid had taught him a valuable lesson. He found a secluded place to hide his horse and was inside the hole beneath the dead cedar long before the wagons came close.

His original plan was to take one shot and kill one man as the wagons moved past his hiding place. But they had helped him considerably by stopping to rest. Now he could pick his targets based on which one of the white men he disliked the most. Rabbit picked a man with a wide belt around the top of his trousers because he had the jerky mannerisms of a squirrel—not that he had anything against squirrels. Squirrel had been riding on the right side of the wagons, and if he resumed that position, he would be within range of Rabbit's six-shooter.

He had caught bits and pieces of their conversations. They were carrying supplies to Fort Phil Kearny and Fort C. F. Smith and touting their good fortune at not having encountered any "heathens." Rabbit smiled, and a dark joy glistened in his eyes.

One of the whites who seemed to be in charge ordered everyone to tighten the cinches on their horses and prepare to move. As luck would have it, Squirrel was the last to mount, and he took up his position to the right of the last wagon. The man pulled a rifle out of its sheath attached to the girth and placed it across his saddle.

Rabbit brushed aside a twig from the opening, cocked the six-shooter, and took aim. He glanced across the trail at an innocuous dead branch curving up out of the dirt, a long stone's throw away.

The drivers cracked their whips over the mules and shouted. With a clunk, the loaded wagons moved ponderously. Rabbit took a deep breath to steady himself, aimed, and slowly squeezed the trigger.

Squirrel rose up in his stirrups, slumped forward over the neck of his horse, and tumbled to the ground, landing with a thud. The rifle clattered to the ground. His horse lurched forward for a few confused steps and then yielded to panic. With tail high, he raced away.

Shouts filled the air. The outriders drew pistols and looked wildly about for the all-out attack they knew was about to happen. None of them was particularly concerned about Squirrel; they were already moving away. The wagon drivers cracked their whips incessantly, screaming at their mules. Finally, the teams managed to achieve a trot, the best they could do with the heavy loads behind them. Wagon wheels clunked and rumbled as the train moved away from Rabbit's hiding place.

He turned his attention to the dead branch across from him, cocked his pistol, and took careful aim at it, resting the barrel of the gun on a root. He squeezed the trigger but missed. Cocking again, he aimed once more. His next shot shattered the branch. In the next instant, a rifle blasted the air and its lead ball cracked into the canvas-covered load of the second wagon.

To the drivers and the outriders, the attack was

on. The mounted guards looked around frantically but saw nothing. To a man, they expected hordes of riders to boil out of the earth itself. The man in charge shouted for everyone to keep moving.

In his hole, Rabbit loosed a long sigh of relief. He knew that the white men could have stopped and perhaps figured out where his shots had come from. For that reason, he had hidden a rifle and rigged it so that, if he hit the trigger stick, a stone tied to a string fell and pulled the trigger of the rifle. He had been so very lucky it had worked.

By now, the five wagons were moving away quickly. He waited until they dropped out of view before he emerged. The man on the trail had not moved, but when he stood above him, Rabbit could see he was still alive. The bullet had entered to the right of his backbone and left a hole in the front of his right chest. He was still bleeding. Nearby lay another six-shooter, and on a strap over the man's shoulder were attached pouches, the kind of pouches that usually contained round bullets.

Rabbit looked south to make sure no one happened to be approaching, Lakota or white. Tucking his six-shooter into his belt, he slid the pouch belt over the man's head and tossed it aside. The man had nothing else he wanted.

There was one more task to be done. Yanking his knife from his sheath, he knelt at the man's head. With a quick swipe, he sliced off the top of the man's scalp, but it was only a small swatch. It was the best he could do with one hand. The man moaned loudly. Rabbit stepped over him and grabbed the pouch belt. After tucking the other pistol into his belt, he retrieved the new rifle. After that, he walked away without looking back. The hair on the scalp he took was thin, but it was a scalp nonetheless. One to add to the others.

Rabbit shook the belt he had taken and heard the soft rattle of bullets. A new supply of powder would have been good, but he did have a new supply of round bullets, another six-shooter, and a rifle. He recovered his hidden rifle and walked east to get his horse. With only one arm, he was having some difficulty carrying all of his captured booty.

For the rest of the day, he shadowed the five wagons after he caught up to them. But he stayed just at the end of rifle range and out of sight. He occasionally propped his rifle on a branch or a rock and snapped off a long shot. He did not care if he hit anything. He simply wanted to harass the whites.

As the sun dipped close to the western horizon, he finally broke off his attack and made camp. He had found a bowl atop a low butte far to the east of the Powder River Road. The bowl was home to a few scrub pines, their growth stunted by the frequent high winds that careened over the rim. But tonight it was calm.

Rabbit watered his horse in a nearby stream that trickled lazily. After that, he built a fire to warm himself and to lift his mood. He decided to go home tomorrow, hoping that in the lodge of his parents he could forget the sense of melancholy that dogged him almost constantly now. For now, he pulled an elk-hide robe over his shoulders, annoyed at the sudden sensation that tried frequently to trick him into thinking the fingers of his right hand were still there. He did not once think of the dead white man he had left along the trail.

———————

Hornsby was restless on his bedroll on the ground in the back of the blacksmith shed. Although the night air brought a definite chill, he took no notice of it. He marveled at how suddenly quiet the fort became after sundown. Except for the occasional snort of a horse or a muffled voice or two from somewhere, it was eerily quiet. It was difficult to fathom that several hundred souls were probably asleep inside the log walls.

From beyond those walls came the wavering cry of some kind of an animal. *An owl*, he thought. The strident wails of coyotes and the deeper howls of wolves were easy to hear from every direction, it seemed. Hornsby wondered how many of those voices were actually coyotes and wolves. Sometimes things were not what they seemed.

He sat bolt upright. That was it!

One of the outriders on Petersen's train had been a trader for a time, traveling into the Wind River country among the Shoshone, he had said. After one transaction had gone bad, he had to run and hide. He had saved himself from an angry Shoshone warrior by hiding in a ravine. A trader! Perhaps as a trader, he could get into the camps on the Tongue River.

Hornsby lay back down. Faces flowed through his mind as rapidly as the cold waters of Piney Creek slid over the rock-strewn creek bed. As before, they stopped with the face of the red-haired white woman atop a bay horse. A red-haired white woman probably, even now, sharing the bed of a Sioux warrior. Hornsby rolled over angrily, finding momentary comfort in the feel of the old Hawken rifle next to him.

CHAPTER TEN

The Visitor

It was the Moon When Leaves Fall. The first day of the Winter Moon was not far off. The air was cold beneath a thick layer of clouds that stretched like an endless gray blanket over the Shining Mountains and east across to where Sky and Earth met.

Along the Tongue River, nearly a day's ride north of the town of log walls on Buffalo Creek, there was suddenly a whirlwind of commotion in Black Shield's encampment. Two young men were dragging a prisoner into camp, along with his packhorse laden with goods.

By the time the terrified white man was brought to the outer circle of lodges, he was surrounded by at least a dozen mounted warriors. A boy was already running among the lodges carrying the news to as many of the old men as he could find.

A man with hard, measuring eyes and the self-assured demeanor of a buffalo bull in his prime met the young men who had captured the intruder.

"Take him no farther," he advised. "He is not a guest, so he should not enter the circle of our lodges. Hold him here until we can send for Rabbit."

The young men, Neck and Little Bird, took the man's advice and motioned with their rifles for the man to sit.

The news spread quickly through the encampment of twenty lodges in the wide gully north of the river. Young sentinels hiding in a grove of trees on the north bank had been watching the lone white man come down a slope from the east. He had not been particularly quiet. They had waited until after he had crossed the river to capture him.

Now the man sat forlornly, encircled by armed warriors, frightened and utterly alone, eyes darting about like a bug on water. A step or two away, a young man had the white man's packhorse by the lead rope.

Goings was sitting outside the lodge he shared with Walks in the Night and Gathers Medicine when the news reached him: a white man was in the camp.

He looked at Gathers Medicine, his Lakota wife, sitting nearby. Together they cast a worried glance into the lodge, where his Cheyenne wife was helping to make a cradleboard. Gathers Medicine nodded in response to the silent request in her husband's eyes and stood to enter the lodge. Goings nodded his appreciation and left to see what was happening.

On the other side of the village circle, Sweetwater Woman also heard the news being shouted. Glancing up from the basket she was weaving to look into her husband's eyes, she knew that the fear in her own was plain. But it was not the fear of a white man. It was the fear of an unknown part of something she once was somehow threatening what she was now.

Cloud looked reassuringly into his wife's eyes for

a moment then leaned over to point at her swollen middle. "Is that little one kicking again?" he asked. "I thought I saw your stomach trying to do a round dance."

She smiled. "This baby is already a better dancer than his father—her father."

Cloud returned her smile. "That," he said, "is not a difficult thing to do." After a glance in the direction of all the noise and activity, he turned back to his wife.

"One white man, alone?" he wondered aloud, as the corners of his eyes crinkled into another smile. "He is either lost, stupid, or very brave. I will go and learn which of those he is."

———————————

Max Hornsby took deep, slow breaths, trying to calm himself. Indians at a distance through a telescope were one thing. Up close, their angry, coppery brown faces turned his insides cold. Sheer dumb luck had brought him to this camp. Three days ago, he was wandering on foot around the rolling hills to the east.

To play the part of a trader, he had to use his only horse to pack the assortment of goods he had been able to procure at Fort Phil Kearny. A day north of the fort, the horse had gotten loose and Hornsby had no choice but to trail him. Tied in among the packs were his old Hawken rifle and his food. Armed only with his revolver, he had doggedly followed the horse until it happened to entangle the lead rope in a sturdy plum thicket.

Several weeks of working, bartering, and begging had resulted in an assortment of goods ranging from metal pots, cloth, hand mirrors, trinkets, and butchering knives. Even a few pieces of rock candy. There were moments, such as when he was stumbling around in the dark looking for the errant horse, when he wondered if he was being driven by pure foolishness. Days before, he had been slightly encouraged when the post chaplain, a man with wild gray-blue eyes, had called his plan to search for the captive white woman the "highest of noble intent."

Now, far from the protective log walls of Fort Phil Kearny, sitting within a circle of solemn-faced Sioux warriors, he did not feel at all noble. And he could not stop trembling.

———————————

Grey Bull hung back in the crowd and carefully observed the white man. He had just arrived to visit with Cloud when all the excitement had erupted. Although the bearded, stocky man was afraid, there was something else about the way his eyes darted quickly, surreptitiously, over the faces in the gathering crowd. Grey Bull touched Cloud's arm as he made his way to the outer circle of people.

"My friend," said Cloud, "is it true?"

Grey Bull nodded, smiling wryly. "Yes. There he is."

"I told my wife this man is either lost, stupid, or brave," Cloud said.

"Something else, too," Grey Bull replied.

"What?"

Grey Bull shrugged slightly, a bemused look on his dignified face. "I do not know. Maybe we will know when Rabbit gets here."

By now, except for the very young, the very old, and those who had better things to do, the camp's entire population was crowding around the white man. Nearly a hundred people. For certain, most of the village's thirty able-bodied warriors were on hand.

Boys from the very young to those on the edge of young manhood were the most curious onlookers. One, around the age of ten, broke from the circle and ran at the white man, poked his bearded face, and scurried back to the edge of the crowd. He had claimed victory, counted coup. A ripple of laughter ran through the crowd, directed at the white man because he resembled a goose on ice as he had tried to stay out of the boy's way.

The laughter and the buzz of conversations faded as three men wove their way through and approached the white man: Grey Bull, Cloud, and Rabbit. Each took his own measure of the man. They had seen many like him: bearded, unkempt, and smelling like they had never taken a bath.

In the eyes of Grey Bull and Cloud, there was coldness, almost an indifference, to the white man cowering on the ground.

In the eyes of Rabbit, however, there was a black, smoldering hatred. Over his right shoulder and around his hips was a tanned deer hide, leaving his left shoulder and arm exposed but covering his right. Thus it was not easy to see that the young man's right arm was missing from the elbow down. This was the price he had paid for thinking that all white men were friendly.

Grey Bull motioned for the white man to stand, but uncertainty and fear rooted him to the ground. Grey Bull glanced at the two young men who had captured the man, and they quickly and firmly yanked the man to his feet and stepped away.

———————————

Hornsby's legs were trembling, and he didn't know what to do with his hands. The thought entered his mind that he probably should not assume a pose or stance that could be misconstrued as defiant. He clasped his hands together in front and stood with his head slightly bowed. Then he reached up and removed his hat, though he didn't know why. He raised a furtive glance to some of the faces, but immediately returned his gaze to the moccasins of the three warriors in front of him.

There was not a bearded face among them, and all—men and women, boys and girls—had long, shiny black hair. One woman wore a gray calico dress, and a couple of men had on blue wool trousers, but everyone else was dressed in hides.

Hornsby could feel the curiosity in the many pairs of dark eyes, and apprehension in some of the children. His quick, fearful glance noted outright distaste on many of the women's faces. But in the eyes of the men, he saw cold, calculating stares. Except from the young warrior with a robe over his shoulder—from the dark stare of that one, Hornsby felt the icy, black shadow of death.

———————————

Grey Bull glanced sideways at Rabbit. "Perhaps we should begin by asking him where he came from."

Rabbit nodded, keeping his eyes on the white man's face. He cleared his throat. "Where—do you come?" he said.

The bearded face jerked up, eyes blinking. "What?" it rasped in surprise.

Rabbit repeated the question. "Where do you come?"

The white man nervously squeezed his hat. "Ah— from the trail. Bozeman Trail, up from Fort Laramie."

The crowd had fallen utterly silent, so the white man's words were easily heard. Nearly everyone knew the Long Knife and white man word for the Powder River Road. *Bozeman.* It had brought many like this one into their lands. Rabbit translated the words.

Grey Bull and Cloud exchanged an inscrutable glance.

In a moment, Grey Bull spoke again. "Ask him why."

"Why—do you come?" Rabbit asked.

The white man coughed nervously into his hand. "Ah—to trade. I am a trader," he said, gesturing shakily toward his pack-laden horse.

Rabbit again translated.

A slight murmur ran through the crowd and faded quickly.

Grey Bull leaned toward Cloud. "As the old ones like to say," he said in a low voice, "'White men use the lie like they use the gun.'"

Cloud nodded, then leaned toward Rabbit. "Ask him if he has been in the town on Buffalo Creek."

"You go Fort Kearny? You stay—in?" Rabbit asked.

The white man blinked and glanced up at Rabbit's face, and then just as quickly lowered his eyes, recoiling from the bottomless hate. He shook his head. "No! No. I did not go to the fort. Fort Phil Kearny. I—no," he replied.

Rabbit stared hard at the white man's face before translating.

Grey Bull smiled wryly at Cloud. "This one is no trader," he said. "Perhaps he is a scout."

Cloud agreed. "But what shall we do with him?"

Grey Bull thought for a moment. "Keep him

under guard for the time being. The old men will need to talk. We will do what they think is right." Then he pointed at the white man's horse. "Someone should take those packs off. That load was not tied on very well; it was not balanced. That is why I do not think this man is a trader. He does not know how to tie on the packs the way white traders usually do."

The white man, his horse, and his goods were moved to a brush shelter at the far edge of the camp and kept under guard. Not to protect him, but to keep him from dong any harm.

By early evening, most of the people had lost interest in staring at the white man. One white man was like another. Only a few boys stayed nearby until well after sundown, hoping for some excitement. They talked among themselves, laughing occasionally and making the man nervous. Eventually, only six or so young men stayed to guard the man, keeping a wide circle around him and the fire, talking as if he were not there.

Meanwhile, three young men Cloud had sent out returned shortly after sundown and reported seeing no other whites or any movement along the Powder River Road. After that, the old men gathered in the meeting lodge.

Sometime well into the evening, Grey Bull and Cloud emerged from the meeting lodge and hurried to talk to the young guards. The old men had reached a decision: in the morning, the white man was to be escorted west to the Powder River Road with his horse and goods and then sent north, out of Lakota country.

———————————

Dawn was cold, gray, and misty. A drizzle floated in the air. Hornsby's fire was out and the cold sliced into his bones, even with his hands tucked under his arms. He had slept fitfully through the night and was numb and stiff from sitting and lying on the cold, hard ground. Hunger gnawed at his insides, and he wished he could trade his horse and goods for a hot cup of coffee. Knowing there was no choice but to wait, a part of him wondered if he would live to see the end of this dreary day.

A shiver turned into an outright tremble as it coursed through his body. Although he didn't look up, he could feel an intense gaze upon him. It had been there all night, making him shiver from another kind of chill.

———————————

Sweetwater Woman walked slowly with her skin of water, casually letting the weight of it swing her arm. A well-worn trail from the river's edge led away from where the warriors were guarding the white man, but she turned in that direction.

Two of the young men were returning to their lodges to sleep as two more replaced them. She stopped about twenty paces away from the small form curled under a blanket. As Cloud had told her last evening, the white man was a pitiful thing. He was no soldier, and perhaps he was a scout, but he had not convinced anyone that he was a trader.

She stared at him in spite of a loathing that welled up inside her. Although she fearfully searched her memory and her heart, she could find no connection to him. Whoever had left her those many years ago near the Sweetwater River had long since slipped from her memory. She knew that in her heart, but she had needed to be certain of it. Sweetwater Woman turned and walked away.

———————

Hornsby looked up to see the woman in the tanned-hide dress walking away toward the line of lodges. Although there was a robe over her shoulders, her long reddish brown braids were plain to see. It was her!

The sight of her momentarily made him forget the warriors nearby. With a snort, he jumped to his feet. Hobbling on stiff, unresponsive legs, he ran toward the woman.

"Lady!" he shouted hoarsely. "Lady! Please! I came to help you! Lady! For chrissake, wait!—"

He felt a sledgehammer-like impact and his breath leaving his chest, and he felt his face slam into the ground.

———————

Cloud stared in silent fury at the white man, who was only now waking. His thumb cocked the hammer of the breech-loading rifle, which he pointed at the bearded man's chest.

Sweetwater Woman was still sitting on the ground, where she had fallen. Grandmother Willow and Gathers Medicine were tending to her and quickly motioned to the enraged Cloud that his wife had not been harmed.

The white man was alone in his pain, writhing, struggling to find his way out of the swirling in his head.

Little Bird had stopped the man from attacking Sweetwater. He spoke to Cloud. "As I said, Uncle, I think he went crazy. He was running after her."

Rabbit spoke from nearby, hatred dripping from his words. "The only good white man is a dead one."

A murmur of agreement came from several of the men as a crowd began to gather.

Grey Bull hurried to Cloud's side. "What do you want to do?"

Cloud's left hand tightened around the barrel of his rifle as he glanced toward his wife. He saw the silent plea in her eyes and lowered his head in confusion. She had always been a gentle person. But at this moment, he did not know if she was pleading for the sake of mercy or for the sake of a white man.

Bear Looks Behind, who had snow-white hair and the passage of many years carved into his face, moved from the edge of the crowd and touched Cloud's shoulder.

"One less white man may make things better for us," he said gently, "but one white man who lives because we choose to let him live might have something to teach his own kind."

The old man nodded toward the white man still writhing on the ground and turned his wise face back toward the angry warrior. "Take him to the hills north of the soldier town. Turn him loose, naked, because he was born naked the first time. But keep his horse and his other things. Those things are a small price for a second life."

CHAPTER ELEVEN

Born Again

Grey Bull and Cloud, mounted on their warhorses, watched the naked white man scurry down the slopes of Lodge Trail Hill. Farther south, beyond Buffalo Creek and some low hills, Taken Alive was leading an attack against the woodcutters from the fort. Cloud could hear the gunfire, the signal to turn the man loose.

The running man's whiteness against the stark shades of brown grass was like the sudden flash of a falling star against a dark sky. And like such a star, he disappeared quickly from sight. Both of the warriors watched as the naked man crouched behind some leafless bushes.

Cloud stared disdainfully at the pile of clothes on the ground.

"My friend," said Grey Bull, "I think that white man came to your camp on purpose."

Cloud's eyebrows arched above his questioning glance.

"I watched him," Grey Bull went on, "when he first came. He was looking at everyone who came to look at him. He was searching for something—or someone."

Cloud nodded and glanced to the southwest. They heard more gunfire, the sound of an intense skirmish. "He did try to attack my wife."

"Does your wife know him?"

Cloud shook his head. "She has never seen him before."

"Little Bird told me he started shouting after he saw your wife. Then he ran toward her." Grey Bull paused, looking southwest after a particularly long exchange of gunfire. "I think he is crazy."

Cloud reached under his robe into a beaded bag hanging from his belt and pulled out the glass he had taken from among the white man's things. It and the old muzzle-loading rifle were his to claim. The other goods he gave away to some of the grandmothers.

He stretched out the shiny glass and aimed it at the white man, still crouching behind the shrubs and looking around.

"I want to remember his face," he said. "If I see him near our camp again, I will kill him."

———————————

For Max Hornsby, it was a bittersweet day. He was alive, but naked and cold. The November afternoon was chilly, and there seemed to be no way to hide from the sharp breeze blowing from the northwest. Hunkering down as low as he could behind some brush didn't seem to help.

Back up the slope, about a hundred yards away, were two Sioux warriors, watching him. Up there near them was the last of his worldly possessions: a coat, shirt, trousers, and long underwear. Not to mention his telescope. His horse, gun, and the trade goods he had scrounged together had been taken from him back in the village. He had been forced to walk the several miles from the Indian camp to the ridge where the two warriors were sitting on their horses.

Hornsby was angry and embarrassed. The last time he had been completely naked was in early July during his bath in the North Platte River.

Gunfire came again from the southwest. He glanced tentatively in the direction of the fort, knowing that he should at least move that way and find better cover if he could. No telling what those young bucks would do on their way back from attacking the wood detail if they found him.

After a quick, frantic look around, he jumped up and sprinted for a grove of pine to the southeast. Thorns scraped his legs, and he yelled out in pain as he tried to sidestep them and stepped on a sharp stone. Hornsby went down in a heap, furious that someone was witness to his misery and embarrassment.

———————————

Cloud smiled broadly. He had been watching the white man through the glass. Pushing the glass back within itself, he pointed toward the sound of gunfire. "Perhaps we should go see how Taken Alive and the others are doing."

Grey Bull nodded, and they loped their horses

down the long south slope of Lodge Trail Hill.

But Cloud's mind raced along faster than his horse. If Grey Bull's suspicions were true, then the "trader" might have come looking for someone. But why Sweetwater Woman, if it was her he was after? She had often spoken, sometimes sadly, of the fact that she could not remember who her first parents were.

Twenty winters ago, she had been found wandering alone near the Sweetwater River, along the Oregon Trail, as the whites called the road that was said to go far to the west, into unknown lands. The Lakota scouts who had found her could not even guess where, or who, to return her to. So they had taken her with them. Summer was nearly over when they reached their people, who were camped near Bear Butte in the Black Hills. There, the lost little red-haired girl was taken in by Star Woman and her husband, Bearface.

For nearly two years, she was silent, and often cried softly at night. Because no one knew her given name, her new mother simply called her Fawn. Suddenly, one day she spoke, and the Lakota words kept tumbling out. It was at that moment, Star Woman liked to say, when Sweetwater became a Lakota.

Cloud glanced in the direction the naked white man had gone, but he could see nothing. The "trader's" face, however, hung in his mind like a lone cloud in an open sky. He would not forget that face. Whoever and whatever the man was, Cloud was certain that he could not be a relative of Sweetwater. The only possibility that made sense was that the man had lost a sister and Sweetwater happened to resemble her.

This morning, she had once again reassured him that she did not know the man who had stumbled into the camp on the Tongue. Cloud believed his wife, so the unsettled feeling in the pit of his stomach was not because of her. Perhaps it was because of all the whites.

They wanted everything that belonged to the Lakota. But he would not let them have his wife. She was a Lakota woman, soon to give birth to a Lakota child. A whole nation of fighting men was prepared to defend everything that was Lakota. Cloud was likewise prepared to defend his family with his life.

He looked again in the direction of the town of log walls, even as more gunfire came from the wood road. He hoped that Taken Alive was giving the Long Knives plenty to think about.

———

Were it not for the women and children in the fort, Hornsby would have simply walked in. He was angry enough to have done that. But he waited instead, shivering inside a sparse stand of shrubbery near the wood road. After the firing had subsided from the west, he guessed that the wood detail would be hurrying back to the fort. And he was right.

Embarrassed and a little hesitant, he emerged from his hiding place when the lumbering, creaking wagons were close. The twelve men in the wood detail were jumpy, as they had just been in a fight with the Sioux and two of their number had been wounded.

"Well, it's for sure you be no damn Sioux," one of the civilian guards said as Hornsby stood with his hands covering his genitals. "What happened to ya?"

Hornsby nodded back over his shoulder. "Indians captured me. Turned me loose, jus' before they came after you. They took everythin' I had."

Sympathy crept into several pairs of eyes that had been on the verge of ridicule only moments before.

"Why'd they let you go?" Claxton, one of the guards, wanted to know.

Hornsby was growing more uneasy by the moment. He shrugged. "Anybody got a blanket or extra coat I can borrow?"

"Here!" A well-worn buffalo robe flew from the first wagon, and the man who tossed it spoke loudly to everyone. "We got two wounded need tending to! This man can tell his story inside the fort!"

Then the man, who had the largest hands Hornsby had ever seen on anyone, motioned him toward the lead wagon. "Get on," he ordered. "No tellin' when them heathens'll come boiling out of the trees!"

Hornsby quickly wrapped the robe around himself and jumped into the wagon. Barely an instant after he was on, the driver shook the long reins and cracked his whip again and again over the rumps of the mules. Hornsby hung on to the top edge of the wagon box with one hand, and with the other tried to keep the robe from falling. He sent a glance or two toward the north, toward Lodge Trail Ridge, but he mostly kept his eyes down and away from the questioning stares he could feel upon him.

Several moments into the jostling ride, he finally noticed that the man curled on the bed of the wagon toward the back moaned with each bump along the road. Then he saw the broken-off arrow shaft protruding from the man's lower left rib cage and, finally, the pool of red that was coloring the bed of the wagon.

Hornsby couldn't pull his eyes away from the sight of the wounded man's blood, and suddenly the face of the young one-armed Sioux warrior came into his mind. The warrior with death in his eyes.

He hunched lower inside the buffalo robe, realizing that he was incredibly lucky to be alive. But there was something else, something he knew he had in common with the one-armed warrior: anger. A jagged-edged, black, and growing anger. Anger that was connected to another image that hung at the back of his mind, like a nagging ache that wouldn't go away: the image of a red-haired white woman in a buckskin dress.

She had turned as he was trying to get her attention, before someone knocked him senseless. But he could still see her as she was turning. He could still see her swollen belly. A belly swollen with child. With an Indian child.

The wood wagons rolled through the west gate of the fort. Work in the pinery had been interrupted by the Indian attack, and the only results from the wood crew's efforts this day were two wounded men. Both wagons stopped near the fort infirmary. Soldiers rushed forward, and many pairs of hands quickly unloaded the wounded men.

Since the establishment of this lonely outpost in the foothills of the dark and brooding Bighorn Mountains, the Sioux had been relentless. Although most of their attacks had been by small groups of warriors pouncing quickly and then, just as quickly, breaking off, the tactics were effective. Since July, there had been casualties and loss of livestock. In one raid alone, two hundred mules and some horses had been stolen. No one, civilian or soldier, dared wander outside the walls of the fort alone. To do so was to invite certain death, or worse.

Hornsby considered these things as he limped toward the blacksmith shed. Only now did he begin to feel the effects of his several hours of naked uncertainty after the two Sioux warriors had turned him loose. His legs were covered with scratches, some of them deep, from thorn bushes. His left ankle was throbbing, and the soles of both feet were tender and sore. He was lucky to be alive. Yet the deepest wound was to his pride as he began to realize that the Sioux had treated him as a nuisance and not as a worthy adversary.

As he reached the blacksmith shed, he suddenly

felt powerless. Hornsby gathered the buffalo robe tighter and leaned against a wall. He was alive only because of incredible good fortune, because the whims of a few Indian had gone one way and not another. He was not alive because of anything that he had done to cause it, except to cover his nakedness and pitifully ask for help.

To chase away the feeling of utter helplessness, Hornsby latched onto the image of the red-haired white woman in the Sioux camp. The pregnant white woman, carrying an Indian whelp!

His breathing grew faster and his lips turned into a thin line as the anger filled him, nearly obscuring the sound of faint rustling nearby. He looked sideways into a softly pinched face and sympathetic eyes. It was Mrs. Carrington, wife of the fort's commanding officer. After a moment, the realization of how he must look to her sank in and his sense of helplessness returned.

Hornsby cleared his throat while making sure the buffalo robe was properly covering him. "Ma'am. Ah, I did not see you come in—that is, I am afraid that I am not very presentable at the moment."

The woman's face softened even more. "That is quite alright, Mr. Hornsby. It is not necessary to concern yourself." She waved a hand around. "This is a harsh land. Sometimes it takes our dignity from us."

Hornsby nodded. "Yes, ma'am."

"Mr. Claxton, from the wood detail, tells me you were captured by the Sioux?"

Hornsby kept his eyes to the ground. "Yes, I was."

"In that case, you are fortunate to be alive."

He nodded slowly. "Yes, I know."

Mrs. Carrington suddenly realized that she was making the man very uncomfortable and turned aside. "Mr. Hornsby, please come to our quarters, as a guest of the colonel and myself. You should not stand here like this. Please. Perhaps a bath and some food. And I think I can muster up some clothing for you."

Hornsby nodded. "That would be very kind of you, ma'am."

He pulled the robe tighter and kept his head down as he followed the woman, trying to ignore the questioning, amused stares cast in his direction. The hem of her dress swished just above the trampled ground, swaying slightly as she walked, reminding him of the fringes on the buckskin dress worn by the red-haired white woman in the Sioux camp.

CHAPTER TWELVE

Grandmother

Sweetwater Woman awoke in the night and knew immediately that the old men and warrior leaders were still in the council lodge—her husband was not sleeping next to her. From across the room came Grandmother Willow's soft breathing from beneath her covering robes.

Sweetwater shifted heavily. As time went on, it was becoming more and more uncomfortable to sleep on her back. On this night, the little being inside her had been especially active, frequently kicking against her lower ribs.

It was cool in the lodge. Sweetwater decided to add wood to the coals in the fire pit and pulled herself up to a sitting position. As she carefully dropped the second handful of twigs onto the glowing coals, muffled voices floated through the night air outside. Soon she heard footsteps coming toward her lodge.

The outside covering was carefully lifted and then Cloud slowly pushed the inside cover aside as well. A smile crossed his tired face as he saw his wife. "Did I wake you?" he asked.

Sweetwater shook her head. "No. Your son—or daughter—did, with some very hard kicking."

Cloud smiled again and retied the inside covering before he moved across the lodge. He handed a robe to Sweetwater because she was naked and sitting with her arms crossed against the chill. After adding more wood to the low flames beginning to flicker, he sat back against a willow chair.

Sweetwater wrapped the elk robe over herself and slid into her chair. Grandmother Willow moved a little and then sat up, wide awake. It was amazing to Sweetwater how quickly the old ones could come awake.

"Grandmother," said Cloud, "I did not mean to wake you."

The old woman quickly waved off her grandson's concern and then held out a palm to the growing fire. "One thing about being old," she said, "I can sleep whenever it pleases me. Do not worry. Besides, is it not nearly dawn?"

Cloud nodded.

"It must have been a talkative night for the old men," the old woman said with a twinkle in her eye.

A soft chuckle came from Cloud. "Yes, they all had something to say."

The twinkle faded in the old woman's eyes. She knew that many important men among the Oglala in the Powder River country had been in the council lodge. There were many camps along the Tongue River this autumn, drawn together by concern and anger over the intrusion of the Long Knives. And since the Middle Moon, the old men and warrior leaders had talked through many nights like this. What they decided would touch the lives of all of the people. It would touch the lives of the invaders as well, those strangers hiding behind their log walls.

So although she could tease her grandson a little about how long the old men talked, it was only to help him forget the weariness in his body. As well as to let him know that the women in his life understood that a warrior often had to endure hardships not directly associated with fighting an enemy.

"I heard that the leader of the Bad Faces is here," she said.

Cloud nodded. "Yes," he replied. "Red Cloud was in the council lodge, and he grows angrier with each passing day."

"At the Long Knives?" Sweetwater asked.

"Yes," he said, "but there is something nipping at his heels. Some of the old men think he has taken much upon himself by trying to speak for all of the Oglala at the treaty meeting on Horse Creek."

"I thought many of the old men agreed with what Red Cloud said to the whites," the old woman said, "because he said we will not sell our lands, that we do not want their towns up here in the middle of our country."

"Many still do," Cloud pointed out. "Red Cloud spoke what was on many Lakota minds that day. But I think that when the whites turned to him, thinking that he was the leader of all of the Oglala, he did not tell them that he was not."

Grandmother Willow nodded as she reached

around for one of her rawhide food cases. "My cousin lived for a summer with her family near Horse Creek," she said. "One thing she noticed is that the Long Knives and the white peace talkers have one man who speaks for all of them. One person tells everyone what to do and when to do it. It is their way, so they think it is the way all people do things. It does not enter their thinking that others have different ways." From the painted case she pulled out a small bag of tea leaves.

Cloud had heard old men make the same observation several times. "Yes," he replied, "and that is why they turned to Red Cloud. Last night, he said that the problem we face with the Long Knives is bigger than the jealousy over who is the leader among us and who is not."

Cloud watched as his grandmother prepared to boil water to make tea.

"I think he is a wise man," he continued. "I think he knows things about how white men think that many of us do not. But there are some of our old men who think that Red Cloud wants to wield his own influence just as much as he wants to drive out the Long Knives, perhaps more."

"Like a white man?" wondered Sweetwater.

Cloud nodded. "Perhaps. But there is something he said last night that many of us think is the thing to do."

Grandmother Willow looked up from her task of carefully placing small stones in the bed of hot coals. When the stones were hot, she would put them in a bowl of water. When the water was hot, she would add the tea leaves. She preferred this method to boiling water in metal pots. "Defeat the Long Knives in one great battle," she said sadly.

A flicker of surprise sparkled in Cloud's eyes, but only for a moment. "Yes," he said, "but how did you arrive at the same thought, Grandmother?"

"A little while ago, we said the Long Knives were different. The only way they may be like us is that they have arms and legs, fingers and toes. They speak, and so maybe they have brains." The old woman paused as she poured water from a flask into a shallow bowl, her lined face concentrating on her task. "Long Knives are not like Lakota warriors," she went on. "Lakota warriors understand courage. Warriors can win a fight by showing their courage. Long Knives think that the only way to win is to kill. It is what they did to the Blue Clouds and Cheyenne at Sand Creek. It is what Woman Killer Harney did to our people on the Blue Water eleven years ago. So the only way to rid them from our land is to kill them. It is not a pleasant thing to consider. But we must not forget: they do not belong here. This is our land, our life. They will not leave, even if they do have the brains to understand that they are doing wrong."

Sweetwater Woman shivered and drew the robe tighter around her shoulders. The thought of what might lay ahead for her husband sent a trembling through her legs. She wondered if the fear had not reached deep inside her, because even the tiny being in her womb was still.

"Red Cloud spoke those same thoughts," Cloud told them, "almost with the same words."

The old woman nodded knowingly as she covered the stones over with hot coals, poking at them with a forked stick.

"Most people who are of the Earth live according to the truth that comes from the Earth," the old woman went on. "One truth is to take only what you need. It is a truth that was not always known, but we know it now. A nation of many people needs more land on which to hunt. We took this land because we were many and needed it. We took it from the Crow people. They fought us, but they understood that we are a nation of many more people. So they moved aside, not because they were afraid, but because they were wise.

"And we did not keep going north to take more and more of their land. We could have because we are strong, we are many. But we do not need to take any more of the land. The Long Knives are different. They take what they do not need, and I think some of us are learning their ways.

"Twenty five years ago, I heard of some Dakota on the other side of the Great Muddy River who killed a thousand buffalo in one day with their rifles. And all they took were the hides to trade to the Long Knives. They forgot the truth of living with the Earth. If the Long Knives keep coming and coming, what other of our truths will they take from us? Yes, I think the leader of the Bad Faces is right: killing is not a pleasant thing, but it is all the Long Knives understand. Those inside the town must be defeated. If we defeat the Long Knives, the others will leave."

After a long moment of silence, Grandmother Willow carefully lifted the hot stones from the hot coals with the forked stick, shook off the ashes, and placed them in the bowl of water. Looking in the direction of her grandson's wife, she smiled gently. "Soon we will have tea," the old woman announced softly.

───────────

Cloud awakened near midday to news that he and Grey Bull had been invited to the village of Crazy Horse, farther down the Tongue.

By late afternoon, they were nearly there. He glanced over his shoulder to see that the sun was still above the western horizon. The days were growing shorter.

They had ridden in silence, for the most part. Grandmother Willow's words were still swirling in Cloud's head, like the summer whirlwind that is born suddenly and lives furiously. He did not know the reason for Grey Bull's silence, but many thoughts had been expressed in the council, any of which was reason enough for deep, silent contemplation.

The air was cold. Breezes slid off the mountain slopes, carrying the biting hint of winter. The first snow was not far off.

They were vigilant, even as they rode in silence,

and constantly watched the skyline, but neither of them anticipated immediate trouble. The Long Knives ventured out of their log walls only to cut wood, not to turn their horses toward the Lakota camps.

Travel along the Powder River Road had diminished considerably since the first days of the Moon When Leaves Fall. Of course, Long Knives and other whites were the only travelers who used the road. Now it was the Winter Moon, and the people along the Tongue hoped that the approaching cold weather could keep travelers off the road altogether. The only danger then would be the Crow raiding parties from the north. They were always in Lakota territory, traveling in small groups, looking for opportunities to harass or help themselves to a good Lakota horse here and there.

Both of them lifted their rifles as a rider topped a hill to the east. But as the dark, distant figure lifted a weapon in a gesture of greeting, Cloud noticed something familiar in the way the man moved. It was Yellow Wolf, the young man with a new rifle. Both Grey Bull and Cloud lifted a hand in greeting as Yellow Wolf galloped his horse off the hill toward them.

The young man slid his horse to a dirt-spraying stop, a half smile curling the ends of his mouth. "They are waiting for you. They sent me to make sure you did not get lost," he teased.

"We are here," said Grey Bull. "I was wondering where you have been, so I guess the talk about you and the daughter of Makes Room must be true."

Yellow Wolf grinned and pointed to the north-east. "All I know is that you are making important men wait in the council lodge. I told them you are probably riding your slow horses today."

Cloud chuckled. He liked Yellow Wolf. "Who are those important men?" he asked.

The young man's expression changed. "Crazy Horse and Hump," he replied, "and some from the Northern Cheyenne, White Elk and Big Nose and his brother, Little Wolf. And a medicine man, Crazy Mule, I think."

"Those are important men," agreed Cloud. "I wonder what they have on their minds."

"I have a feeling we will know that soon," said Grey Bull, urging his horse into a faster walk.

Soon all three were loping their horses along a flood plain. Around a bend, they could see the thin columns of smoke from the fires of Crazy Horse's village.

———————————

Grandmother Willow put away some dried meat into one of her painted rawhide food cases. Finishing her task, she leaned back against her chair and lightly cleared her throat.

Nearby, Sweetwater Woman looked up. "Grand-mother, you finished, and I did not help you."

The old woman waved off the young woman's

concern. "Do not worry," she said. "I know there is something on your mind, and I wanted you to think clearly before I ask you about it."

Sweetwater smiled. The twinkle in the old woman's eyes reminded her of her mother, Star Woman—that is, the only mother she could remember. Not far away was the lodge of Star Woman and Bearface, the only parents she knew.

The earliest memories she had of childhood were of riding on her mother's hip and holding on tightly to a handful of buckskin dress so she would not fall. She could also remember clearly sitting on her father's shoulders as he walked through the camp. She had never really worried that she could not clearly remember her life before her cozy childhood in her mother and father's lodge—until now. That lost white man, if he was lost, had stirred up a yearning to know. Whatever and whoever he was, he had come from somewhere. Yet the chances of that "trader" knowing anything about her were the same as a hailstone lasting from one day to the next after a summer storm. But his coming had unsettled her, even though the only thing they shared was the color of their skin. Beyond that, his heart was different. Like all white men, he probably looked down on the Lakota. He probably thought his kind was better.

Since the white man had been captured, she had searched her memory again and again. But there was nothing that was clear and real, only murky feelings of being among many, many people and of being cold, hungry, and alone. Nothing that made her want to go back to what she was before she became Lakota.

"The first memory I have of being a child," said the old woman, gently breaking into Sweetwater's thoughts, "is of my mother singing me a sleeping song."

Sweetwater listened as the old woman sang a soft, lilting lullaby that sounded almost like the song of the doves. It was a short song.

"That is all I can remember," Grandmother Willow said sheepishly. "It is all I ever heard because I was asleep before she finished."

Sweetwater smiled. "I remember things about my mother and father and being a small girl. But before that, there is really nothing."

"You were meant to be the daughter of Star Woman and Bearface," the old woman assured her. "You just came to them in a different way. Life is like that. Sometimes it corrects the silly mistakes it makes. Sometimes."

"What is it you wanted to ask me, Grandmother?"

"I was wondering if you would think of letting me give your baby a childhood name," the old woman said wistfully.

"Yes," Sweetwater replied immediately. "Your grandson and I have already talked about that."

"Good," whispered the old woman. "Now I cannot wait for my first great-grandchild to come."

CHAPTER THIRTEEN

The Black Stone

If power were a drum, it would have been beating loudly in the village where Crazy Horse lived. One lodge in the very center of the village stood taller than the rest. Around it, older boys and young men waited to picket the horses for the warrior leaders as they arrived; consequently, an impressive array of horses filled the middle of the circle of lodges. The feeling of power and might was like the air itself: it could not be avoided. Inside the tall council lodge were gathered Lakota and Northern Cheyenne leaders, fighting men in the physical prime of their lives. With them were the old men who had seen many, many battles and wore their exploits in their eyes. Physical power mingled with the power of experience. On this day, that power would be brought to bear on the one thought on all their minds: how to drive out the Long Knives.

On the north side of the lodge sat the old men, because North was the home of winter and it was the most difficult season of the year. As a group, the old men had seen many difficult winters. On their side were deep wrinkles and old scars and the insight of hard-earned honor, wisdom, and patience.

On the opposite side sat the warrior leaders. Everyone in this lodge on this day was a man of experience and reputation and had earned the right to lead other men.

Without experience and a strong reputation, no one could lead other men. But no matter their reputations, they were all still on the journey to achieve the level of knowledge that would give them the right and privilege to sit on the north side.

Crazy Horse and Cloud were among the youngest of the warrior leaders, and today neither one would speak. Both knew that their knowledge and experience, in comparison to the company they were in, was like a pebble against a boulder.

Worm, the father of Crazy Horse, and High Eagle were joined by another medicine man, the Cheyenne Crazy Mule.

After each of them spoke and reminded everyone of their responsibilities to all the people, especially the helpless ones, Worm—the eldest of the medicine men—lit his pipe and offered a prayer:

> Father Sky, have pity on us.
> Grandmother Earth, you who wait for us all to
> return to you. Have pity on us.
> Our relatives in the West, the Buffalo People,
> who live in the place of power. Have pity
> on us.
> Our relatives in the North, the Elk People.
> Have pity on us.
> Our relatives to the East, the Black Tail People.
> Have pity on us.

Our relatives to the South, the Owl People.
Have pity on us.
Great Spirit Grandfather. We raise our voices
to you in humility. We thank you for the
wisdom and the courage You have given to
these strong men, here gathered. We ask
that You help them so that our peoples
will live and endure. We ask this in the
name of all our relatives.

After that, the three pipes belonging to the medicine men were lit and passed from man to man. After all had smoked, the talking began.

White Elk, a Northern Cheyenne much venerated among his own people and well known to the Lakota as well, was among the first to speak. Although he spoke in his own language, all of the Lakota in the lodge could understand him. Likewise, all the Northern Cheyenne could understand and speak Lakota. This was a consequence of a strong alliance between the two nations, generations old.

"I have listened to the young men tell their stories, as all of us have, about this and that attack against the Long Knives. If you listen closely, very closely, they are telling us something different about how battles are fought today. They are not the same as when we fought battles in our youth. Things have changed, but it was not the firearm that brought the change, as some might think. The change was brought because the Long Knives are not warriors; they are killers. They do not fight for honor, as we did when we were young. They fight to consume everything in their way. If they do not like something, they kill it. If—if we are to prevail against them, we have to change as well. By that, I mean when we fight them, we fight to kill. That is the thinking that will help us drive them out."

After a moment, Bear Looks Behind labored to his feet. "My friends and relatives," he began, "I have just heard some good and wise words. Things have changed. I myself do not think of the Long Knives as honorable enemies either. We do not know them as well as we know the Crow and Shoshone, because they think differently. So we must fight them differently. Although there is no honor in fighting Long Knives, they still must be fought and driven out. Once they are gone, we can have healing ceremonies to cleanse ourselves of the ugliness they have brought."

Grey Bull was the first of the warrior leaders to speak. "My grandfather told stories of how the firearm drove our people from the lake country many generations ago. Firearms were given to our enemies by the white men, he said. Our ancestors had none. Today, now, we have firearms also. The reality is that not every fighting man has one, and only a few bullets at that. I think we have allowed that to become a greater problem than it really is. Their rifles may shoot greater distances, but one good man among us can fire many arrows while the Long Knife reloads. To me, it does not matter whether we defeat them in one great battle or a hundred small ones. It does not matter whether we defeat them with or without firearms in our hands. What matters is to defeat them, to drive them out."

"All of our fighting men must agree that we have an important duty," said Hump after Grey Bull took a seat. "That is to make the Long Knives' fear of us grow every day and every night. We cannot let them rest. Every time they set foot outside the walls of their town, whether it is the one on Buffalo Creek or the one up north of the Greasy Grass, we attack them. It is our duty to make life difficult for them." He paused for a moment to gesture toward the younger leaders in the lodge. "I have asked my friends and fellow warriors to count the young men in our encampments. We think there are nearly five hundred. Those five hundred fighting men can scatter themselves and fight in small groups. They must hit hard and fast. That is how our leaders must think, and I know that many of them do already."

Sometime after sunset, women brought food to the council lodge to feed the old men and the warriors. When the meal was finished, the talking resumed and went on into the night.

Cloud and Grey Bull returned to their own encampment the next morning. They carried the power with them. They, and many of the younger men who listened to the good words spoken and who sat in the presence of wisdom, were like the finely crafted arrow with its sharp point sent from the strongest of bows.

From a hill above the river, Rabbit had watched Grey Bull and Cloud ride away from the winter village. His father told him the two had been summoned to a meeting. The valley was buzzing with news that Red Cloud was the focus of some kind of disagreement among the various village councils. Big Voice was afraid that those disagreements, if true, would favor the Long Knives somehow. Rabbit paid little attention to such talk. He had his own issues with the Long Knives that did not need anyone's blessing or interference. Urging his horse into a lope, he headed for a gully hidden in a stand of pine far above the river. He had lately become quite adept at finding such lonely and out-of-the-way places.

A month or so ago, he had asked his mother to make a rifle case for him, one that would enable him to carry a rifle over one shoulder or tie it onto his horse. But he also wanted the case to cover the rifle completely. At first, he had disdained the rifle, but he changed his mind because of its far-greater range compared to his six-shooter. Furthermore, he discovered that by putting a patch over his right eye, he was developing good accuracy shooting left-handed.

When his mother finished, it was a fine case. She had taken the trouble to decorate it with beads. The case would be strong and durable because it was made from elk hide. Rabbit carried the case bundled insight his shirt and thought about his mother as he rode up the long slope. He was out of sight of the encampment now, and he stopped briefly to assure himself that no one happened to be following or was in the area. But he could see nothing moving in the cold afternoon.

He was careful each time he visited the hideout he had fashioned at the head of the gully. Every time he came, he approached from a different direction. There was good reason for caution other than secrecy. Scouts had reported seeing Crow north of the river.

Riding down into the gully, he tied his horse to a branch that bent across the opening of the cave. It was the same mare he had ridden in the raid that took all the Long Knives' mules. Cloud had given her to him. She was not tall, but she was fast. Yet as good as she was, she was not trained as a warhorse. He wanted a good warhorse, one that was trained specifically to function in battle. Neck had one that he was training, a sturdy buckskin. Rabbit had watched him working the horse a few times and had casually inquired if it might be available for trade. "For the right kind of trade," Neck had said. Rabbit knew he could work a trade because Neck had one old muzzle-loading rifle and desperately wanted a better one. Rabbit had a better rifle. As a matter of fact, he had several.

Taking another look around and listening intently for several long moments, he ducked into the narrow cave. No wider than two men standing shoulder to shoulder, it curved back the length of the height of four. He carefully moved aside what appeared to be a tangle of brush, which concealed the opening. A day of work had accomplished that. Light poured into the dim hole, revealing what appeared to be nothing more than an indiscriminate pile of more brush and dry grass. Carefully pulling that aside, Rabbit uncovered his cache of four hide-wrapped bundles. Three contained two rifles in each and the fourth, smaller bundle contained the all-important powder and lead balls and percussion caps. All of it he had acquired from his successful ambushes along the Powder River Road.

One of the rifles was different, and he suspected it was a newer version the Long Knives would be using in the future. It was a breechloader. The top of the breech ahead of the hammer opened upward from the back, on a hinge. But the most amazing thing was the bullet. This rifle did not have to be loaded through the muzzle. It had a long, large metal case at the end of which was an elongated bullet with a round end. The length of it was the width of his hand, and it fit snugly into the opening when the breech was lifted.

Rabbit took the new decorated rifle case out of his shirt and slid the breechloader into it. He had given his mother a string that was the length of the rifle, and she had done a marvelous job. The rifle fit perfectly. When the end flap was pulled over and tied, it completely covered the rifle. No one would know it was different. The twenty-two bullets he had he would use judiciously, but he felt confident they would be easier and easier to obtain from the whites. He was good at that.

He selected a rifle for his trade with Neck, along with a supply of powder and round bullets. Before he hid his cache again, he sat for a moment and stared at the rifles, remembering how he had captured them. Dark images played in his memory, along with the sounds of gunfire and screams of terror and pain.

Before he was through, he would have many more weapons.

———

Black Shield had not attended the meeting at the Crazy Horse camp because an old injury always flared when cold weather came. With this in mind, Grey Bull and Cloud scratched at his lodge door the evening after they arrived home. The old man welcomed them warmly. His wife had a pot of elk stew simmering over the coals, and the men talked even as they ate.

Black Shield listened to their news. He was especially curious about everyone who had been there, and happy to hear that his old friend White Elk was well and still full of opinions as well as wise insights.

"He and I hunted often together, when we were much younger, of course. We also traded horses, though I think he got the best of me each time." His eyes twinkled at the memories. Then he reached behind him and pulled out a quiver beautifully decorated with dyed porcupine quills and bristling with arrows. "I wanted to show you something," he told them.

The old man carefully pulled out two arrows and handed one to each of his visitors. "Look at the points," he said quietly.

Both of them were amazed. Grey Bull shook his head in wonderment. "Uncle," he said, "I have not seen one like this since I was a boy."

Black Shield solemnly nodded. "I made those many years ago. I still make those points now and then, just so that I do not lose the skill," he told them.

Cloud slowly twirled the arrow between his fingers as he admired its black, shiny point. It was obsidian, also known as black stone. The craftsmanship was masterful. The triangular point was as long as from a man's middle knuckle to the tip of his finger. It was thin, fluted so that it was even from back to tip, and the edges were still sharp enough to scrape the hair off a buffalo hide.

Cloud had never seen one this fine, so exquisitely made. "There is a terrible beauty in this thing," he observed.

Black Shield slowly nodded. "Keep them. I give them to you. Something to remember me by," he said.

Both Grey Bull and Cloud were astonished. The arrows were gifts they would treasure always.

Cloud cleared his throat. "My father knew how to do this. He taught me when I was a boy. But I have not made a point like this since I was sixteen. I mean a point made of stone. My skill was never this good."

"Me, too," said Grey Bull. "I can make them if I take my time."

"But how many of our Lakota men can still do this?" asked Black Shield. His tone indicated that there was something more behind the question.

"We make them from iron now," Grey Bull answered. "I think the younger men would not know where to begin to make an arrowhead from any kind of stone."

"Yes," said the old man. "Now our tools for making arrowheads are the white man's hammer and chisel, and the file. Or we melt iron in the fire. I have seen men argue over the iron bands around the wooden barrels."

The two visitors waited in respectful silence, knowing that there was a reason Black Shield had brought up the loss of the skills to make stone arrowheads. They did not have to wait long.

"When I was a boy," the old man began, "there was news that came from our Sicangu relatives living along the Great Muddy River. That time, we were just west of the Black Hills, just beginning to look in this direction. But we already knew about this country. I will get back to that. Anyway, the Sicangu told about some white men with fancy clothes, firearms, and long knives who traveled in boats up the river. Imagine that—they were going up the river, against the flow. Now that is a white man for you. So the white man has always been part of my life. There was almost a fight when the white men on the boats took a

Sicangu prisoner. It came to nothing because they let him go. But it was a standoff. The Sicangu had bows and arrows against the boatmen. I think the Sicangu would have killed them all. I sometimes wish they would have." The old man paused and sighed deeply. "But that would have only delayed them a while, I think. When that happened with the boatmen, there was a large village of Oglalas who were there that summer. Many of them saw the white men, too. They had gone to the Sicangu to make a gift of the black stones. That is the story I want to tell you."

The old man paused as his wife poured peppermint tea into metal cups for her guests. As he waited, he took a chunk of obsidian out of a case, a piece the size of a man's fist. "I have had this for over thirty years," he said, holding the piece up for them to see. Then he passed it over to Grey Bull. "Every time I look at that, it reminds me of how I became a man."

"Do you mean, Grandfather, that you went to look for the stone?" asked Cloud.

The old man nodded, pleased that something of the past had not entirely been forgotten. "Yes," he replied. "My friend and I traveled west from the Black Hills. We were seventeen that year. We crossed over these mountains south of Cloud Mountain and descended onto a wide plain that took us to mountains farther west. Young men who had gone before gave us directions and told us what landmarks to look for. Cloud Mountain was an important one. But we also had to stay alert because the people who lived here did not want us in their country. It was an adventure, but a dangerous one."

"My father told me that the black stone came from one place in a strange land where the water boiled out of the ground," said Grey Bull.

Black Shield's eyes twinkled. "Yes, he was right. Did he ever make the journey to search for the stones?"

"No, but my grandfather did."

"Then remember his story," advised the old man, "because no one will ever do it again. That is sad, because that journey to find the stone was the best way for boys to become men."

"Was there a mountain of the black stone?" Cloud wanted to know.

"We found a mountainside," recalled Black Shield. "From it, we chipped several pieces like that one there. On the way home, we finally ran into trouble. Some people, probably Shoshone, saw us and chased us for days. But we lost them in the area south of Cloud Mountain. We killed one of our horses because we had to run them day and night. From then on, we took turns riding and running. But we made it home.

"That journey taught me much about what I had to do, what I could do, when life and death come face to face. But when the white man came with his things and we began to make lance points and arrowheads from iron, it was no longer necessary for young men to make that journey. Oh, once in a while after that we traded for the black stone with people who could get it. But that was it. I make the journey only in my memory now. Although neither of you have done it, I hope that you remember what I told you. Remember what your grandfathers told you."

"I will not forget," promised Cloud. "I am glad you told us, Grandfather."

"There is another reason for the story," the old man continued. "The white man came with his things, some or many of which we all use in our homes, like those cups, knives, cooking pots, and blankets and cloth. Many, many things. But he also caused us to change our ways. No one among us makes stone arrowheads, because iron is easier to acquire. The white man did not tell us to make iron arrowheads and iron lance points. Those things we did because it was easier. What other ways will we change or forget just because something is easier? I think one day all Lakota men will have guns, perhaps several apiece, and we will no longer make bows and arrows at all."

Grey Bull nodded and slowly twirled the arrow in his hand. "I think I see what you mean, Uncle. Where one thing changes so easily, other things can, too."

"Yes," replied the old man, "that is what I am afraid of. In the past few months, there has been much talk about how we should lead the young men and who should have the power to tell others what to do. That is dangerous. No one among us ever had the power to tell anyone what to do or to decide something for all the people. Now we are arguing over *who* should have that power. When did we decide to change that? Or was I asleep when that happened?"

"What shall we do, Grandfather?"

Black Shield picked up the chunk of stone and gazed at it for several long moments. "Do not forget the old ways," he said. "They are what made us into the people we are. If we cast aside the old ways, we are throwing ourselves away, and the Long Knives will not have to go to the trouble of defeating us. We will have defeated ourselves."

Cloud would remember those words for the rest of his life. And each time he looked at Black Shield's arrow or held it in his hands, he would see the wistful and pleading expression in that old man's eyes.

CHAPTER FOURTEEN

A Lost Soul

Max Hornsby snipped the protruding end of the last nail he had pounded into the draft horse's shoe and wearily straightened before he led the animal to the holding pen. His back ached fiercely, and he was immensely relieved to know he had shod the last horse for the day. He took a deep breath, rubbed the back of a hand across his mouth, and slowly began putting away the tools. Slattern, the blacksmith he worked for, did not want tools left lying around.

The task finished, he trudged wearily toward the water bucket and basin in the smithy's shed to wash his face and hands. After that, he collected his mess tin from under his bunk in the back of the room and sat down, waiting for the supper bell to ring.

He finished eating in the enlisted men's mess. It was a concoction of some sort of stew that was vaguely pungent. He suspected it might be one of the oxen that had dropped dead a few days ago.

After swishing his tin in a pan full of greasy water, he returned to his bunk. From a square tin, he took out the makings for a cigarette, rolled one, and lit it. Watching the smoke bend in the air, he pushed aside the images that forced their way in. Vivid images of smoke rising from campfires in the Sioux village.

Life as a blacksmith at Fort Philip Kearny was nothing to write home about, and he didn't. At least, he didn't talk of his meager existence since his botched attempt to rescue the white woman. Instead, when he wrote to his mother, he described only the obvious things about the fort: its contingent of soldiers and civilians, the sawmill, and the somewhat-regimented life inside the walls. He purposely did not mention the Indian attacks, or certainly his own brush with death. His mother would have been horrified if he had told her. For all intents and purposes, Henrietta Hornsby probably thought her son was a grand part of the civilization of the vast uncharted frontier that lay west of the Hudson River.

Hornsby finished the cigarette and lay back on his bunk. It was one he had built himself and padded with straw. A thin wool blanket covered the straw, but the buffalo robe a teamster had given him—on the day he showed up naked at the fort—helped keep him warm at night. He had also built the wall that closed in the back corner of the shed that was now his living quarters. Luckily, there was room enough for a small stove, as heat was a priceless commodity during these cold November nights. He suddenly remembered he had to bring in wood for the night.

"Hornsby!" A hard knock swung his door open following the shout.

"Here! I am here!"

Slattern, a beefy, square-shouldered man with thick forearms, stood in the doorway. The rail-thin man next to him was one Hornsby recognized as some kind of civilian contractor, but he couldn't remember his name.

"Max," said the blacksmith, "Jennes here is looking for a brave man."

Hornsby sat up. "Well," he drawled, "you be looking at the wrong man."

"This is serious," insisted Slattern. "Some couriers have to make the ride to Fort Laramie. The colonel will authorize only four soldiers, so Jennes needs at least one more guard. Are you up to it? It means extra wages."

"For extra wages, I can be brave," Hornsby told the thin man.

"Good," said Jennes in a high-pitched voice that matched his frame. "You be leaving at dawn. I can supply a horse, rifle and ammunition, a bedroll, and food. I will pay when you get back in one piece. Otherwise, I may not know which piece to pay, if you run into trouble and the Indians get you," Jennes giggled at his own thin humor, "if you get my drift."

Hornsby knew damn well Jennes was hedging his bet to make sure anyone he hired completed the trip, hence the task, before he would dole out money.

"Well, there is the rub," protested Hornsby. "The only thing I desire in this life is a good rifle. Not a woman, not riches, just a damn good rifle. They have rifles at the trading post at Fort Laramie. I know that for certain. Trouble is, I got no money. So the wages up front would be appreciated—if you get my drift."

"Ya got some pay coming," said Slattern. "I will draw that for you, if that will help."

"For sure," said Hornsby. "My thanks to you."

"Tell you what," chimed in Jennes, "I can give you half."

"That will do. Thank you as well."

"Then we have a deal," returned the contractor. "Meet me at dawn at the lower corral. All you need will be waiting."

―――――――――

Sweetwater Woman finished mixing the last bowl full of dried and pounded elk meat together with the dried choke-cherries, also pounded. To it, she added enough rendered fat to hold the mixture together. Cloud had announced that he was leading a group of young men south along the Powder River Road in a day or two, and that meant he would be gone for days. The pemmican was the staple for hunters and fighting men when they took to the trail. She wanted him to have plenty of it along, enough for more than a few days, in case his outing took longer than expected. She knew it would; it always did.

She was alone inside the lodge. Cloud was outside next to the door, making arrows, and Grandmother Willow was off visiting somewhere. Sweetwater was grateful for the unexpected privacy. There was much on her mind.

Her sleep had been fitful for many nights, partially due to the baby growing inside her. At least that was what she allowed her husband and Grandmother Willow to believe. She was afraid to tell them the other reason, perhaps the real reason: she was beginning to doubt that she really belonged here.

Finished with her chore, she packed away the pemmican into several bags that Cloud would take. Then she went out. "I am going over to see my mother," she told him, brushing his cheek with a hand. "I have not seen her for a while, and she likes to watch my stomach wiggle."

Cloud nodded and watched his wife waddle away slowly, her elk robe around her shoulders.

Star Woman greeted her daughter effusively. "Come, come inside, it is warmer in there," she said, holding the door aside. "Your father went fishing. At least, he went hoping for fish."

Star Woman's hair was nearly white, though her narrow face was surprisingly free of wrinkles. She smiled easily and was thin and energetic.

Sweetwater Woman carefully sank down and leaned back against the willow chair. "Is that peppermint tea I smell? If it is, I would like some."

The older woman studied her daughter's face as she poured tea for both of them. After she took a seat, she watched a moment longer. Something was not right.

"If Grandmother Willow's prediction is correct, you have about a month longer," she pointed out.

"Yes," Sweetwater said, absently staring into her cup.

Another moment of silence ensued. "Daughter," said Star Woman, "is there something on your mind?"

Tears welled up in Sweetwater's eyes. Star Woman immediately moved over and embraced her daughter. She hoped that it was the pregnancy creating this sudden mood of melancholy, which often happened with mothers-to-be. "Tell me," she said.

Sweetwater dabbed at the tears. "Mother, I am so afraid."

"Do not worry. Everything will be fine. There is no better midwife than Grandmother Red Shawl, and you have been healthy all this time. And you will be a wonderful mother, I know it!"

"Those are not the things I am afraid of."

"What is it then?'

Sweetwater drew a deep breath and exhaled, then sipped her tea. "Mother," she said softly, "I think I would like to know who I really am."

"You are Sweetwater Woman," her mother replied, "daughter of Bearface and Star Woman."

Sweetwater glanced almost apologetically at Star Woman. "But I did not grow in your womb like this baby is growing in mine. This baby will know its mother, and I will never know the woman who gave birth to me. Is that so much to ask?"

Star Woman sighed. "You can ask it, and life may

answer you, or it may not. The trouble with asking is that we may not always like the answer."

"Ever since that white man came," admitted Sweetwater, "I am having these—these thoughts. They will not leave me alone! What am I to do?"

"What are the thoughts?"

"I want to go looking to find what I can. Perhaps the chance of finding anything is small, but I feel I must try."

"Where would you begin? I have heard there are so many of them, the whites, that they cannot be counted. A greater truth is that the Great Spirit sent you here, to us. Why would you leave us?"

Sweetwater Woman leaned her head on her mother's shoulder and wept softly. "I do not know. I do not want to leave. What shall I do?"

"For now, cry all you want. Maybe your tears will wash away the thoughts that are bothering you."

Sweetwater waited until her eyes had cleared before she went home, and it helped that evening had come so neither her husband nor Grandmother Willow noticed that she had been crying. Although she knew the old woman suspected something, she said nothing. It was not so easy to fool her.

Two mornings later, Cloud rode away with his young men, south toward the Powder River Road. She prayed silently that he would return safely.

Hornsby hefted the muzzleloader, the same type issued to the soldiers at Fort Phil Kearny. This one was new.

"This one just came not two weeks past," said the post trader. He pointed to the waxed-paper wrapping in the crate behind the counter as proof of an honest sales pitch.

"Something new comes with it, too." He tossed what looked like a small roll of paper onto the counter. It landed with a clunk.

"What is it?"

"Ball and powder, both in that container. You tear off the end and the powder comes out, already measured for you. Then you pour it down the barrel and tap in the ball. All you need is pockets, not a powder horn and shot bag."

"If all this is not more than the money in my pocket, we can likely work us a deal," Hornsby said.

"That is what I like," returned the trader, "an optimist. I expect we can work a deal."

Later, with a new rifle in the crook of his arm, he walked around the grounds of the outpost. He could not afford the new powder-and-shot containers, though he had managed to scrounge powder and balls at Fort Phil Kearny. Just in case, he had brought it along and was glad he did. But he did buy more powder and shot and percussion caps. Once again, he felt adequately armed, though this time he vowed that the only way this rifle would be taken from him was from his dead fingers.

Fort Laramie was a direct contrast to Fort Philip Kearny. There were no walls here, and the buildings were larger. One of them, the officers' quarters, he thought, was called Old Bedlam. He was afraid to ask why. To the north was the North Platte River, and everywhere else beyond the buildings was open prairie. Furthermore, there were more than a few Indians around, which made him a little nervous.

"Pay them no heed," the trader replied when Hornsby asked why Indians were here. "Them bucks is peaceful, at least today."

Still, he wondered if some of these sullen-looking Sioux might have been involved in the attacks on Fort Philip Kearny. In fact, he would be willing to bet money they were.

He bought more tobacco and passed the time drinking strong coffee in the dry-goods store. The large clumps of sugar in the bottom were to his liking. One of the couriers had said they would start back in the morning if they didn't have to wait for the dispatches they were expecting from the east. Hornsby didn't mind waiting. Anything was better than breaking his back in the blacksmith shed.

As it turned out, however, they did depart the next morning: two couriers, four soldiers, and one other guard besides Hornsby. The rifle he had been issued several days ago looked old and worn in comparison to the one Hornsby had purchased. If there was trouble, he decided to use up the army's supply of powder and shot first.

The plan was to stop overnight again at Fort Reno,

at least six days of riding away. From Fort Laramie to Fort Reno was the most secure stretch of the Bozeman Trail; however, after that, those heathens could be anywhere.

═══════════

Cloud's new glass revealed eight riders before they came within rifle range. It was a good glass. It could reach out farther than the other one he had. Hunched between two low boulders on the lip of a flat butte, he had spotted the riders when they were still dark specks on the land. Now he could see them. Four were Long Knives and four were not, but he knew they were from the log town. They had to be scouts, or at least messengers of some sort. Or message carriers, more likely. There was communication between the Long Knife outposts along the Powder River Road, and small groups occasionally went as far as Fort Laramie and back. He and his young men would heed Hump's words and make life difficult for these riders. There was plenty of time to set up an ambush.

They had spent many hard days out on patrol and were on their way home when he spotted the riders. Due mainly to the cold weather, Cloud guessed, few whites were on the Powder River Road. All of the landscape was thoroughly familiar to Cloud, even to the point of recognizing certain trees and rock formations. Cloud could not begin to guess how many times he had traveled and camped in this area. As a matter of fact, they were along that stretch of the trail where Rabbit had been wounded.

An idea to hunt for fresh meat had to be put aside until it was seen what would develop because of the approaching riders. He left his lookout post and joined the others, all of them gathered around a fire against a rock wall below the butte. The wall reflected the heat nicely.

Yellow Wolf looked up from between the folds of his buffalo robe. "Meat roasting over that fire would be good. See any elk or deer?" The others—Little Bird, Goings, Taken Alive, Good Hand, and Rabbit—nodded in agreement, good-natured smiles creasing their brown faces, except for Rabbit's; he was always serious these days. Good Hand was the new one of the group, the seventeen-year-old-son of Neck. Like his father, he had a skill with horses.

Cloud shook his head. "No, but eight riders are coming up the trail. Four are Long Knives."

All of the men were instantly alert, especially Rabbit.

"No need to hurry," said Cloud. "If they stay on the road, there is a good spot up the trail."

"The road dips into a low spot, and there is good cover because the sagebrush is thick," said Rabbit quietly. "There are rocks, too."

Cloud nodded. "Yes, that is the place I had in mind."

Staying in a dry watercourse they had used before, they rode fast and kept out of sight of the trail. Arriving at the site suggested by Rabbit, they hid the horses well off the road to the east. Good Hand would stay with them.

They all carried rifles now, even Rabbit, and, except for him, they also carried bows. Rabbit's backup weapon was the six-shooter Cloud had given him. Each of the others had at least forty war arrows with wickedly sharp points. Little Bird was the deadliest with the bow. More than once, Cloud had watched him hit a sitting jackrabbit at sixty long paces.

The plan was simple. Goings hid on the east side of the road, and Rabbit and Taken Alive on the west. Farther down the trail, Cloud and Little Bird were on opposite sides of the road. Cloud was anticipating that when Goings and the others opened fire, the riders would turn around to head back south. If that happened, and he was sure it would, he and Little Bird would be ready.

A cold breeze bothered the land, and somewhere in the folds of the foothills, a bull elk whistled. Otherwise the land lay silent. The eight riders were in two lines, rifles held across the withers of their horses, no doubt expecting trouble because they were north of the Powder River outpost.

———————————

Corporal Francois Decouteau was one of the two soldiers in the lead. Hornsby didn't like him. The corporal assumed authority over the civilians, and Hornsby was not certain that was part of the arrangement. Like him, most of the others, including the three other soldiers from the Second Cavalry, simply tolerated Decouteau. He had seen action at Vicksburg in the war over slavery, he had said, but Hornsby had his doubts. No matter, they were less than two days from Fort Philip Kearny. He was not looking forward to going back to work for the blacksmith, however. But the new rifle resting across the saddle helped him feel better about life in general.

Hornsby kept a sharp eye on the terrain. Nothing big was moving anywhere, though the usual hawks and eagles prowled the skies. A bull elk whistled; the thin, almost wheezing notes came intermittently.

He reached up to fasten the top button on his overcoat when he saw Decouteau twist, a quick jerky motion. Hornsby saw something fly from the back of the soldier's coat, and then heard the *boom* of a rifle. Decouteau flopped sideways like a rag doll and was on the ground. More booms.

Hornsby heard a hollow *crack* as one of the couriers screamed. Another *thwack*, and the horse ahead of him screamed in pain. The gunfire was from up the trail. Instinctively, they all yanked their horses around to go back down the trail. The sudden noise and confusion panicked the horses into a gallop.

Hornsby thought he might have reached safety as he saw a thick clump of sagebrush ahead. He felt a tug at his hip and heard a *whump* and then the blast of a gun.

In an instant, he reached the horrific realization that they were surrounded. In his peripheral vision, he saw another soldier tumble out of the saddle. Without conscious thought, Hornsby turned his mount to the right, kicking him viciously to make him run faster. He heard low humming noises followed by gunfire. Later, he realized they were the sound of near misses, very near misses.

He leaned low over the neck of the horse. All he could think to do was to get as far up the slope as he could, even if he had to wear out the horse to do it.

Cloud watched four of the riders running away to the west. One was following another, but the other two were widely separated from them and each other. All of them were nearly out of range. Along the road, three of them were dead, he assumed, as well as a horse. Somewhere, there was a fourth dead, or wounded and hiding.

He stood and walked north after he reloaded his rifle. The gunfire from Goings, Taken Alive, and Rabbit had been heavy and fast. He wondered when they had learned to reload so swiftly. The ambush had been effective to the extent that they had taken out some of the intruders. Still, it bothered Cloud that four had gotten away.

All of the men were converging carefully on the area where the dead men and the dead horse were, though the bodies were somewhat scattered. Cloud and Little

Bird came to the body of a soldier, his blue eyes staring in perpetual panic. Little Bird removed the belt and the bullet case. He found the rifle in the grass back up the trail.

Cloud felt bad about the horse. Several paces away, he found the next body, someone who was not a soldier. Up the trail, he saw Goings bending over the body of another soldier, then stripping it of the six-shooter and bullet pouch. Taken Alive was looking around in the brush for the rifle and found it.

The fourth casualty was harder to find. He had either gone down away from the trail or he was only wounded and was crawling and hiding.

"There is one more!" Cloud yelled to the others. "Be careful!"

No sooner had the echo of his shout faded away than a man jumped up from behind some brush, a six-shooter in hand.

Boom!

The civilian jerked backward and went down in a heap, struck squarely in the middle of the chest. Everyone except Rabbit stared in momentary confusion. He was walking toward the dead soldier, reloading his rifle as he walked. Stopping above the body, he fired once more, shattering the man's arm at the right elbow. Saying nothing, the young man turned and walked away.

Watching Rabbit, Cloud understood why the gunfire had been so fast. It was the rifle, a new type. It had a mechanism that opened from the top and could be reloaded very swiftly, even by a one-armed man.

The others exchanged silent, puzzled glances and then turned to stare at Rabbit as he walked away toward the horses.

CHAPTER FIFTEEN

Alive and Cold

Cold forced them to hunker down inside a narrow gully. Four men sitting in a circle, almost nose to nose. Cold and miserable fear. Private Herman Kennard shivered, not only from the cold, but from the images in his mind that he could not drive away. He had been next to Corporal Decouteau and heard the hollow pop of the Indian bullet tearing into the man's chest. How an instant in time could be caught in a man's mind, he didn't know.

"Are you certain we should not have a fire?" he asked hopefully.

"No!" Max Hornsby was emphatic. "Them damn Sioux are at home anywhere, even in the dark!"

"I didn't see them come up the slope," insisted Private Holman. "Mr. Conklin and I watched from some trees while we rested the horses."

Evan Conklin was the other civilian guard. He nodded in agreement.

"Well, it is a fine choice," said Hornsby, "be alive and cold or warm and dead."

"I expect the cold might kill us as well," protested Kennard.

Somehow the survivors of the attack had managed to find one another after their mindless flight up the slope. But one of the horses had slipped down an embankment during the mad gallop and broken an ankle. It was Conklin's horse, but Hornsby talked him out of shooting it, because the Indians would hear the shot. So somewhere out there was an injured horse they had had to leave behind. The remaining three horses stood only a few feet away, their reins clipped together. Hornsby had appointed himself the horse holder and grimly hung on to the lead line. Being unarmed in this godforsaken country was bad enough, but being on foot was just as much a death warrant.

"A fire throws light farther than you think," Hornsby warned, "even a little fire."

"We could cover it somehow," Kennard persisted. "Besides, what about bears? I hear they is still not in their dens sleeping. A fire would keep them away, right?"

Hornsby relented. "Yes, alright! But we use only the driest wood we can find, small twigs."

In a few minutes, the small fire was burning brightly, though it only kept the cold at bay. But it was enough.

"Keep an eye on the horses," said Hornsby. "If they get nervous, we do not waste any time putting out the fire!"

As long as there had been daylight, they had huddled in a grove of aspen and watched to see if the Indians would come up the slope. They were immensely relieved to see them riding away. But, of course, the heathens could be planning to double back in the dark. So they had climbed as far up the slope as they could until they had rock walls behind them to guard their backs. The deep, narrow gully was a fortunate discovery.

Coyotes yapped all around them and wolves howled. Stars twinkled in the cold, cloudless sky.

"What do you suppose they will do to us?" asked Holman.

"Who? The Indians?" said Conklin.

"No, back at the fort. Likely they will not be pleased. We lost four men and all the dispatches, and the guns, and five horses. Nothing to brag about."

"Well, Holman," said Kennard, "I expect they will decorate you for just being alive."

"Are you joking?"

"There is one small detail," chimed in Conklin. "We still have to make it back to the fort for anyone to do anything to us."

"How we going to do that?" worried Holman. "We are not going down to the Bozeman Road, are we? Them Indians'll be waiting for us!"

"No," said Hornsby. "We stay up high, out of sight. We got a little food and we have ammunition. Take us longer, but up high, we have a better chance to see what might come at us, Indian or beast."

"What about the corporal and the others?"

"What about them?" returned Hornsby. "They are dead. Nothing we can do to change that."

After a minute or two of awkward silence, Conklin cleared his throat. "Mr. Hornsby is right about everything.

Hell, we should not have this fire going. He knows because he has gone up and down the Bozeman a time or two. I hear he even had his own fight with them damn Indians."

Hornsby chuckled derisively. "Hey," he said, "I came out on the short end of that affair. I just want to stay alive, like all of you. That is why I put up a fuss about the fire."

"Can you tell us," asked Holman, "about your fight with the Indians?"

"No," replied Hornsby. "Nothing to brag about. They let me live is all I can say. Just like today. They could have come after us. Hell, did any of us here fire our guns in anger today? Sometimes things happen in ways you cannot figure until long after it is over."

Holman shook his head. "There was no time," he said pensively, "no time at all. Makes me wonder why I joined the damn army."

"Why did you?" asked Kennard.

"Got in a fight with my brother," replied Holman. "I licked him good. My father licked me worse and then sent me packing. Jake was his favorite. I headed straight for Jefferson Barracks and signed up."

"Where you from?"

"Saint Charles, Missouri. But I thought they would send me east."

"That war is over," said Kennard. "The army is done killing rebels, so now we go killing Indians."

"Hey," said Holman, "ever wonder why they sent

us here to kill Indians? This is their land, right?"

"Yeah," agreed Conklin. "I expect that is why they fight us so hard. Got to admit, fellas, the Indians is good fighters. And they ride like they was born on a horse."

"You got that right," pointed out Hornsby. "When I got to Fort Laramie the first time, back in July, I saw those that were around there. But they reminded me of dogs with their tails between their legs. These up here in this country, there is something about them. Wild, is all I can think of. I saw two of them once, on their horses, galloping flat out. Never seen anything like it. None of us can ride that way."

Kennard snorted. "Yeah, well, think about this now, gents. They just rubbed out half of us, and here we are admiring those buggers when the next one you see up close will probably kill you in a heartbeat! In a heartbeat!"

"Sure and true!" Conklin chuckled. "Sure and true. But this is their land, and they will not let us rest in peace as long as we are here."

The cold air seemed to grow heavier as the night wore on, forcing them all to lean in closer to the low flames and close their eyes against the smoke. They talked intermittently, nodding off now and then until dawn brought a hint of light to the eastern sky. After the morning grew brighter, they built up the fire until it was roaring, and they soaked up all the heat they could before they buried it.

They rode when the terrain allowed. The two soldiers doubled up on the biggest of the horses. They were less than two days from the fort when they were ambushed, but Hornsby guessed it would take them three days to reach the outpost. It took them four.

For three more nights, they endured the bone-chilling cold, and on the third day, they ate the last of their hardtack and bacon. Their brush with death made them jumpy. Once, they nearly fired at a cow elk crashing out of the brush when they frightened her. It took them a moment or two to recover their nerve.

They spoke no further about the ambush and the men left behind, but each of them could not help but think of those few heart-stopping beats in time and feel guilty for not doing more.

Late in the afternoon on the fourth day after the ambush, they reached the sentinel hill on the knob south of the fort. They hid in the brush and called out to the sentries, not wanting to be shot by mistake. After the sentries signaled the fort, the four survivors rode wearily down into the valley, glad to be still alive.

Second Lieutenant George Grummond gestured toward the chairs in the sparse room as Privates Kennard and Holman entered. They were relieved at not having to stand at attention. Grummond studied them. They were disheveled, their uniforms a little worse for the wear. But it was the hollowness in the eyes that he noticed immediately.

He had seen that look before, from men who had seen death up close.

"I trust you have had time to eat?" he asked.

"Yes, sir," replied Holman, "we have. Thank you, sir."

"Men, I want you to relax. This is not an inquisition. I simply want a report. You can begin by relating what exactly happened. I know you were attacked by Indians, so I want details."

They nodded in unison. Holman cleared his throat and glanced sideways at Kennard. "You—you can go first."

Kennard gathered his thoughts. "We were about two days south," he began, "no more. The trip was no trouble, up—up until then. I saw nothing. I guess none of us did. They started firing, and even then, I could not see them."

"Heavy and rapid firing?"

"Yes, sir. That it was. The corporal got it first. After that, we turned to—to find cover. We did not get far. They was behind us, too."

The lieutenant looked toward Holman. "Private Holman, what happened next?"

Holman's lower lip trembled. "I saw the courier go down and then—and then Desantis, I think. Somehow we all got turned up the slope, and we kept running our horses. The other courier, his horse was killed. Four of us scattered and kept going up the slope. We found cover in some rocks."

"They—they got him later, I think," added Kennard. "The other courier, I mean. Milward. I heard a shot when we got up to some rocks."

"I see," said the lieutenant. He took a few minutes to finish writing, pausing to dip his pen occasionally. He looked up. "Is there anything else you can think of, either of you?"

The privates shook their heads.

"Thank you. You have no duty for two days. If you feel the need, I suggest you talk to the chaplain. He is available. That is all for now."

Lieutenant Grummond sat for several minutes after the two weary soldiers left the room, his lips compressed into a thin line. *If it was necessary to take the risk to send dispatches to Fort Laramie*, he reasoned, *then it should have also been necessary to send more than four soldiers.* He glanced down at the report he had written to make sure the ink was dry, but also to fashion another argument to take to Colonel Henry Carrington. *Seven hundred men*, Grummond fumed silently, *and we sit inside these walls and let the sneaky little devils out there pick us off one or two at a time.*

He closed his leather folder and stood. It was time to face the most cautious field officer he had ever had the misfortune to serve under. After a deep breath, he headed for the door.

On the other side of the parade field, Hornsby put the reins of the horse into Jennes's hands. He patted the rifle in its scabbard. "All the powder and shot is there, too. The bedroll is on the cantle, as you can see. I did consume the food you supplied."

Jennes nodded grimly. "All the powder and shot? You mean you never got off a shot?"

Hornsby glared at the narrow face. "No, not a one."

"Well, I was just asking," the man retorted, "not accusing." He counted coins and handed them over. "The other half of your wages. Sorry to hear how it turned out," he said. "I lost my couriers. Come see me if you be interested in the job."

"The life expectancy of anyone who goes out of these walls is short," Hornsby replied. "That is not exactly a drawing card. I will give it some thought, though."

At least here I have choices, he thought wryly as he lay on his bunk and smoked. "Work until my back breaks or put myself in the sights of an angry heathen with a gun," he said out loud. "Mother would be proud."

He finished the cigarette and started to doze. Outside there were sudden noises, loud voices shouting commands, scuffling footsteps, and the creak of saddle leather and jingle of iron bits. *Perhaps the cavalry is riding out for revenge*, he thought. But after he listened more closely, he realized that people had arrived. A lot of people, from the sounds of the commotion. He sighed and pulled the buffalo robe over him. He would find out sooner or later, and later would be good.

—————————
=========
—————————

A knock at the door stopped the colonel in mid-sentence. "Yes, what is it?" he asked impatiently.

The young blonde-haired orderly opened the door and peered in cautiously. "Sir," he said tentatively, "the sergeant asked me to inform you that a relief column has arrived."

"Indeed?"

"Yes, sir!"

"Very well. Thank you, Corporal."

Carrington turned a bespectacled look back toward Lieutenant Grummond. The argument was not old. They had had words before, over strategy, tactics, and operational orders.

"We are within the spirit and the letter of our orders, Lieutenant," the colonel said wearily. "We were sent here to build outposts. We have done that. We were sent here to protect civilians using the Bozeman Trail. We do that."

"Not in my opinion, sir."

"What might that opinion be?"

"We react, sir, more than we anticipate. I think it is our responsibility to prevent civilian travelers from being harassed and killed. Sadly, we show up more after the fact."

"What you are implying is next to impossible, Lieutenant. We simply cannot escort each and every wagon or group of wagons on the trail, primarily because

213

we do not know when they will come north. In any case, you will agree that civilian traffic has diminished to a virtual trickle."

"I agree, sir, but it has diminished as a consequence of the Indian attacks. If we were to send out regular patrols, large patrols and heavily armed—"

"Lieutenant," the colonel sighed, "we are not here to wage war as an offensive force. We are here as a protective force."

It was Grummond's turn to sigh. The argument was the same as before, even with the same words and gestures. "Sir, I interviewed Privates Kennard and Holman regarding the attack on the courier detail several days ago. What they told me indicates that the enemy carried out a determined and well-planned action. We cannot allow that to be uncontested!"

As the colonel lifted a hand in protest, another knock at the door interrupted him. "What is it now?" he demanded.

"Begging your pardon, sir," said a deep voice. The man in uniform who stepped through the door looked tired. The overcoat draped over his arm was dusty. "I have just brought in a troop. I believe a dispatch was sent by courier only days before we left Fort Laramie."

Carrington and Grummond saw the captain's insignia on the man's shoulders.

"Unfortunately, Captain, those dispatches never got through."

"Then that would probably explain the bodies we found along the trail, sir." The man stepped to the opposite of the colonel's desk. "Captain William Fetterman, sir, reporting for duty."

The man offered a salute, which the colonel casually returned.

"Happy to have you here, Captain. This is Lieutenant Grummond."

As the two younger officers shook hands, the colonel studied the new arrival. His hair was dark, and his thick handlebar mustache made him look older than he probably was. But the air of self-assurance was just as obvious as the physical characteristics, and it grated on the colonel.

"You mentioned bodies, Captain?"

"Yes, sir. We found them yesterday. All of them dead of gunshot wounds and scalped. Two civilians and two soldiers, one a corporal."

"Very well. Thank you for bringing them back. We have a post cemetery. Is there anything else?"

"No, sir. I will see the adjutant to see to quarters for the new men."

Grummond stepped forward. "I can help with that, sir," he said to Fetterman.

Alone after the door closed behind the two officers, Carrington suddenly felt the weight of his responsibilities get heavier, and he was certain it had something to do with the arrival of Captain Fetterman.

CHAPTER SIXTEEN

The Singing Medicine Man

Grandmother Willow's yearning for fresh elk roast was enough for Cloud to carefully check his hunting bow and arrows. The stout ash-wood bow was longer than the war bow, though it was also backed with a layer of buffalo sinew. It was bigger and stronger so that it could fire a heavier arrow. He shook his head as he inspected the iron points on the arrows, remembering Black Shield's story.

From the back of the room, Sweetwater Woman watched him as she braided sweetgrass. It was his hunting equipment that he had taken down from the lodge poles. With a well-worn whetstone, he was touching up the edges of the arrow points. At least he was not going out to fight the Long Knives again, and he had promised her he would be gone only a day. He would be gone by the time she awoke in the morning. She hated that moment when she rolled over in their bed and saw the empty space where she knew he had slept. It matched the emptiness she was feeling more and more. Now even his physical presence could not seem to dissipate the feeling, as it once had.

She finished the braid and laid it in the case nearby. "So High Eagle is going with you?" she asked.

"Yes," he replied without turning away from his task. "He said he needs to do something to loosen up his joints. But I know he wants to talk to me about something."

"Where will you go?"

"I thought to the Little Goose Creek area."

"That is near the Long Knife town."

"Yes," he turned and smiled at her, "it is. I thought of going north because Rabbit said he saw a herd of elk up near there. But he also said he saw the tracks of what he was sure were Crow horses. The Long Knives stay inside their walls, and even if one wanders out, I would rather face a scared Long Knife than a sneaky Crow any day."

She smiled in spite of herself.

"We will be home by dark, with or without an elk," he assured her.

———————

He decided on the Little Goose Creek area because a few elk were still moving down from the high country and that valley was their main passage.

He awoke to a dim but warm lodge and looked at the fire pit. The short, knotty piece of thick pine he had placed on the coals had burned down. It had not burned with a high flame, but as the heat nibbled it down, it keep the lodge comfortable. And because it was a mere chunk of glowing ember now, he knew it was near dawn.

He dressed quietly so as not to wake either of the sleeping women and slipped out the door with his things. He was not surprised that High Eagle was waiting outside with his horse and hunting bow.

Still on the early side of morning, they crossed Big Goose Creek, and by mid-morning, they came to Little Goose Creek. Their horses, including the big Long Knife horse he used to pack game, moved briskly. The air was crisp and exhilarating, and Cloud felt good.

They came into the tall pines that filled the air with their scent and found a likely thicket where they could wait. After tying the horses and preparing their weapons, they covered themselves in their elk robes and sat against a dead stump and spoke in hushed voices.

"It is days like this that make life worthwhile," said High Eagle.

Cloud nodded in agreement.

"I was born at the front of the Winter Moon," the medicine man went on. "Your child will be born at the back, I think."

"That time is drawing closer," said Cloud. "I think it is harder on my wife than she lets on."

"Women are strong, or they could not be mothers and grandmothers," High Eagle pointed out, "but carrying a child is hard on them. But, Nephew, I think it is not carrying a child that is a worry for your wife."

Cloud was looking around, peering between the branches of the thicket. He turned. He knew that men like High Eagle did not make idle statements, and the man had invited himself along when Cloud had revealed his plan to hunt. He had something to say. "What do you mean?"

"Some time ago, I saw something around your wife. I thought it was a bad spirit trying to get at the baby. They do that sometimes. So I prayed in the sweat lodge for her and the baby. But I do not think it was a bad spirit."

"What is it?"

"I think it is something that is part of her. A part of her that has become like a shadow. That is why I could see it, I think."

"A part of her?"

"Yes. Sometimes feelings can become so strong that they are easily perceived. Like anger or happiness. And sometimes feelings like doubt, uncertainty, or fear. Has she said anything to you at all?"

"No, nothing like that. But she has been a little quiet lately, like she is deep in thought."

High Eagle nodded slowly. "Stay close to her, even if you do not speak to her. But resist the urge to ask too many questions. In fact, do not ask her any questions at all. Just be with her and keep yourself calm and centered. It will be good for her."

"Thank you, Uncle, I will do that. Perhaps I have been gone too much of late. But I will do as you say."

"Life can be a strange thing. That is the only thing I know for certain," said the medicine man. "Hard times come and go, but they do make us strong. And I fear the winter coming will test us severely."

"You mean because of the Long Knives?"

"Yes. Several days ago, I asked Grey Bull to ride

with me to Buffalo Creek. The Long Knives have built something inside the town and are using the creek for something more than drinking. The water does not like it. When I drank from the water, I felt as though something was twisting and turning inside of me." High Eagle's eyes narrowed; he was still bothered by the incident. "Whatever it was, it is something that will cause death and grief."

Cloud thought for a moment as he poked at the grass near his feet. "Death and grief for who?"

"I am not certain. Only that I felt spirits in turmoil from their town. Sometimes when a life is over suddenly, the spirit is surprised and does not want to go over to the other side. It was something like that."

"You think some of them inside the walls have died?"

"No, it is not that. I think perhaps some of their spirits sense they will die and do not want to go."

They sat in silence for several moments, feeling the cool air on their faces and taking in the uplifting scent from the pine trees.

"You think they will ever leave, Uncle?" Cloud wondered.

"Yes, they will," High Eagle replied resolutely, "but I am afraid that will not be the end of the trouble with them."

They were silent again for a long while. The forest seemed suddenly to pause, and the silence all around them grew deeper. Then, in a while, Cloud heard a bird flying overhead, and somewhere far above the treetops, an eagle shrilled.

"That has never happened to me," he said, "whatever that was."

"Once in a while, it is possible to feel the heartbeat of the Earth," High Eagle replied. "And once in a while, we can sense that pause in between the beats. Like just now. It reminds us that silence is good, it is necessary. We can use that silence to gather ourselves, and then move again with power and purpose."

High Eagle reached into the bag at his belt and soon took out a pinch of red willow tobacco. He offered it to the sky, the four directions, and the earth. "I would sing a song, but I would spoil our hunt," he whispered. "I think there is something moving up there, down through the trees toward us."

"I hope it is something of this world," said Cloud, smiling.

The old man smiled. "It is. We should take your horse and stalk with it. The other two can stay here together, so they do not become nervous and make noise."

Cloud and High Eagle moved out of the thicket and walked slowly up the incline, staying close to the side of the horse. The mare's ears perked up, and she peered intently into the trees. Something was there.

"You think it might be a bear?" asked Cloud in a slow whisper.

High Eagle shook his head. "Watch your horse.

She will tell us."

Although the mare's nostrils flared as she tested the wind, she gave no indication of anything more than intense curiosity. So they continued to proceed slowly. After they had covered a hundred paces or so, something moving through the trees snapped branches as it went.

They waited, arrows nocked on the taut bowstrings, keeping the horse between them and the noise.

It came out of the shadows and into a narrow clearing, pausing to lift its nose to scent the air. The distance was too great for an accurate shot, so the hunters waited motionlessly. Cloud slowly and gently stroked the mare's neck. She had already spotted the elk and was watching it intently.

Satisfied that the horse was no danger, the cow moved along a narrow rise, and Cloud immediately saw why it was alone. She had an injured leg, probably an old injury, because he could see nothing to indicate that it was recent. But her limp was pronounced.

Cloud was prepared. He had tied his quiver to the front so that the opening and the arrows were at his right hip. If he needed a second arrow, he could slip it out easily. One arrow was already on the string, and he was ready to draw. If the cow kept moving along its present course, she would cross in front of them at about forty paces or less. That is if they did not give themselves away somehow. So far, the cow did not appear alarmed. She limped along the rise.

High Eagle relaxed and slowly lowered his bow,

trusting in the younger man's marksmanship to bring home meat. He touched Cloud on the shoulder and whispered, "If you move here," he pointed to a spot near the mare's left leg, "you will have a good view and a good shot."

Cloud nodded. They moved in unison, slowly, very slowly. High Eagle took the lead rope and stood by the mare's neck and shoulder while Cloud took two steps to his right. Their movements barely caused the air to stir.

Coming to a tree near the rise, the cow veered left and went behind it, momentarily blocking Cloud's view. When she emerged from behind the tree, she was still behind a low thicket of sumac stalks, and a few paces farther away. Cloud decided she would still be within his range once she cleared the sumac. In a step or two, she did.

Cloud's draw and release was deliberate. This was not a battle where warriors used a lightning-fast draw and release. A hunt called for accuracy rather than speed. Flashing across the clearing, the arrow buried itself deep into the right chest of the unsuspecting cow. She jumped to turn away from the sudden jolt of pain, but her injured front leg caused her to lose balance, and she crashed to the forest floor. By the time she was up, Cloud's second arrow was already on its way, and it hit not more than a hand's width from the first.

There was no jubilation in either of the hunters as they watched the cow crashing through the forest. Now it was time to follow the blood trail she would leave. But first, High Eagle once again offered tobacco and sang a thanksgiving song for the life of the cow.

They found her not far from the thicket they had hidden in where the other horses were waiting. Cloud left a bundle of sage where she lay, and they set about the task of gutting the big elk.

By the middle of the afternoon, they had the carcass tied securely and balanced on the packhorse and they started for home. They stopped at Little Goose Creek to wash the blood from their hands in the icy waters.

"The spirits told me something else," High Eagle said, speaking in a normal voice now that the hunt was done. "They told me that a hard winter is coming. A winter with much cold and deep snow. So hunting as often as we can will be good."

"Maybe a hard winter will drive the Long Knives away," Cloud said hopefully.

"I would pray for a long, hard winter, but there is no way to draw a line and make winter harder on their side than it would be on ours."

"We will survive," replied Cloud. "This is our land, and we have seen hard winters before."

They rode in silence for most of the rest of the way home. The old man would occasionally sing, though not at the top of his voice. Some of the songs were nonsensical, like a hand-game song. But some were songs to honor the deeds of warriors long gone. Thus they rode on, the silent hunter and the singing medicine man.

High Eagle decided not to reveal something else

the spirits had told him. He was afraid it might push Cloud just enough off center to contribute to the problem rather than overcome it. Cloud, it had been told, would come near to death on a day when the ground was frozen and ice covered the land. Instead of telling him, High Eagle decided to make some protection medicine. Even now, he carried it in his bag, and before the day was over, he would give the bundle to Cloud.

—————————

Because the days were short this time of the year, the darkness caught them on the trail. But they knew the trails well—or at least the horses did. So they simply rode, and the horses found the way home.

A few dogs announced their arrival, and Grandmother Willow was pleased that her grandson had fulfilled her wish. She happily whipped out her favorite butcher knife and sang a song in praise to the spirit of the elk as she helped cut up the carcass. She sent one hind quarter to the lodge of Sweetwater Woman's mother and father and the other to her cousin Blue Medicine Woman, who was older than she was—some said nearing ninety years. The woman was old enough not to remember how old she was. Nonetheless, she was grateful for the meat and profusely thanked Cloud when he brought it over to her.

Grandmother Willow's generosity did not stop there. She gave one quarter of a side of ribs to Black Shield and his wife and another quarter of ribs to Big Voice and his wife. And she found people to give the two front quarters to. The kidneys, liver, and tongue were almost immediately cooking over the fire, to be shared with anyone who wandered near. For the side of ribs she kept for herself and Cloud and Sweetwater Woman, Grandmother Willow had a special purpose.

Tomorrow, she would ask her grandson to dig a pit and prepare a large bed of coals. Over the coals, she would roast the ribs, turning the entire side slowly on a huge spit. It was her favorite way to cook elk ribs. Then she would invite all the women who were in their term of carrying babies to come and eat with her grandson's wife. It was her way of giving strength to the little ones so they would be ready to come out into the world.

High Eagle watched the activity with a smile. Although it was dark and the air chilly, the warmth around Grandmother Willow's fire was from more than the flames. A large contingent of children watched as several old women helped. All too soon, the work was done, and people reluctantly turned back toward the warmth of their own lodges.

The medicine man reached into his bag and pulled out a much smaller bag, one made from the skin of a bighorn sheep. Inside were objects he had prepared for Cloud's protection. He joined the younger man sitting near his grandmother's fire. "This is for you," he said, holding out the small bag.

Cloud reached for the bag, an unexpected gift. Yet he was puzzled by the solemn expression deep in the old man's eyes. "What is it?" he asked.

"Protection," replied High Eagle. "It is necessary. More than that, I cannot say. Wear it around your neck until I ask for it."

Cloud nodded solemnly and tied the bag around his neck. He knew better than to ask what was in it, though he was more concerned as to why he needed it. Judging from High Eagle's demeanor, Cloud thought he probably would never know that. But because of the medicine man's demeanor, he would do exactly as he was told.

"Tell anyone who asks that I gave it to you and that there is a purpose for it. Beyond that, no one will know, not even you. And when it is time, I will take it back."

Cloud fingered the bag and felt something beyond the physical aspects of the contents, but he could not describe the feeling.

"It was a good hunt today, Grandson. Thank you for taking me along."

"You have given me much to think about," Cloud replied.

He watched as the old man disappeared into the darkness. Before he could think of the bag around his neck, a slender young man came out of the darkness from where the medicine man had faded into it. A young man with a strong step and a smile on his face. It was Little Hawk, Crazy Horse's younger brother.

CHAPTER SEVENTEEN

A Good Plan

Cold though the pushy breeze was, the four men on the ridge beneath the old, bent cedar tree were oblivious to it. Their collective intensity seemed to protect them from the biting cold as they watched two dozen mule-drawn wagons rolling two by two toward the slopes darkened by a pine forest. More than thirty mounted Long Knives rode guard.

Crazy Horse, Cloud, Little Hawk, and Lone Bear knew every rock and shrub on the hill, and the old cedar was like an old friend. They had used this lookout point many times. This time, there was a sense of urgency.

Lone Bear, the closest friend of Crazy Horse, nodded toward the wagons. "They go into the trees. They have axes and a kind of long blade, I think for cutting down trees. Other times, they gather up dry wood. They have been collecting more dry wood now, because of the cold weather. All of those people inside their houses need wood to stay warm."

"And that means they will be going back and forth from the town to the forest more often now," said Cloud.

"I think the best time to attack is when they are going west," said Crazy Horse, "when they are still in the open and before they cross the creek."

228

Cloud agreed. "There, the sentries on the hill below can see them, see us attacking, and signal the fort. After that, the Long Knives will be sent out to help the woodcutters."

"Yes," said Crazy Horse. "After the Long Knives come out, we usually break off and it is over. Sometimes we kill or wound some of the woodcutters, or the Long Knives with them, and sometimes not. But I think the thing is to let the rescuers come out well away from the town, and attack them. The trouble is, we cannot bring all or most of our fighting men into this area, because such a large force will be easily seen."

"Once they are seen," said Cloud, continuing the line of logic, "the Long Knives will not come out of the fort. They will stay inside the walls and fire at us with their big wagon guns."

"Lone Bear and I have a thought," Crazy Horse told them. "The ambush has worked well on the Powder River Road. We think it can work here. We have not tried, except for a few times, and not very hard. Yet if we can coax a large column of Long Knives out of the fort, the thing to do is attack them with a small force. They will not be afraid of a few of us."

"That does not sound like an ambush," Cloud pointed out.

"The ambush has to be away from this area. Those of us that attack will have to lead them into the ambush," Crazy Horse replied.

Cloud nodded thoughtfully. "Yes, that could work."

Lone Bear motioned toward the wood wagons, now nearly to the forest. "They have been going for wood nearly every day."

"Good!" exclaimed Cloud. "Today we leave them alone. Tomorrow, we attack and break off immediately after the Long Knives come out. Let them think we do not want to engage them. Let them think we only want to harass them."

It was agreed. The next day, Crazy Horse, Cloud, Lone Bear, and Little Hawk returned with eight more men. Cloud and Crazy Horse would remain on the hill to observe as the others attacked. Their observations would be useful for planning a larger ambush.

The pattern was the same as before. Ten men charged after twenty-some wood wagons and opened fire as they went, spreading out to force the whites into a wide and moving field of fire. Owing to skittish Long Knife horses and the superb horsemanship of the Lakota fighters, none of the attackers were hit; none of the wagon men or the mounted Long Knives had an easy shot. On the other hand, none of them were hit either, because they had quickly stopped the wagons and used them as barriers, firing from behind them. Nevertheless, Lakota bullets slammed into the wagons, splintering holes in the boxes.

Response from the Long Knives at the fort was slow, but they did come. Cloud counted thirty mounted men, not as many as he had anticipated. He was disappointed.

"I thought they would send more," he said.

"I did not know you wanted to kill them all at once," Crazy Horse said, grinning.

Cloud shook his head. "As many as we can is the best we can hope for. The truth is, we do not know how many of them will come out. It may be more the next time, or less."

That night, Crazy Horse, Little Hawk, and Lone Bear spent the night in the council lodge in the village of Black Shield. Cloud and Crazy Horse explained their plan to Grey Bull and Hump. Crazy Horse sent a rider to his own camp and to the others along the Tongue with a message for the fighting men, along with a bundle of arrows including one of his, one from Cloud, Grey Bull, and Hump. With those arrows, anyone would know that the messenger was speaking for the men whose arrows he carried. The message was simple: there would be an attack against the Long Knife town, and all good men would be needed.

A little more than one hundred and fifty men arrived at Black Shield's camp early the next morning, armed and ready to fight. As they rode toward Buffalo Creek, Grey Bull and Hump talked with the warrior leaders and explained the plan to them. They rode north of Lodge Trail Hill and left most of the warriors to hide and wait behind a ridge. One or a few of them could watch from the ridgetop. If the attackers were successful, they would be leading the Long Knives to the valley below that ridge. The ambushers would hide when they saw the soldiers chasing the attackers, then open fire when the Long Knives were below them in the valley.

Among the ambushers was Rabbit, with his breech-loading rifle. As the day wore on, he could see that everyone was growing impatient. The initial enthusiasm changed to boredom and then to more and more grumbling. The spotter sent to watch on the ridgetop fell asleep for a while, and Rabbit was relieved. Rabbit found a young pine tree somewhat out of the wind and tied his horse to it and sat down to wait. He could not understand how anyone could not realize that the largest part of an ambush was waiting. And there was no way to tell how long they would have to wait. As the morning wore on, he kept warm as best he could beneath his buffalo robe, stayed apart from everyone else, and wondered where Grey Bull and Hump had gone. If anyone could reorganize the ambushers, it was them.

Little Hawk and Lone Bear led the attack on the wagons, joined by Yellow Wolf and a contingent of young men known for their superb riding. They charged the wagons and then retreated for cover, but they kept up a steady fire from covered positions, giving every indication that they would not break off the attack this day. The sentries on the hill frantically signaled to the Long Knives in the town.

Like the day before, thirty mounted Long Knives galloped out of the west gate of the log outpost. Meanwhile, the men with the wagons were grimly defending themselves. The boom of their rifles and those of their attackers echoed off the slopes to the west. Some of their mules had been wounded, their frantic braying adding to the din of shouts and gunfire. As the relief column came into full view of the wagons, Cloud and Crazy Horse charged from behind the sentry hill with six men. Shortly after that, Little Hawk signaled his men to break off, and they made their way around behind the ridges to join Cloud and Crazy Horse. As they did, they saw another Long Knife column approaching. It had apparently gone behind the sentry ridge on the northeast side without being seen by any of the Lakota.

Ponderously, it seemed, the relief column wheeled right, leaving the wood road to pursue the attackers.

Crazy Horse and Cloud's warriors watched the column of Long Knives riding carefully down a long, steep slope, the same slope the Lakota had descended without difficulty. To their surprise, the broad valley below them was full of activity. Another column of Long Knives was in pursuit of several warriors. Cloud and Crazy Horse immediately realized it was Little Hawk and his men. One soldier left the column to pursue them. He retreated, however, when someone nearly hit him and his horse with some good long-distance shooting. Once on the valley floor, the column pursuing Crazy Horse and Cloud moved into a high lope on the more even ground. After they crossed Buffalo Creek, the two columns, more or less, converged into one.

Hump and Grey Bull were waiting on the south-facing slope of the ridge, on the opposite side of where the ambushers were positioned. They had ridden a good distance down the slope and assumed the young men below the ridge were in position and waiting. They could hear gunfire, some faint and some loud. In a while, they could see specks moving on the valley floor, darting about. Then a dark line came into view, telling them the plan was working.

Crazy Horse, Cloud, and the others had assessed the effective marksmanship range of the Long Knives pursuing them: they were not impressed. Clearly, they were not skilled enough to fight while mounted. Many of them stopped their horses to take aim, and when they fired on the move, their aim was worse. Therefore, it was not so risky for the Lakota to stay within overall rifle range just to keep the Long Knives engaged. It worked. One man, they noticed, galloped his horse far ahead of his column— the only one anxious to press the attack, it seemed.

Cloud and Crazy Horse angled slightly north to approach the ambush ridge from the west. It was not as steep a slope, and they did not want to create an unnecessary barrier for the Long Knives. Halfway up the slope, they were joined by Grey Bull and Hump, both pleased to see that the plan was working.

Rabbit heard faint gunfire, and so did some of the other ambushers. Almost at once, just about everyone rushed to the top of the ridge, until they were dark silhouettes against the skyline, and they saw the Long Knives coming, so the boredom they had felt before instantaneously turned to impatience. Everyone wanted to kill Long Knives and take scalps. They galloped down off the ridge, some of them firing.

Rabbit stayed near his tree, holding on to the lead rope of the warhorse he had traded from Neck. The gunfire from the valley was coming closer and closer.

Cloud knew they had the Long Knives exactly where they wanted them. The ambush ridge angled down to the west, and the trees were sparse. It was obvious that no one was on the slope or on the ridge. The Long Knives kept coming. Suddenly, another one of them raced ahead of the column.

Closer and closer rode the Long Knives, closer to the ridge, and then everything fell apart. To Cloud and Crazy Horse's surprise, the ambushers had left positions and came down the ridge. The Lakota had had the Long Knives surrounded, but only briefly.

The Long Knives, though somewhat strung out, galloped behind a protruding hill and turned back south for the safety of their outpost. A few of the Lakota pursued them but ran out of ammunition. Crazy Horse, Cloud, Hump, and Grey Bull watched helplessly as the Long Knives regained the valley floor and galloped away.

Only two Long Knives had been killed. One was the second of the two who had outraced the column. He briefly exchanged fire with the first of the onrushing ambushers. He was hit in the flurry of return fire and fell from his horse. After the rest of the Long Knives had gotten away, several frustrated young men went back to his body and shot it full of arrows.

Cloud watched them from a distance, some of them shouting victory cries. He was disappointed. Victory cries over one dead man while all his comrades had escaped?

There was nothing to be done. Hump rode into the middle of the milling, jubilant young men and fired his rifle into the air. As startled faces turned in his direction, he made a hand gesture that indicated that everyone was worthless.

"Go home!" he yelled. "Go home and hide behind your wives and mothers. Maybe they will teach you to fight like good warriors! Go home!"

─────────────

The next evening, Hump, eyes still flashing with anger, stood before a gathering of old men. His friend Grey Bull, still angry as well, sat nearby. Red Cloud was among those in the first row.

"I can blame the young men only so much," said Hump. "Many of them are very young and very inexperienced. From some of us, they are hearing that fighting Long Knives is a way to glory. From others of us, they hear that we must fight as one or the Long Knives will defeat us and take our lands. Then they hear that fighting them may not be necessary at all, that we will talk with them and make them hear our words. No wonder some of the young men are confused. So when it comes time to do something, they run around like moles blinded by the sunlight. Let me tell you this: I would rather ride into battle with ten good men who think as one and are committed to duty and not glory! Ten such men are better than ten thousand blind and confused moles.

"However, unless those of us who should have the experience and the wisdom think and speak as one, there will always be confusion. I think even some of us here, in this lodge, must decide if we should chase after glory or stand for the people.

"That is all I have to say, my friends."

The rustle of clothing against the door was the only sound in the lodge as Grey Bull and Hump left. In the silence that followed, not a single man lifted his eyes to look around.

———

Several miles away, almost at the same moment, an officer stood at rigid attention in a room lit by an oil lamp. But there was no remorse in his eyes, only bored contempt.

Colonel Henry Carrington, hands clasped at his back, paced in front of Captain William Fetterman. "The least of the offenses you committed, Captain, was an inability to maintain tactical control of your command, the consequence of which was the death of an officer and an enlisted man. In this instance, I can provide firsthand testimony, because I was there!"

"Colonel, it is unfortunate, but Lieutenant Bingham took it upon himself to pursue the Indians alone. Had I been able to communicate with him, I would have ordered him to stay with his men."

"Well, it is rather easier to be precise in one's analysis after the fact, is it not? Hindsight can offer lessons, however. Perhaps you should keep that in mind. Keep that in mind, because this is a different enemy, Captain. They are not predictable, and they do not fight in formation. However, there is another issue here, one that I will diffuse here and now, before it gets out of hand."

The captain stared straight ahead. "I do not understand, sir."

"You will, you will. For weeks now, you and others have questioned not only my authority, but my experience and my honor. There is a set of orders on my desk, Captain, given by Brigadier General Saint George Cook of the Department of the Platte. Those orders state clearly that I am in command here. That means whether I am sitting at that desk or at the head of a unit in the field. Because you are the chief critic, I am reassigning you, effective immediately. Tomorrow morning at nine o'clock sharp, you will arrive here, in my office, and you will read those orders I allude to. And you will do precisely the same at nine o'clock every morning thereafter. That, Captain, is the only duty you will have at this post. You are hereby relieved of field command until I say otherwise. That is all. You are dismissed!"

The captain sat at the table in his quarters, slowly sipping whiskey from a glass. He didn't bother to stand to answer the knock at the door. "Enter," he said in a hoarse whisper.

Lieutenant James Powell and Captain Frederick Brown stepped into the dark room. "William," said Powell, "mind if I light a lamp?"

"As you wish."

Powell brought the lighted oil lamp to the table as Brown joined them, scraping a chair against the floor.

"We can just about guess what happened," Powell said, "but you can fill us in, if you do not mind."

Fetterman shook his head. "Hell," he snorted, "with a hundred men—no, with only eighty men, I can ride through every heathen village up there on the Tongue. That is the depth of my experience!"

"What did the colonel do to you, William?" asked Brown.

"I am relieved of duty," Fetterman told them, "for inability to maintain tactical control."

"What happened out there yesterday?"

"I will tell you what happened," Fetterman spat. "I saw firsthand the sorry ability of those Indians as combatants. They have no organizational cohesion and no tactics to speak of. All they do is ride and shoot! Any organized and well-planned offensive against them would be swift—if we had a commander with operational experience."

"We know that, William, and we have been arguing to take the fight to them until we are blue in the face, you know that," Powell insisted. "But nothing will change unless we have a new post commander."

Fetterman lifted his glass. "Gentlemen, the best of luck to us all on that score!"

On a bench above the Tongue River, a fire crackled and burned brightly, casting its heat toward the circle of faces around it: Cloud, Crazy Horse, Hump, and Grey Bull along with Little Hawk, Goings, Taken Alive, Lone Bear, and Little Bird.

"Patience," said Grey Bull. "Someone has to teach all of our young men the value of patience. Otherwise, my hair will turn white."

"We came close today" was Hump's opinion. "The Long Knives did everything I thought they would. And maybe they can be counted on to do it again."

"Can you be certain of that?" asked Cloud.

"No, not entirely," returned Hump, "but I have been thinking about what happened yesterday. I think the Long Knives think they won. So maybe they are full of themselves. In a way, that is good. That way, when we attack the wood wagons again, the chances are they will chase us again. But I saw something else, too. One man was way ahead when they were chasing you. He is the one that was killed. In their way, one man leads them all when they do battle. One man tells the other Long Knives what to do, and they have to do it. So if he decides to chase us, the others have no choice but to follow."

"The plan was good," interjected Crazy Horse. "It worked once, and it can work again. And if what my friend just mentioned is true, we have to influence that one man. He is the head of the snake."

"I am in favor of trying again," Cloud affirmed.

Grey Bull tossed a stick into the fire. "The truth is, we have to keep trying. We have too much to lose."

CHAPTER EIGHTEEN

Old Bones, Old Ways

For the life of him, Rabbit could not understand why some of the Lakota people insisted on living near Fort Laramie. His uncle, his mother's brother, High Pine, had been one of those. Although, since last year, after the Long Knives tried to imprison those they called "loafers," High Pine had moved his family north. Now he was in the camp of the Bad Faces with Red Cloud.

Rabbit had lived with his uncle's family near the fort for nearly two years. He had spent many days on the grounds of the outpost and managed to learn the language of the Long Knives. Most fascinating was the seemingly endless line of wagons that stopped at the fort during the summers. They came from the east somewhere and were headed for somewhere in the west. Those wagons were filled with white men and women and children. They were not always clean and were always busy, and some of them did not stop talking. Still, because he knew some of their language, he had been able to trade for things, such as a mirror, a piece of red cloth, and a small skillet. His aunt and uncle's lodge was full of the things of the white men: blankets, cloth, utensils, cooking pots, and two four-legged chairs, so a person could sit above the ground.

As a teenage boy full of curiosity, he had been oblivious to the impact the hundreds of wagons and thousands of white people were having on his own people. Those wagons and people came through each summer— and still were. His own opinion of the Long Knives began to crumble after two Lakota were hung—they were said to have harmed some "innocent" whites. But if the Long Knife commander at the fort had not suddenly become suspicious of the "loafers" and decided to send them to prison, Rabbit would likely still be living near the whites. He had happened to come north after that time, to stay with his parents. That had spared him from being rounded up with the other "loafers," some of them in chains, including women and children, his uncle and aunt among them. Crazy Horse, Cloud, Spotted Tail of the Sicangu, and even Red Cloud had taken action. They led warriors against the Long Knives and rescued the "loafers." After that, Rabbit did not go back, and his uncle and aunt moved north—without their white-man things.

Now he could not understand why he had ever felt any kindness toward the Long Knives and the other white people. He was stupid for thinking there was anything good about them.

Rabbit had all these thoughts as he rode home leading a packhorse carrying the deer he had shot. There was some risk in hunting alone because some Crow had been seen and chased back north only a few days ago. But he had the breech-loading gun, and he was becoming faster at reloading. Besides, he was angry enough to fight the whole world. Fighting was not too much on his mind this day, however; fresh meat for his mother and father was.

It was the afternoon now, and he came to the ridge above the camp and passed by two sentinels huddled under buffalo robes beside a tree. He nodded in response to their waves and rode down the slope. Stopping at his parents' lodge, he called out to them. They emerged and smiled when they saw the deer. Big Voice took the lead rope for the packhorse and untied the carcass. Rabbit helped unload the carcass and then took his horse to the river to drink. On his way back, he heard loud voices arguing near the outer circle of lodges. He paid no attention, however, until he heard his name shouted.

"Hey, Rabbit! Over here!"

Turning, he saw Yellow Wolf with Good Hand, the son of Neck, and a few others he recognized, though he could not remember their names. One of them was wrapped in a finely decorated elk robe and had shells tied into his braids.

Yellow Wolf motioned for Rabbit to join them. Almost immediately, Rabbit could sense a mood, or perhaps it was just the cold edge to the afternoon air. No matter, he liked Yellow Wolf. So he dismounted and led his horse over to the group of seven or eight young men.

"My friend," Yellow Wolf said, "we were just talking about what happened three days ago, about the ambush and the fact that it did not work. You were there, and so was I. What do you think?"

The young man with the shells in his braids was

older, but not by much. He gazed mockingly at Rabbit. At his shoulder was a stocky young man wearing an angry scowl.

"We were told to wait, to hold our fire until the Long Knives crossed below us," Rabbit recalled. "Someone started shooting too soon, and we did not make a good surround."

"That is not what we heard!" said No Horse, the scowling young man.

Yellow Wolf stepped forward. "You see, that is the problem! All you can say is that you 'heard' this or that. We were there! Where were you?"

The finely dressed young man snickered. "We chose not to take part in all that foolishness," he said.

Rabbit took a step forward. "Who are you?" he demanded.

The young man looked at Rabbit with disdain. "I am Woman's Dress," he said haughtily.

Rabbit smiled. "That is a good name for you," he said calmly. "Now I can understand why you were not there, because you probably did not want to get your clothes dirty."

Those standing with Yellow Wolf snickered a little.

No Horse tossed off his robe and took a step toward Rabbit, placing his hand on the war club under his belt.

Rabbit held his ground. "You want to fight me? Yes, I will fight! But first, I want to hear from your friend

Woman's Dress here," he said, with ridicule dancing in his eyes. "I want to hear this 'great warrior' tell us why he thinks fighting the Long Knives is foolishness."

Uncertainty crept into the eyes of Woman's Dress. He blinked, but was not about to lose face. "The foolishness is in Cloud and Crazy Horse, the men you follow. They are only after the glory. They want to be important men, so they go against the Long Knives. Many of us know the Long Knives will leave, whether we fight them or not. So your warrior leaders are taking advantage of you to make themselves important."

Yellow Wolf and Rabbit exchanged glances and shook their heads. Rabbit took a deep breath and went nose to nose with Woman's Dress. "Who tells you these things? Because I do not think you are smart enough to think of them yourself."

"There are many wise men that see how things really are," Woman's Dress said weakly.

Rabbit smiled, but it was not a friendly smile. "Did one of them give you your name or did you give it to yourself?"

No Horse moved in a blur and shoved Rabbit to the ground. Rabbit rolled over, leaving his robe on the ground, and was quickly on his feet, a war club in his hand. The young man paused to stare at the stump of Rabbit's arm.

"Come ahead," Rabbit hissed, waving his club, "do not let this stop you, unless you are a coward, like your friend!"

Although No Horse was bigger, Rabbit was much faster, and he fought from the darkness in his soul, which made him fearless. He blocked several blows, absorbed some, and landed a few of his own. Eventually, the head of his club caught the young man squarely in the chest and made him stagger backward until he fell. Rabbit jumped astride his stomach before he could rise again and smashed the stone head of his club into the ground with a vicious blow next to the young man's right ear.

Chest heaving, Rabbit pushed the club against the man's throat. "Be glad I have only one arm, otherwise I could really hurt you," he hissed.

Rabbit gathered up his things and led his horse away, followed by Yellow Wolf, Good Hand, and two others. Woman's Dress did not bother to help his friend up.

―――――――――

That evening, Big Voice cleared his throat as he dropped a handful of twigs onto the hot coals in the fire pit. "I heard what happened," he said.

Rabbit nodded. "Do you think the Long Knives will ever go away?" he asked.

"I do not know. But we cannot allow them to think it will ever be easy for them to take anything from us."

White Hill Woman handed plates of roasted deer to her husband and son. "There is a hunter in our lodge," she said lovingly, "and so we eat well."

"Thank you, Mother."

After they had eaten, Big Voice pulled out a flat bundle, unwrapped it, and revealed an unpainted rawhide shield covered with tanned hide. "This was made by Two Crow," he said. "He sent it over, finally. It is made of the rawhide from the buffalo's hump, the strongest part. It was twice this big, or more, before he heated it slowly in the ground beneath a fire for ten days. It shrunk and became thick." He thumped the shield. "Arrows and lances cannot go through, and it may even stop a bullet. It is yours, a gift from your mother and me."

Rabbit took the shield and saw that a special sleeve had been attached to the back, a sleeve to fit snugly over his right arm. He knew his mother had done that. He was taken aback. Never did he think he would carry the shield of a warrior. Laying it over his crossed legs, he caressed it. "Thank you," he said

"You must paint it," Big Voice told him. "Paint it with colors and a design that suits you."

"I will," Rabbit said brightly. "I will."

Curiosity, Max Hornsby decided, is what had gotten him into trouble. As a matter of fact, it always had. He had been curious about ink, so he had stuck the end of Minerva Porch's braid into the inkwell on his desk. The ends of her red hair were black for months. To atone for his transgression—his curiosity, really—he had to mop the schoolroom every Friday after school for two months.

The roll of the deck of a schooner on the open sea was never to his liking, much to his father's disappointment. Although he was curious why Hiram Tidwell's right arm was more muscular than his left, and he ended up learning the blacksmith's trade from the man. Then he was curious about what lay beyond the western horizons, far beyond the Adirondacks, in that mysterious Great American Desert he had heard so much about. So in spite of his mother's softly sobbing protests, he decided to satisfy his curiosity.

At Saint Louis, he heard about Fort Yankton in Dakota Territory, and at Fort Yankton, he heard about Fort Laramie. At Fort Laramie, he met a man named Highsmith who was taking wagons north into Montana Territory and dropping supplies at three outposts along the way. Two days from Fort Philip Kearny, Hornsby's curiosity had taken him from one hilltop to another and another, until the image of a white woman came into his telescope, the last thing he had expected to see in a land inhabited by savages.

He no longer had the telescope, of course, and the woman was still with the Indians, as far as he knew. Pausing for a moment from his task of sharpening the blades of a whipsaw, he once again pondered his future. Up north near Virginia City was where the gold was, or so he had heard. Between here and there, however, were Indians, a group of people he had come to grudgingly respect. They were nothing to be trifled with. Home was an alternative that seemed more and more sensible. At least there he could walk down the street and not worry about being adequately armed.

Whatever he decided, he was certain of one thing: he would always be curious about the white woman in the Indian village. What was her story? How had she gotten there? He sighed, shook his head, and resumed his task.

———————

"They did not come out yesterday," Lone Bear said. "And they may not come out today."

Once again, on the ridge with the old cedar, Cloud and Crazy Horse and their young men were watching the wood road.

"They did not post sentries on the hill below us," Lone Bear went on. "Something has changed, I think."

Crazy Horse nodded, deep in thought. In a moment, he spoke, turning his back to the stiff breeze blowing from the north. "I think we should change something, too. We should stay away from here, perhaps for a few days. We can send scouts to watch, to hide and watch alone. If the Long Knives think we have pulled back, maybe they will come out. Meanwhile, we can stay home and stay warm."

Cloud grinned. "It would be good to stay warm."

"But we should agree to meet in a few days," suggested Crazy Horse. "Then we can ask Hump and Grey Bull what they think."

They rode off the ridge, hurrying to get into the thick pine forests that blocked the wind. But even without the wind, the air was colder than it had been for several years. Usually, the Moon of Frost in the Lodge was the month with the deep, deep cold, not the month of the Winter Moon. They tied their buffalo robes tighter and rolled up the ends to cover their ears. They rode through the forest without speaking, watching their breath mist and billow in the cold, cold air and thinking of the cozy lodges waiting—especially when the snow began to fall.

As the sun dipped behind the jagged western ridges, old men were arriving in the village of Black Shield. The increasing cold prevented everyone but the habitually curious from peeking out their doors each time they heard hoofbeats and footfalls on the cold ground. Before evening passed into night, a blanket of snow covered the ground and several horses were picketed around the council lodge. Any word about old men gathering this night had been passed by only the old men themselves and a few trusted messengers. They had agreed to meet just after sundown, not to keep the gathering a secret, but to prevent curious onlookers.

A thick bed of coals in the fire pit gave off a pale orange glow of light, a hue often seen in lingering autumn sunsets, and enough heat to pamper old bones and new aches.

Black Shield's wife and daughters provided bowls of hot buffalo and elk soup seasoned with wild turnips. The old men sipped and slurped the soup, mumbling their appreciation. They finished with cups of tea or strong black coffee laced with sugar.

Amenities out of the way, eight old men leaned back against their willow chairs and turned their attention to the issue that had brought them together on the coldest night so far this season: the often-bothersome issue of change.

Black Shield, though an elder, was not the oldest in the lodge. That distinction belonged to Ghost Bear, who had silvery white hair and many of his teeth. He was near eighty winters old. Next was Bear Looks Behind, followed by Attacking Eagle, Two Horns, Black Horse, No Tail, Kills Crow, and Black Shield. Everyone waited for Ghost Bear to speak first.

"My friends and relatives," he began, "I have to talk first because good food always makes me sleepy. I am glad to see you all, and glad to know you are as bothered as I am about things that have been happening." He paused to gather his thoughts as he held his palms to the fire, his eyes half closed.

"We have all seen things in our lives," he went on, "and we all know that things change. We changed from walking hunters to hunters on horseback after our people crossed the Great Muddy River and came this way. Some of us live in canvas lodges now instead of lodges made of buffalo hide. Some of us wear clothing made from cloth. Some of that cannot be helped. And we can sleep in canvas lodges and wear shirts made of blue cloth, but we are still Lakota in our thinking and in the ways we do things. Our thinking and our ways made us strong." He paused to take a deep breath and softly clear his throat.

"If I have a good bow," he continued, "one that is powerful and sends an arrow farther than other bows, I would not cast it aside because I think there is a better bow somewhere. I would keep that bow. It seems to me that some among us, and perhaps it is only one or two, want to change how we do things, as far as how the people should be led and who leads them. That troubles me. I will say it clearly because I am an old man: it seems to me someone wants to control our people the way the whites control their people. They have one man that everyone must follow. I do not like that. That is not our way. There, I have spoken."

A chorus of monosyllabic affirmations uttered several times by each man flowed through the room like the distant rumble of quiet thunder. Old heads nodded in agreement.

"I agree with my friend," said No Tail in a voice like stones rolling over stones. "The people have always decided who to follow or when to stop following. That is the way it should stay. That is the power the people have, and we should remind everyone that it is still that way."

"We can do that," said Attacking Eagle, "but there is something else that we must consider. This reminds me of the big wasp that came into my lodge this summer. He came and buzzed around. I did not want him to sting me, so I held the door open so he could go out. But he stayed in, flying around and scaring everyone. He just would not leave. When he landed on my leg, I swatted him. Then I told him, 'You should have gone out when you had the chance.'"

Laughter rolled through the lodge.

"So that is the question," said Bear Looks Behind, "and the answer, I think. But how do we swat the wasp in this situation?"

"We do what is necessary," Black Horse stated emphatically. "In the old days, we had ways when someone got out of hand."

"Is this thing bad enough for us old men to do something?" Bear Looks Behind asked. "Is it bad enough for us to invoke something old that has not been done since I was a young man?"

A contemplative silence filled the room.

Ghost Bear cleared his throat. "We are old men," he intoned. "We have grown old as Lakota. When I was a boy, strong young men walked in fear of criticism from frail old men. Why? Because then, old men did not bend the ways that made us what we are. Then, old men stood up for what was right, for the Lakota way of doing things. Now should we do any less? Look around, we are the keepers of the ways. Who will do what is right if we do not show them the way? Think about it, my friends."

Once more, old heads nodded in acknowledgment

of the words and wisdom of Ghost Bear. The affirmations were spoken once more, but more quietly this time. The old men were not afraid or timid. Their quiet manner was an indication that they took their responsibility seriously.

Outside the snow fell on this last night of the Winter Moon. The horses picketed around the council lodge were all blanketed in white. A deep cold descended. The smoke flaps on every lodge were nearly closed, open only enough so smoke could rise into the frigid air. Dawn would chase away the darkness and bring the light of a new day in the Middle of Winter Moon, regarded by many as a month in which everything could be good or everything could be bad.

CHAPTER NINETEEN

Rainbow around the Sun

During the night, the snow stopped, and in the morning light, it was a tattered white blanket over the land. But the cold persisted. Footsteps on the ground squeaked. Dogs curled up against the lodges to keep warm.

A few of the old men spent the night in the council lodge, and others slept in the lodges of relatives. Black Shield came to ask Cloud to provide armed escorts for three of the old men who had the farthest to go home. Cloud was puzzled at the request, but it explained all the horses picketed around the council lodge. But Black Shield gave no further explanation.

By mid-morning, a dozen young men rode out with the old men. Cloud was curious and was tempted to drop in on Black Shield for an unannounced visit but decided against it. He wanted to spend the day, in fact the next several days, with Sweetwater Woman. Besides, the reason the old men had come to the village of Black Shield would be revealed sooner or later. He amended his thought: *might* be revealed. Some of the old ones could be secretive to the point of frustration for everyone else.

Grandmother Willow found her winter moccasins, bundled herself in a buffalo robe, and went out to experience the first bone-chilling cold of the season. "The cold makes my bones ache, but aching bones remind me that I have lived a long life," she liked to say.

Cloud arranged the iron spit over the fire and hung a pot of water over the deep, hot bed of coals in the fire pit. He wanted tea. Sweetwater Woman was busy folding and putting away summer clothes and pulling out the rawhide cases with the winter dresses for her and winter shirts and leggings for Cloud. She worked quietly and did not seem to be aware that her husband was in the lodge.

He leaned back against the chair and suddenly felt the medicine bag High Eagle had given him roll on his chest and he recalled the medicine man's advice.

"I walked down to the river this morning," Cloud mentioned. "Already the edges are beginning to freeze. That is early. Someone told me a hard winter is coming, and I think they might be right."

Sweetwater kept at her task and did not reply. Cloud leaned over to see if the water in the metal pot was beginning to boil and sat back.

"The next time you go out, you can open the smoke flaps a little wider," she said softly. "I cannot see any smoke in here, but my eyes are stinging a little."

"Yes. Yes, I will."

With two women in the lodge, it was always neat and orderly. Cloud always made sure that his tools and weapons were put away, hung high on the lodge pole at the back of the room. Behind the fire pit was a large, flat river stone as wide as his two hands side by side. On the stone were braids of sweetgrass and bundles of sage wrapped in red cloth. It was the altar. Behind him, hanging below his weapons, was his pipe in its quill-decorated bag. It was his father's pipe actually, made of black pipestone—the gray shale—from the White Earth River valley.

"Will you go somewhere today?" Sweetwater suddenly asked.

"No, no," he replied. "I will stay home today. I will be home for several days."

She nodded absently and glanced toward the pot over the coals. "The water is about to boil." She pointed to a small painted case leaning against the dew cloth. "The tea is in there."

He moved from his chair to get the dried peppermint tea leaves out of the case and stole a glance at his wife. She was staring into the low flames, one hand on her abdomen. "I can make enough tea for both of us," he offered.

After a long moment, she turned to glance at him briefly and turned away again. "Yes, tea would be—would be nice," she said.

Her eyes did not have their usual spark, he noticed.

He slid the pot to the end of the spit and dropped a handful of leaves into the water and sat back. When he looked, Sweetwater was still staring into the flames. "After we have tea, maybe we can take a walk," he suggested.

Without looking at him, she slowly nodded.

"Yes, good. We will do that," he told her.

She kept staring into the flames.

Cloud could think of nothing further to say or do except to wait for the tea to steep.

———————

Since the middle of the Moon When Leaves Fall, the summer encampments had started moving to winter locations, breaking up as they did. That is, winter encampments were smaller. A forty-lodge summer village became two with twenty lodges for the winter until fresh grass was available for the horses in the spring, beginning in the Moon When Geese Return.

Therefore, many winter villages were located along the Tongue River valley. There, the people could take shelter from the cold winter winds and, being not far from water, horses could find grass. Most of the encampments were Lakota, of course, but there were also a few Northern Cheyenne, and at least two were Blue Clouds, or Northern Arapaho.

Two wide gullies away from the village of Black Shield, two riders and one packhorse laden with fresh meat approached a village of eighteen lodges on a bench southeast of a ridge. They stopped to chat briefly with young sentinels standing over a fire and then rode into the village.

Grey Bull and Hump stopped at the council lodge, picketed their horses, and paid a visit to the lodge of the headman. They sought his permission to make a feast for all the young fighting men in the camp.

"There are ten young men here," the headman told them.

With the help of several women, a feast was prepared. A boy was asked to find each of the ten young men and invite them to the council lodge to listen to Grey Bull and Hump. All ten came, partly out of curiosity and partly because very few men among the Lakota had the strong reputations that these two visitors had.

The message from the two venerated warriors was simple: patriotism and choices. Each wore a shirt made of the tanned hide of the bighorn sheep in a color that nearly matched that of the new snow and was decorated to represent their deeds in battle. Rows of locks of hair wrapped in red hung from their sleeves. And each man held a red-wrapped ceremonial lance to which were attached the tail feathers of eagles in a neat row from top to bottom. Each lock of hair and each feather signified a deed performed in combat. To one day wear such a shirt and carry such a lance was the goal, the hope, of every young fighting man.

"Years ago," began Grey Bull, "my friend here was leading some young men like you against the Crow. They were on the edge of Crow lands, south of the Elk River. One day, they saw a Crow scouting party across a ravine. For a while, the two groups just watched one another. Finally, the leader of the Crow shot an arrow, and it hit in the bank just below the Lakota warriors. They took the arrow and looked at it, at the markings. But my friend did not know the man whose mark was on the arrow. So he took one of his own arrows with his mark on it, drew his bow, and sent it toward the Crow. After the Crow looked at the arrow and recognized the mark, they knew who it belonged to. They knew the kind of man the arrow belonged to, the kind of fighter he was. So they left. They just rode away."

The young men sent glances at Hump, who sat looking down with a bemused smile.

"Two of the young men with him that day were Cloud and Crazy Horse," Grey Bull continued. "Ask them, they will tell you the story. There was a time when our enemies were honorable. We knew them, we fought them, and we respected them. Things have changed. Those old enemies are still there, but now there is a new one, one who came long before any of you were born. I myself question if the Long Knives are true human beings. But whatever they are, they are trouble. We have to do something about them. By we, I mean you and me and my friend here and all of the fighting men the Lakota have, as well as our friends the Northern Cheyenne and Blue Clouds.

"To defend the people is the calling we have all answered," he went on. "It ends when we die of old age or on the battlefield. So my friend and I have decided that we want to talk to all the young men who want to listen. For the next several days, we will go to all the villages along the Tongue. Now it is time for my friend to talk."

Hump nodded and rose to his feet. He was a solid, muscular man. Holding on to his feathered lance, he cleared his throat and glanced at the circle of upraised, young faces. "My friend and I are warriors," he began. "Our people expect it from us because it is their right. Our families expect us to provide for them, so we hunt. They expect us to protect them, so we face the enemy when it comes. It does not matter who the enemy is. It matters that our people are safe. It matters that they live safe and happy. And we cannot say we will face this enemy but not that one."

He paused and let the expectant silence deepen for several moments. "My friend here and I will honor our calling until the day we die," he went on, "and maybe we will die honoring it because we have enemies.

"We have always had enemies. Before the Long Knives came, the worst and the best thing about our enemies was that they kept us strong. There is no best thing about the Long Knives, not even a little bit of a good thing. They are not really an enemy. They are a scourge, a blight. They are a prairie fire that consumes everything in its way. To face this scourge, to endure this fire, all of the fighting men must stand to defend the people. We must choose to defend, and then we must choose to follow those men who have faced the enemy many times."

Two or three of the young men had been in the spoiled ambush, and they nodded almost imperceptibly.

"You young men are our way to victory because you are strong," Hump continued. "Your bodies are strong and your fathers, uncles, and grandfathers have done their best to prepare you. Now your will must be strong. We cannot defend our people without you, and we cannot defeat the enemy without the will to win."

Hump paused once more. "You have much to think of," he said, his tone softening. "You have a choice to make."

He lifted his hand and spread his fingers. "When the hand is open," he pointed out, "the fingers are separated." Then he made a fist. "When it is closed, the fingers are united. That is how we must face this enemy."

———

Hump and Grey Bull carried their message up and down the Tongue River valley to all the camps and to all the young men who came to listen. Their years of experience had taught them an important principle: winning the heart of a warrior is halfway to winning the battle. When the warrior gives his heart to a cause, he will endure the most terrible of hardships in pursuit of victory.

In spite of days of biting cold, Grey Bull and Hump completed their mission to win the hearts and minds of the young men. In ten days, they had visited most of the camps and had spoken to more than two hundred men. Their logic was simple. Those among the older warriors with certain attitudes and loyalties could not be changed, so Grey Bull and Hump bypassed them. Both men had learned that those who argued about small issues could not see the bigger, more important danger, so those men were not necessarily the best hope. The best hope was the young men, who were still untainted by the exigencies of innuendo and politics.

The last meeting was in the village of Black Shield. On the same day, Crazy Horse came to see Cloud about the rumors flying around like snowflakes whipped by the wind. All the rumors were about their old friends Hump and Grey Bull.

"I think I can see what they are doing," Cloud said thoughtfully. "You or I could not do the same."

Crazy Horse agreed and then said, "I wonder if they will tell us what they are up to."

That night, his curiosity was answered somewhat.

Hump and Grey Bull were waiting in the council lodge. Crazy Horse and Cloud were greeted with enigmatic smiles and the lingering aroma of elk stew. Black Shield was also there.

"My friends," said Grey Bull, "I saw a rainbow around the sun days ago, which meant that the weather would change, and it has. I cannot remember it being this cold in recent years. But I think something else has changed. For one thing, we have a town full of strange people over there along Buffalo Creek, and they have taken root like a bad boil. Remember what it was like last winter when they were not there and some of our people camped along Buffalo Creek to hunt elk in the mountains? That is how I want it to be again! So we have to dig out that boil!"

Hump chuckled. "That is the best way to describe them—a bad boil. My friend is right, we have to dig it out. And we think we should keep attacking them through the winter. Usually, we settle in for the winter. We think it would better not to do that. We should keep after them, at least while there is feed for our horses to stay strong."

"Fighting in the winter is very hard on men as well as horses," Crazy Horse reminded them. "How many of our men would be willing?"

"We have tried to do something about that very thing, but it is hard to know," admitted Grey Bull.

"No matter," returned Crazy Horse. "Whether one or a hundred come behind me, I will go, and I know my friend here feels the same."

Cloud nodded his affirmation.

"Good!" said Hump. "We were hoping you would feel that way. But somehow, we knew you both would. We were counting on it!"

Cloud thought about the meeting with Grey Bull and Hump as he sat in his lodge the next morning. He decided to wait to tell his wife and grandmother. He almost did not notice that Sweetwater Woman had bundled herself against the cold until she announced that she was going to visit her mother and left. Soon after that, Grandmother Willow came in with a bundle of firewood.

"I saw her walking toward her mother's lodge. She needs good food, she needs to be strong now that her time is getting near," she told Cloud. "Fresh meat would be the thing."

Toward the middle of the day, Sweetwater still had not returned, so Cloud prepared his weapon and told his grandmother he would hunt. "I know a herd of black-tailed deer live in the hills above our summer camp where there is shelter and food. I will go there."

She noticed he had chosen to take only his rifle.

"It is loud, but I do not have to be as close," he said. "I should be home by dark."

———————————

Wind was only a whisper, allowing cold to wrap itself around every stalk, every branch, and around everything that stood or moved on the land. Snow had fallen off and on throughout the day, sometimes lightly and sometimes heavily. Now the land was mostly white, except for vertical walls of rock. Rabbit was looking for a good spot to stop and make a fire. He wanted hot tea.

The sun went down just as he was searching along an embankment he was familiar with farther up the valley from the encampment. He found his spot, a small eroded bend in an old creek bed. As he was about to dismount, he heard a slight noise that made him remove his mitten and reach for the six-shooter. The mare's ears bent forward, and she was looking toward what looked like a section of the embankment that had broken away to the creek bed.

Rabbit waited and heard the sound again.

The mare was alert but not alarmed, so Rabbit was certain it was not a mountain lion or some other dangerous four-legged. He urged her forward, and she moved without hesitating. Slowing cocking the hammer of the six-shooter, he let the mare walk slowly, ready to grip with his legs if something should suddenly frighten her.

A slight movement in the fading light caught his eye. The mound of earth against the embankment had moved, or something behind it did. Then he heard the sound again and recognized it as a soft sob, a woman's sob.

He stopped and studied the mound of earth, waiting for something to move from behind it. Then he realized that it was not a mound of earth at all. It was someone sitting against the embankment, covered with a dark robe. The sob came again, unmistakable this time.

"Sister," he said, throwing caution aside, "are you there?"

He heard the sudden intake of breath and saw the woman's head jerk up.

"Do not worry," he said reassuringly, "I am a friend." He assumed that it was a Lakota woman, and, if so, she would understand. Or perhaps she was Cheyenne or Blue Cloud.

"I have lost my way," said a childlike voice. "I am cold."

Rabbit put away the six-shooter and slid off the horse. When he came close to the woman, he knew who she was immediately. "Sister," he said gently, "I was looking for a good spot to build a fire. Where you are sitting is good. I will try to be fast."

From his horse, he took his spare buffalo robe and draped it over hers. Questions flowed through his mind as he gathered fuel, but he said nothing. Working swiftly and expertly, he soon had a fire going. When the twigs were engulfed, he added larger pieces. It was not long before the embankment reflected the light from the bright, hot flames.

She spoke not a word the entire time and simply stared into the fire. When the tea was brewed, he offered her some in his only cup. She nodded her appreciation as she took it. Rabbit noticed that she was prepared for the cold. She had heavy mittens and winter moccasins. Next to her was a bundle.

"I am going home," he explained. "We can go together."

Sweetwater Woman nodded. "Yes, that would be good."

"We will leave when you are ready. Can you—can you still get on a horse?"

She nodded. "I think so."

As she sipped her tea, he looked around and found a downward slope in the old creek bed with a low bank. He would put the horse beside the bank and the woman would find it easier to mount.

He kept the questions to himself and waited

patiently while she sipped her tea. When she was ready, he covered the fire. After he took her and the horse to the bank and helped her get on, he led them off into the deepening night. But the sky was clear over the eastern rim of the earth, and the orange sliver of the moon began to grow.

There was activity in the encampment. Rabbit could hear it as they came closer. In the growing moonlight, he saw men and horses gathered in front of the lodge of Cloud and Sweetwater Woman.

Her only words had been in response each time he had asked after her comfort. Rabbit could not sense if she was happy to be home, but that was not for him to know.

Cloud turned at the sound of slow footfalls, and Rabbit could see the others, included Goings, Taken Alive, Little Bird, and Yellow Wolf. All of them were preparing to ride out—to search for the woman, he could only assume. Nearby were Grandmother Willow and Bearface and his wife.

"Cousin," he said to Cloud, "I have brought her home."

Cloud and Bearface moved forward and helped Sweetwater Woman down from the horse, and Star Woman and Grandmother Willow helped her into the lodge.

Cloud turned to Rabbit, questions in his eyes.

"North of here, I found her," he told his cousin. "She said nothing, but I think she is not hurt."

Cloud grabbed Rabbit's shoulder, relief etched on

his face. "Thank you. I will always be grateful to you."

"There is no need," Rabbit replied. "You saved my life. You risked yours to save me. Now I am glad I was the one who returned something that is precious to you."

CHAPTER TWENTY

Something Coming

Sweetwater Woman was awake when Cloud returned to the lodge after watering his horses the next morning. The morning was still new when Grandmother Willow had whispered to him, "Go check on your horses, go for a walk. Take your time. She is awake, but she will need to get herself together."

Sweetwater Woman greeted him with a quick, nervous smile. Cloud returned her smile and was then momentarily surprised when Grandmother Willow began taking up her buffalo robe and mittens.

"My cousin needs help with the yoke of a dress she is making," she told the couple. "I may be gone until sundown." With that, she rustled through the door and was gone.

Cloud tied the inside door to prevent the cold from leaking in and turned around, trying to hide his nervousness. There was much he wanted to say, but he did not know where to begin. He took a seat across the fire from her.

"I am glad to see you," he said meekly. She was nervous, too; he could tell.

"It is—it is good to see you," she said in a near whisper.

He sighed openly. "When I came home at sunset, I—"

"One day, I hope you will forgive me," she interrupted. "I went to visit my mother. She gave me a bundle of food, dried meat, for you. I came out of her lodge and it was snowing. Only a few people were out. I went north, thinking no one would see me in the snow. Not even the sentinels saw me."

"Where were you going?"

"Looking for something that is not there," she answered without hesitating. "I—I wanted to think. I kept walking because it felt good to have silence all around me. Since that white man came, I have been thinking about—about my life before I was found and brought here. More and more, I wanted to know so badly. It was all that was on my mind."

"Yes, you seemed to go somewhere, to someplace I could not go," he said.

"Then I realized the answer was not out there in the cold, or anywhere. The answer was in me. So I turned around. When it snowed again, I lost my way. I sat down against a bank, where Rabbit found me."

Cloud listened with a lump in his throat, and his heart beat a little harder. "I wish I knew what to do to help you," he said, sounding like a boy. "If you want to stay with you mother and father until—"

"No! No!" Her voice was firm.

A weight lifted from his chest and he felt moisture growing in his eyes.

"I know who I am," she said. "My mother said I

was meant to be the daughter of Star Woman and Bear-face. And so I am. I was also meant to be the wife of the good man I see before me."

All he could do was nod until he found his voice. "And I was meant to be the husband of the woman I see before me, the woman who fills my dreams. There is nothing to forgive."

He moved across the room and took her in his arms. For many, many heartbeats, they clung to each other, weeping softly together.

In the afternoon, they went to visit in the lodge of Star Woman and Bearface. Like all Lakota sons-in-law did, Cloud sat quietly and respectfully in the presence of his mother- and father-in-law. But he had known them all his life and sincerely liked them. He listened to the happy conversation between mother and daughter. Like a proper guest and good son-in-law should, he ate every morsel of food Star Woman placed in front of him, even when he thought there was no more room. Toward sunset, they took their leave and walked the few paces to their own lodge.

As they walked, Sweetwater Woman felt a strange sensation, a slight cramping, but it did not come a second time.

The following morning, in spite of the cold, except for the babies in their cradleboards, everyone in the encampment watched the Tongue River valley come alive with warriors. Here and there, an old man sang a Strongheart song, and women trilled as their fighting men joined the procession. Many waved to their wives, sisters, daughters, mothers, and grandmothers before they blended into the throng.

Cloud held his wife close and thought he felt a kick from beneath her buffalo robe. He let go reluctantly and swung up onto his buckskin mare. Grandmother Willow gave him the braided lead rope to his warhorse, a tall, muscular bay. His two bows and quivers of arrows were already tied to the neck rope of the bay. Sweetwater handed him his encased rifle, honoring an old tradition that symbolized a blessing from the keeper of the home to the protector of it.

Then she spoke words that went back beyond the reach of memory. "Remember, it is better to lay a warrior naked in death than to be wrapped up well with a heart of water inside."

"I will remember," he promised as he rode away.

Sweetwater Woman stood with her mother and Grandmother Willow and watched the nearly endless stream of men moving up the valley.

The flow of men and horses had started from the upper villages and followed the river, growing in strength as they passed each camp. Most of them were Lakota, but the Northern Cheyenne were noticeable, and there

were even a few Blue Clouds. Of the Lakota, there were
Oglala, Mniconju, Sicangu, Hunkpapa, and even some
Isanta Dakota. By the time they passed the last camps
on the upper reaches of the valley, they numbered several
hundred in all. Many, if not most, were leading a warhorse, and all were equipped for battle. Half, perhaps, had
a firearm of some kind, whether a rifle or a six-shooter,
and each had a bow, and many had a spare, and a quiver
bristling with arrows. Necessarily, the men were bundled
against the biting cold.

Leading the procession were several medicine
men, including High Eagle and the Cheyenne Crazy
Mule. Behind them rode Grey Bull and Hump.

Before they reached the foothills, the fast-moving
procession turned left toward the southeast. The change in
direction put the sharp breezes from the north at the backs
of the riders. Soon they were on the Powder River Road.

Already far to the south, scouts were on the ridges
and high points from which, looking through a field glass,
they had unobstructed views of the log town and the
immediate surrounding area. Hump and Grey Bull had
sent them. They had already endured a bitterly cold night
in order to be in place when daylight came.

Cloud noticed Rabbit not far behind him and
slowed his horses until he was riding side by side with his
cousin.

"I have never seen anything like this," said Rabbit. "I have never felt this way."

"It was like this when we went up north against the Crow three years ago," recalled Cloud.

"It probably was not this cold," Rabbit guessed.

"No, but the mosquitoes ate us alive. I do not know which is worse: having your blood sucked or having it freeze."

Rabbit grinned from beneath the coyote-hide cap his mother had made for him. "What do you think will happen today?" he said, turning serious.

Cloud chuckled and shook his head. "Maybe nothing. Maybe we are freezing our noses off for nothing and all we do is wear out our horses. When the sun goes down, we will look back on the day."

"I have not been able to sleep very well these past few nights," Rabbit admitted. "Two nights ago, I woke up and my mother was sitting by me, just—just watching me. We talked a little. She went back to her bed. But I could tell she was worried about something."

"Mothers worry about everything."

Rabbit nodded. "Yes, but she woke up because she had a dream, she said, a dream about rifles and six-shooters on the ground in a row on a hilltop."

They rode in silence for a while, listening to the sharp thud of hooves on the cold ground. After a moment, Cloud pointed to the long hide bundle Rabbit had tied to his warhorse. "I hope that is full of bullets and powder," he teased.

Rabbit smiled. "Gifts," he said.

"Gifts?"

Rabbit nodded, smiling mysteriously. "Gifts," he said again.

———————

As Cloud pondered the meaning of Rabbit's enigmatic smile, eight old men had gathered and were standing in a sheltered gully not far from one of the encampments but still well hidden from prying eyes. They kept warm around a fire as they waited for three more. In a while, the three others appeared and dismounted.

"I do not see any food," the first of the three joked, "so this is probably not a feast."

Only his two companions laughed.

The eight old men formed a circle and invited the three into the center. Tentatively, the three entered, and the circle closed around them.

"What is this about?" the first man asked suspiciously.

The oldest of the eight cleared his throat. "If we cannot rely on the honor of men, then we grow weak," he said. "And if any man makes himself bigger than the ways that have sustained us from our grandfathers' grandfathers' time, the same will happen."

The first of the three glanced at his two companions and then turned to the old man. "Our ways are good, but they were born in a time very far past, when no one knew the troubles we would face now," he replied resolutely. "Sometimes we need to change."

"Things do change, and we can decide to change when it is for the good of all and not for a few, or one."

Dark hints of anger appeared in the eyes of the first of the three. "I have nothing but the welfare of the people in my heart!" he blustered.

Another of the old men spoke. "Then make certain you serve that first and yourself last."

"I will not be scolded!" the first of the three shot back.

"Those are the words of arrogance," someone from the circle said. "A humble man would not speak that way. Arrogance needs the satisfaction of power, and even to be worshipped, and it will seek it and find it in the wrong places. Anyone who stands for the people must first rid himself of arrogance."

"Who are you to tell me this?" demanded the first of the three.

"Only old men," replied the oldest man. "We are only old men who have walked a hard road." So saying, he drew his bow from its case, and the other old men did the same.

Stepping forward with a grim set to his mouth, the oldest man suddenly struck the first of the three across the face with his unstrung bow, making him grunt in surprise and pain. "Do not forget the old ways!" warned the oldest man.

Before the surprise and astonishment on the face of the first of the three faded away, the second old man stepped forward and struck him as well. He, too, warned, "Do not forget the old ways!"

And so it went. The other old men stepped up to deliver a blow and the warning. The two other men stepped in to help ward off the blows directed at their companion, but it did not stop the old men.

In the cold silence after the last blow was struck, only the shuffling feet of the old men could be heard as they were walking away. Not a one turned to look back.

The first of the three stood, astonishment frozen on his face. A little blood trickled from a cut above his eye. His companions were equally dumbstruck. None of them spoke. There was nothing to say.

───────────

With only a few brief stops, they came to Prairie Dog Creek around midday, and there, Hump and Grey Bull put the first and last parts of their plan into place. Hundreds of men were deployed on either side of a narrow ridge northwest of Lodge Trail Hill. Deep gullies and narrow-cut banks provided cover—not the best, but it was enough. Once again, the ambushers were expected to wait, not knowing when, or if, they would see Long Knives coming over the hill. There were more ambushers this time, and many of them were seasoned veterans.

The immediate problem was staying warm in the bitter cold. Some of the men were already out foraging for fuel, looking for dry wood and dry buffalo dung to burn. Anything to build even the smallest fire, just to provide the illusion of warmth, at the very least.

Rabbit found Little Bird with a group standing out of the wind down in a gully around Hump. Hump was giving final instructions to the men who were to attack the wood wagons.

Rabbit moved up behind Little Bird. "I have something for you," he said into Little Bird's ear.

Turning, Little Bird saw the shiny muzzle-loading rifle along with a bag of powder and bullets. He was stunned.

"The white man I took it from does not need it any longer," Rabbit said, his eyes twinkling. "I know you will use it well."

Little Bird could only nod at first. "I am grateful," he said.

Rabbit had brought along two other rifles besides his breechloader. One he gave to a man named Wing, and the other to Stands Alone, a quiet man with three daughters. Wing had only a six-shooter, and Stands Alone had only a bow, until now.

Once the ambushers knew where they were to hide, Grey Bull and Hump sent a large group, perhaps forty, to attack the wagons. Crazy Horse and Cloud were to lead the attack against the Long Knives again and draw them into the ambush.

Everything began as planned. A column of Long Knives came out of the fort to go to the aid of the wagons under attack. Hump and Grey Bull watched from the west rim of a ridge east of Lodge Trail Hill, though they could not see the fort itself. If Crazy Horse and Cloud were able to draw the Long Knives across Buffalo Creek and through a thin grove of trees, they would have a clear view. Once that happened, they would signal scouts on a knoll southeast of the ambush site. They would then signal the ambushers.

Grey Bull and Hump heard the faint cracks of distant gunfire, sporadic at first, but they seemed to be a little louder each time.

"I think the Long Knives are taking the bait, again," Grey Bull said matter-of-factly.

Each of them stood on the lee side of their horses, field glasses trained on the meadow north of Buffalo Creek. First, they saw dark specks, seeming to float almost playfully over the ground, more obvious when they moved across the snow cover. In a while, a dark line followed.

Grey Bull grunted in satisfaction. "Here they come!"

North of the grove, the specks went out of sight behind the intervening southern slopes of the end of Lodge Trail Hill. The dark line turned to follow them. After mounting their horses, the two warriors put the horses into a high lope until they reached the knoll and the waiting scouts.

"They are coming!" said Grey Bull. "You go to the west side of the ridge, and you to the east side. Everyone is to stay out of sight, especially the men on the west side of the ridge!"

Wheeling their horses about, the scouts went down the slope. At the bottom, the two young men split off from each other in the meadow south of the ambush ridge. Hump and Grey Bull circled the knoll to the east and dismounted. Leaving their horses on long lead ropes and carrying the other end of the ropes, they burrowed down in the grass where they could see the top of Lodge Trail Hill. There was nothing to do but wait. The plan was for Crazy Horse and Cloud and their men to lead the Long Knives down Lodge Trail Hill toward the ambush.

Gunfire was still sporadic but growing louder. The Lakota appeared on the ridgetop and stopped at the lip of the northeast slope. Crazy Horse and Cloud were the last to appear and then sent the others down the slope. Bullets erupted on the ground around them, and the two war leaders picked their way down the slope as well.

Long Knives appeared. The column turned northwest along the ridgeline. Many of the men near the rim fired at the Lakota who had now reached the meadow at the bottom and stopped. The deep boom of the Long Knife rifles reverberated in the cold air.

Grey Bull realized he was holding his breath.

"Go down!" whispered Hump, trying to will the

Long Knives off the ridge. "Go down!"

They did not. Instead, the head of the column turned left and the rest of it followed like a lethargic snake.

The two men behind the knoll watched the column until the last of it disappeared behind the west side of the ridge. Grey Bull turned to his friend and shook his head in disbelief. Hump angrily smashed a fist into the ground.

In the meadow below them, Cloud and Crazy Horse and the others stared at the empty ridgeline. First, Crazy Horse, then Cloud, urged his horse up the slope. When they reached the top, they saw the last few Long Knives drop from sight.

Cloud sighed. "I guess I was right. We will freeze our noses off for nothing."

"It is not over!" spat Crazy Horse. "This is not done yet!"

From the east came hoofbeats on the breeze. Hump and Grey Bull were approaching at a lope.

Dusk revealed the glow of nearly a hundred campfires in the forest south of Little Goose Creek, an easy ride west of the ambush site. Shelter and wood for fire was of prime necessity. Makeshift sleeping shelters had been hurriedly but skillfully constructed. Men stayed close to the fires, waiting for word about what the leaders would decide to do. Most of the talk was about what did not happen. Just over ten days past, overanxious young men had spoiled an ambush. Today the Long Knives themselves had prevented one by simply leaving. Some of the fighting men speculated that perhaps the Long Knives had spotted them somehow.

"No," said one man. "It was too cold for them on the ridge."

"It was not their day to die," another philoso-phized.

"This morning, we rode out like a buffalo bull in heat," one young Mniconju joked. "Now we have to cool ourselves down."

"It will be so cold tonight, it will freeze off, and then you will not be a bull anymore," teased a battle-scarred veteran. "But do not worry, there is always the next time, and then you might wish you had never been born."

The young Mniconju laughed thinly but did not reply.

But the primary mission this night was to stay warm. Foragers tramped through the forest gathering wood for the fires and to improve their windbreaks.

At one camp deeper in the forest, two roughly dome-shaped shelters stood side by side and a fire burned high. Here were gathered nearly a dozen men, among them High Eagle and Crazy Mule, the Cheyenne.

"We cannot turn back now," High Eagle told everyone. "There is something moving, something com-ing this way."

Crazy Mule nodded slowly in agreement, though

he said nothing. His face beneath the bear-hide cap was partially hidden in the shadows. "I cannot say exactly what it is," continued High Eagle, "but it is strong."

"We will not turn back," Hump said firmly. "The plan we made was good. The one thing we all can see is that the Long Knives can be led away from their outpost. I think it is possible to do it again."

Cloud looked across the fire and caught the introspective gaze of Crazy Horse, who was nodding in agreement.

"Yes," Hump said, looking around. "We will do it again."

CHAPTER TWENTY-ONE

Lodge Trail Ridge

Max Hornsby decided that the officers' mess was very well appointed, much finer than the enlisted men's mess. The last time he had seen a linen tablecloth was in his mother's kitchen. But his attention to the finery was quickly diverted by the smell of cigar smoke and the presence of Colonel Henry Carrington and several of his officers. Hornsby assumed a noncommittal air as soon as he stepped inside the door.

"Come in, Mr. Hornsby," exuded the colonel. "Come in and have a seat."

Hornsby moved to the chair indicated by the colonel, which was to his immediate left. He nodded a greeting to the men in the gathering as he went: Captains Frederick Brown, Tenador Ten Eyck, and William Fetterman and Lieutenants James Powell, George Grummond, and William Bisbee. He had seen them enough to know who there were, but had had no conversations with anyone but Bisbee, who now regarded him with a bemused smile. To the right of the colonel was the old mulatto whose name he could not remember. That old man had hard eyes. Hornsby removed his overcoat and took a seat.

"Pardon me for prevailing upon your time," the colonel apologized and then gestured at the men around the table, "but after breakfast this morning, we seem to have fallen into a very interesting—shall we say—discussion concerning our adversaries." Carrington glanced to his right. "According to Mr. Bridger here, they are mainly Sioux, I believe."

Fetterman, the one with the cigar, leaned forward. "We are told you have had some experience with the Sioux. Is that correct?"

"Yes, I did," Hornsby replied. The captain had very intense eyes.

"Mr. Bridger is of the opinion that there are upward of several thousand warriors. What is your opinion, Mr. Hornsby?"

Someone had sold someone a bill of goods about his "experience" with the Indians. "I saw one village just north of the Tongue, 'bout thirty miles north of here," he explained. "Noticed maybe two dozen or so warriors."

"Large village?" asked Lieutenant Powell.

Hornsby shook his head. "'Bout thirty lodges, maybe more. But I cannot say if that is large or not. It is the only one I ever saw."

Carrington turned to the old man Bridger. "Is that usual, James?"

Bridger nodded slowly, pursing his lips. "Yeah, for a summer village. They move for the winter, break up into smaller villages. If the boy here saw two dozen warriors, they was pro'bly two dozen more he did not see."

The colonel stroked his chin. "So the question is, gentlemen, how many of these villages are in the Tongue

River valley and elsewhere? That is difficult to ascertain. Owing to the lack of direct intelligence, I am inclined to accede to Mr. Bridger's knowledge of Indians. He has spent a lifetime making it his business to know about them, I might add."

Captain Brown waved a hand. "Sir," he said to Carrington, "I have a thought. Although I am not long for this posting, I must press the point that it would be possible to gather direct intelligence." He indicated Hornsby with a gesture. "This man has been to the Tongue River basin. He has a familiarity with the area that we do not have. Perhaps, sir, it would be wise to hire Mr. Hornsby as a scout so that he can reconnoiter the area and report back. Then you would have direct intelligence to plan a campaign—"

"Captain Brown!" exclaimed Carrington. "I commend you for an excellent flanking maneuver. Howsoever, we have been over that much-trodden ground. Besides, as you were kind enough to point out, your tenure here at this post is becoming shorter by the day. Therefore, tactical operations here are no longer your concern. Furthermore, need I remind you, Captain, that as quartermaster, they never were!"

Brown threw up his hands, but before he could lodge a protest, Fetterman stepped in.

"Nevertheless, sir," he said evenly, in spite of the intensity in his eyes, "Captain Brown does raise a valid issue! We have the strength to take the offensive! If the only obstacle is direct intelligence, I think we might have a solution here—in the person of Mr. Hornsby."

Carrington looked at Hornsby with a fatherly gaze. "Well, I believe Mr. Hornsby might have something to say about that, Captain. He is a civilian and someone who is not attached officially to the post in any way. He is here of his own volition. Let us not assume, gentlemen, that he would be disposed to anything you might suggest."

"Mr. Hornsby," said Fetterman, "I understand you were with the courier detail that engaged with a war party last month."

"Yes, I was."

Captain Brown slid his chair back and went to the stove in the corner of the room behind the colonel. "Pardon me," he said to Hornsby. The captain opened the stove and put in two pieces of split wood.

"How many did you encounter at that time?" Fetterman persisted as Brown returned to his chair while trying to be as quiet as possible.

Hornsby waited as images, mostly flashes and blurs, slid through his mind's eye. "Hard to say," he finally responded.

"Well, I am sure that it had to be a considerable number of them," allowed Fetterman, "given that half the patrol was killed."

Hornsby recalled the gallop up the slope away from the trail until his mount began struggling up the incline. By the time he had dismounted and ducked behind a boulder—or was it a tree?—he was likely more than half a mile from the ambush. He tried to recall how many Indians he then saw when he looked back down the slope. No more than five or six.

"Hard to say," he repeated, staring down at the white tablecloth. "I saw five or six. Maybe the other men in the detail can recall something else."

Lieutenant Grummond jumped in. "Sir," he said to Fetterman, "I took a report from the two privates who survived that ambush. They could not recall clearly seeing any particular number. But I think their statements support what Mr. Hornsby said."

Captain Fetterman leaned back. "If you will indulge me further, Mr. Hornsby, may I ask how long you have been here?"

"Since July, Captain. I came with up the Highsmith train and decided to stay."

Lieutenant Bisbee spoke up. "Mr. Hornsby had seen a white captive with the Indians, a woman. He wanted to investigate that, I believe."

Fetterman, relighting his cigar, turned to look at Hornsby. "Indeed! What happened on that score, Mr. Hornsby?"

"I did see the woman," Hornsby told him, "but I was unable to talk to her, so I know nothing about her."

"Other than the fact that she is, indeed, there in the village," Fetterman pointed out. "That is commendable, Mr. Hornsby."

The captain turned to Colonel Carrington. "Sir, is there anything we can do about this situation that Mr. Hornsby has verified? Probably at considerable risk to himself, I would wager."

Max Hornsby suddenly felt like one of the steers in the cattle pen selected for slaughter and relentlessly herded into a corner. He was worried that the men in the room were forming the wrong idea concerning his experience and ability. Although he had notions of coming west to become a "frontiersman," he was a long way from achieving that distinction. Furthermore, that fanciful notion was fading fast.

Carrington poured himself more coffee from a blue pot. "Mr. Hornsby did make a request in July asking for a rescue mission, as I recall. Under the circumstances, I denied it. Consequent to that, I asked Mr. Bridger about the issue of white captives among Indians. Turns out, it is not an uncommon occurrence. Whatever circumstances may have brought them to the Indians—raids more often than not, in my opinion—I am told that more than a few acquiesce to their lot, strange as that may seem."

Captain Fetterman refused to divert from the issue of taking the fight to the Indians. "Be that as it may, Colonel," he said. "I think that an offensive against the Sioux, or whoever they are, is imperative, as I have recommended officially. Now comes Mr. Hornsby, who seems to be uniquely qualified to validate those recommendations."

"Here, here!" said Brown.

"Yes," said the colonel, "I did read your recommendations, Captain Fetterman. You certainly made use of your time while you were nonassigned personnel."

Fetterman knew he had pushed the issue as far as he could. He decided to heed Brown's cautionary glance from across the table and keep his mouth shut. But he promised himself he would continue to press the issue at every opportunity.

Max Hornsby, meanwhile, felt a tightness growing in his throat and finally decided to set the record straight. Gathering his nerve, he glanced at Carrington and then fixed his gaze on the white tablecloth. "Truth is," he began, "I stumbled onto that village up there along the Tongue. I thought I could walk in there and—and do something. They captured me, and I spent the night sitting in the rain. I did see the woman and I tried to talk to her. That sure as hell upset them! They almost killed me, and I still do not know why they turned me loose."

"Do not belittle yourself, Mr. Hornsby," said Brown. "It did require a certain amount of backbone to do what you did. I commend you."

"Thank you, but mostly I felt stupid. And as far as the ambush last month," Hornsby went on, "well, everything happened fast. Things happened so fast that none of us who survived had a chance to fire back at the Indians. Hell, we could not see them."

A silence descended, and Max Hornsby felt himself being scrutinized.

"You are an honest man, Mr. Hornsby," said Lieutenant Powell. "I admire honesty in a man."

Carrington stood. "Gentlemen, I believe we have duties awaiting all of us and we have taken up enough of Mr. Hornsby's time."

Chairs scraped on the wooden floor. Hornsby turned and suddenly realized that the old scout had been staring at him with an unfathomable gleam in his old eyes. After a slight nod, the man stood and walked from the room.

Carrington extended a hand. "Thank you, Mr. Hornsby. I apologize if we caused you discomfort in any way. And I just realized that we did not have enough manners to offer you coffee. Please forgive me."

"Nothing to trouble yourself over, Colonel."

"You are well spoken, Mr. Hornsby. May I ask where you are from?"

"Maine. My father was a schooner captain until the war forced him to retire five years ago. My mother still teaches piano."

The colonel nodded thoughtfully. "Indeed, indeed. If you would permit a word of advice: go home as fast as you can."

Hornsby saw sincerity and concern in the colonel's eyes. "The thought has crossed my mind, Colonel."

On his way to the blacksmith shed, Hornsby heard the footsteps and knew who was hurrying to catch up: Captain William Fetterman.

"Mr. Hornsby," said the captain, "most of us with Colonel Carrington this morning would very much like to speak with you further on several topics."

Hornsby felt the tightness in his throat again. "I doubt I could be much help to the army, Captain Fetterman," he protested.

"On the contrary," Fetterman asserted, "I personally believe you to be thoroughly valuable. You have experience that I would like to draw on."

Hornsby nodded. *Better to get this out of the way, whatever it is,* he thought. "Captain, as soon as the weather breaks, I am heading south to Fort Laramie to then find the fastest way home. So if you are bound to have this talk, let us make it soon."

Fetterman smiled and extended his hand. "Then let us make it tomorrow evening. We can meet in the officers' quarters. I have a bottle of cherished Irish whisky for the occasion."

Hornsby was glad for the warmth of the smithy's shed when he walked in.

Slattern tossed him a look and kept on hammering on a wagon rim. "Them officers is an interesting bunch, I hear," he said, hoping for some indication as to why Max Hornsby had been summoned by the colonel.

Hornsby doffed his coat and hung it on a peg. "That they are," he said laconically. "That they are."

Snow had fallen during the night, but the sharp cold had kept it powdery, enabling busy breezes to form long, undulating fingers of white and float them over the ground. Hump and Grey Bull had decided that the warriors would stand down for the day. The snowfall had prompted that decision. Overnight the snow had probably covered most of the tracks left by the warriors and the Long Knives the day before. By leaving no new tracks today, they hoped the Long Knives might think that the Lakota had given up. All in all, the relatively minor issue of tracks aside, Hump was simply going with his gut instinct, which was fine with Grey Bull.

Their camp had been improved. Wide, sturdy windbreaks had been erected so that the two of them could comfortably visit with the steady stream of warrior leaders who came throughout the day. For each group, Hump patiently scratched out on a bare patch of ground the plan he and Grey Bull had refined.

The ambush was still the thing, but now, important details were added. Hump was convinced their basic plan was sound. "Yesterday," he told the warriors, "my friend and I watched the Long Knives leaving from Lodge Trail Hill. Their manner told me that they decided to leave on their own. That is, they did not see any of the hidden ambushers. If they did, they probably would have galloped away."

He pointed to a sketch he had drawn on the ground.

"This is the ambush ridge, the same one, because it is on the trail, and they know the trail. So we will bring them to the trail. But," he pointed to an intersecting line, "this is what we did not think of yesterday. The decoy warriors will ride past this point, past Prairie Dog Creek. Past the creek, they will cross in front of each other, like this." With his hands, he imitated horses crossing, one in front of the other. "I think enough of the ambushers will see that. Those that can will tell everyone else. That is the signal to attack."

"All of this will work," said a battle-hardened warrior leader, "only if the Long Knives go down close to Prairie Dog Creek—if they come out of the town, and if they follow from there."

Hump agreed. "Yes. We have a plan for that, too." He pointed to the south end of the ambush ridge. "Now," he said, "when the Long Knives are all the way down at Prairie Dog Creek, the signal will be given. When that happens, the ambushers on the south end—no matter which side of the ridge—have to close the trap behind them, here. That means they have to get to here, south of the narrow point, before the Long Knives do, because they will turn around once we attack and they will try to go back."

"Lodge Trail Hill is the thing," another warrior said. "There is no way to circle behind them, even if they come that far again. How will we bring them off that ridge to the ambush?"

Hump leaned back and drew his buffalo robe

higher around his wide shoulders. "My friend and I have considered that, too," he pointed out. "The warriors attacking the wood wagons are important. The ambushers are important. To be sure, nothing will work if the ambushers do not wait for the signal. But they will have no one to fight, like yesterday, unless the Long Knives are led to Prairie Dog Creek."

Hump looked around at the expectant faces. "My friend and I have decided that the decoys will be ten: two from the Blue Clouds, two from the Northern Cheyenne, and six from the Lakota. They will be the most reckless and most daring, men who have already proven themselves, ten men who are not afraid to thump death on the nose. We have picked the leader: Crazy Horse. He will pick the other nine."

Lone Bear, Crazy Horse, and Cloud were back at their fire, having just returned from letting their horses graze on a good patch of grass in the trees. They were checking powder and bullets when Yellow Wolf rode up and dismounted.

"From the look on your face," teased Cloud, "No Two Horns must think you are good enough for his daughter. Did you have to promise him a hundred horses? Or was it Gets There First? I forget."

Yellow Wolf sat down at the fire, ignoring the gibes. There was something in his demeanor that sent a chill through Cloud.

"What is it?" he cautiously asked the young man.

"When the sun goes down," Yellow Wolf said, "Hump and Grey Bull want to see the two of you."

Crazy Horse nodded and rolled a few lead bullets around in his palm. "I have four," he said to Cloud. "How many do you have?"

"Twelve," Cloud told him, "but I have two bows and two quivers, almost sixty arrows, I think."

"I have over forty arrows," said Crazy Horse after a moment.

"I will give you four of my bullets," offered Cloud.

Crazy Horse was quick to reply. "No, no. Four bullets is a good sign. Four is what I need. It is the medicine number."

Then he shot a quick glance at Yellow Wolf. "What does he want to see us about?"

"Something about tomorrow."

Precisely as the sun went down, Crazy Horse and Cloud arrived at the camp of Hump and Grey Bull. Both the older men were eating and were boiling coffee. Their fire was high and bright.

Grey Bull pointed to the spit. "There is meat," he told them. "Rabbit shot a deer."

Removing his mittens, Crazy Horse sliced off two pieces of deer flank and handed one to Cloud. "I think it was the right thing to do, to wait today," he said to Hump. "I do not know why, but I think it was good."

"I will tell you why," Hump was quick to reply. "We had the time to think about yesterday, so we have some new plans."

"Good," said Crazy Horse, grinning. "I think we should all surround the log town tonight and send fire arrows over the walls."

Both Hump and Grey Bull chuckled, and then their expressions turned serious. "Here it is, my friend," Hump said to Crazy Horse. "There will be ten decoys tomorrow, ten of the best we have, the craziest and the bravest. You will lead them, and you will pick the other nine: five more Lakota, two Cheyenne, and two Blue Clouds."

Crazy Horse licked his fingers after he finished his meat. "I do not know if I am brave, but I never thought of myself as crazy," he said softly.

He looked up to see Cloud grinning at him. "But you are," he pointed at his friend, "crazy, I mean, so you will be one of them."

Then he turned to the two older men. "I think it will be good," he told them. "Yesterday taught me a few things. One is that we stayed too far ahead of the Long Knives. Tomorrow, we have to be close enough to see how many have blue eyes. We will do that; you can count on that."

"Let us know who else you will pick so we can send word to them," said Grey Bull.

"After my friend there, I want my younger brother. Little Hawk is crazier than both of us. From the Cheyenne, we should have Little Wolf and Wolf Left Hand. The others, I will think on it and let you know."

For the second night, fires burned brightly in

the forest south of Little Goose Creek. They burned high because the night was bitterly cold and the men huddled beneath their heavy buffalo robes were confident no enemy was about. Tomorrow, they had been told. Tomorrow, they would try the Long Knives again.

Word had circulated through the camps faster than a stiff breeze: Crazy Horse was picking the best men to ride with him to lure the Long Knives over Lodge Trail Hill. Including him, there would be ten.

Men came to the camp of Crazy Horse, all bundled against the cold, many hoping to be picked as one of the ten and others only to learn who had been selected. By late evening, nine men had been given an arrow from Crazy Horse's quiver, an arrow marked with blue from the dream he had as a boy.

As the excitement died away and the warriors went back to their camps to burrow into their robes, Cloud saw his friend ride away. Crazy Horse had a habit of going off to be alone, especially during a time like this. Cloud had never asked him about the dream. One did not ask such things. But High Eagle had some thoughts that he shared with Cloud.

Crazy Horse, High Eagle said, had been given a difficult path, one he was bound to walk without explaining to anyone. And there was a reason Crazy Horse never described his deeds in battle, the "telling of victories" that warriors were expected to do. There was a reason he always dressed plainly, almost shabbily sometimes. There was a reason he was a quiet and humble young man when he walked through the village and then became a reckless whirlwind on the battlefield. That reason was his burden to bear alone. Although he could not and would not talk about that reason, there was an outward sign: before battle, he painted blue hailstones on his chest and the lightning mark across his face. The hailstones and lightning represented the basis of his power: the Thunders. Crazy Horse was a Thunder Dreamer, and a Thunder Dreamer had to the live his life as an example to others. In a real sense, his life was not his own. Cloud shuddered at the thought of that daunting responsibility as he watched his friend ride away to think and meditate in silence on some hilltop somewhere. He sent a prayer with him.

Cloud suddenly realized he was caressing the medicine bundle High Eagle had given him. On this cold night, it felt warm to his touch.

Then his thoughts turned to home and to Sweetwater Woman.

———

Grandmother Willow heard the stirring under the sleeping robes.

After a soft grunt, Sweetwater Woman sat up slowly. In the glow of the night coals, her eyes darted side to side. "Grandmother," she whispered loudly, "I think something is happening."

CHAPTER TWENTY-TWO

An Icy Calm

Even before Lakota eyes could see the dawn breaking, the small blue jays saw the light approaching and greeted it with their soft *kah-kay-kay*. Shortly after that, Hump and Grey Bull rode through the camps. "Wake up now," they called out without shouting. "Wake up now!"

Many fires had been kept burning through the night. The aroma of coffee and peppermint tea wafted into the air as preparations were made. Weapons checked and rechecked the night before were tucked into belts, tied onto horses, or slung across the backs of anxious men.

The cold had not relented through the night, and in spite of it, many fighting men took the time to paint the symbols of power and medicine on their faces and bodies. Cloud painted the fingers of a left hand vertically over the bottom half of his face in red. This he did in honor of his father's father, a Crazy Dog warrior who never retreated in battle. Crazy Horse painted the yellow lightning mark from top to bottom over the left side of his face.

A deep voice called out softly to him as two Northern Cheyenne came out of the growing light. Crazy Horse and Cloud recognized the two brothers, Little Wolf and Big Nose.

"My friend," greeted Little Wolf, a smile on his usually intense face, "I have a favor to ask. I am honored that you asked me to ride with you as one of the ten, but I would like that honor to pass to my brother, Big Nose. He deserves it more than I."

Both men were seasoned fighters, their achievements and honors known among the Lakota as well as the Cheyenne.

"I will take my brother's place with your permission," Big Nose asserted.

Crazy Horse nodded. "To share this with either one of you is good. It will be as you ask," he said to Little Wolf.

"Good!" smiled Little Wolf. "When this day is over, we will count bullets and arrows and see who has killed the most Long Knives!" Touching his brother's shoulder and waving to Crazy Horse, he spun his horse and rode away into the gray dawn.

Eight men appeared one by one in the span of heartbeats. All of them were bundled against the relentless cold, and all were prepared to thump death on the nose. The ten were ready.

Hump and Grey Bull appeared as well, at the head of the large group that would attack the wood wagons. Crazy Horse and Cloud mounted and stopped for a quick word. Horses snorted here and there and some stomped the cold ground, feeling the nervousness and anxiety of their riders.

Hump seemed relaxed, almost carefree. "I have a feeling this is the day," he said resolutely, looking proudly at each of the decoys in turn. "Even in the best days of my youth, I was not as good as any of you," he told them. "Whatever happens this day, we thank you for your willingness. Bring us the Long Knives. Pull their beards and poke them in the eye if you must. Bring them to us!"

Hoofbeats drumming on the cold ground, Hump, Grey Bull, and their warriors departed toward the log town, moving not with misguided urgency, but with a determined certainty. The decoy warriors followed.

———————

A soft cooing song filled the lodge, along with the warmth of the low fire and the soothing presence of women. At the back of the room, Sweetwater Woman leaned back against her chair. The old woman directly in front of her gazed calmly into her face as Sweetwater breathed deeply while the pain slowly diminished.

"Good," said Red Shawl reassuringly. "Good. You are doing well, Granddaughter. Life begins with pleasure for the man but is sanctified by the woman's pain. That is the way it has always been, because we are the givers of life."

Behind Red Shawl sat Star Woman and Grandmother Willow, ready to help at the moment of birth. On the other side of the room, another old woman tended the fire and another poured a special tea into a cup and passed it to Red Shawl, the old midwife.

"Drink this," she said, passing the cup to Sweet-water. "It will help loosen your hold on the baby."

———————————

High Eagle learned the night before that among the Mni-conju, there was a dreamer who sometimes could see the future, a young man with the mannerisms of a woman. Knowing where the Mniconjus were camped, High Eagle went searching and found him sitting alone at a fire. Beneath his buffalo robe, the young man wore a flowing black dress.

"I was curious what you might see ahead for this day," he said to the skittish young man.

"I have not looked. No one has asked me," the dreamer replied apprehensively.

Some of the Mniconu recognized High Eagle and took an interest in the conversation between the Oglala medicine man and their dreamer.

"I am asking," High Eagle said courteously. He threw a stick on the ground near the fire. "This is a young, fast mare, given to me as a gift last autumn. She is yours if you will look."

By now, several Mniconju had gathered, some to make sure that High Eagle had good intentions.

The dreamer snatched up the stick. "I will look, but this horse is mine even if nothing is revealed to me," he asserted nervously.

High Eagle nodded. "You have a horse."

Finishing his coffee, the dreamer stood suddenly and walked with quick steps to his horse and mounted. He was a small man. Unfolding a wool blanket, he covered his head and kicked his horse into a slow trot. Without guidance from its rider, the horse crossed a small frozen stream and trotted into a wide gully. Leaning forward, head covered, the dreamer swayed with the motion of the horse. At a sudden steep incline, the horse turned of its own accord and headed in a different direction.

High Eagle and several of the Mniconju watched. Twice the horse changed directions. Then, still without guidance from the dreamer, it crossed the stream and returned to the fire.

After a moment, the dreamer pulled the blanket off his head, cupping his hands into a basket. "I have a few Long Knives here," he announced.

High Eagle snorted. "A few soldiers are not worth one good horse," he said.

Staring at the medicine man, the dreamer covered his head with a flourish and kicked the horse. Once again, the horse walked back and forth several times in the gully and returned.

Shrugging off the blanket, the young man held his hands against his chest. "I have more Long Knives," he said.

"How many?" High Eagle wanted to know.

"Twenty," replied the dreamer.

"A victory over twenty is not worth freezing our testicles," High Eagle protested. "And they told me you have a power. What happened to it? Did it freeze along with your testicles?"

Anger flashed in the dreamer's eyes. Covering his head with the blanket once more, he urged his horse into a high lope until they disappeared into some low, broken hills. He was gone for a long time. Just as the Mniconju warriors were beginning to shoot accusatory glances at High Eagle, the horse came loping back.

The dreamer jumped to the ground, his arms straining, struggling to carry a heavy load. From beneath his blanket, he called out in a muffled voice. "I have a hundred! A hundred in the hands!" Then he fell to the ground.

One of the Mniconju standing nearby let out a yell. "It is time to go!" he told the others.

As the Mniconju fighters rode off, High Eagle helped the young dreamer to his feet. He was slight in build with a pleasant, almost womanlike face. "You do have a power," the medicine man told him. "Now you must find a hidden place. You must stay away from the fighting to come. Build a fire and stay warm, hold in your mind what you saw. Do that until the fight is over!"

———————

As the new day grew brighter, those going after the wood train eventually turned southeast, bending south of a ridge until they reached Buffalo Creek before it bent to the east, and making sure to stay out of the line of sight of the sentries on the lookout post to the south. They found mounds and rises, clumps of grass, and every eroded cut bank to hide in or behind and settled in to wait for the wood train. This was still in the early part of the morning.

Black Horn, one of the leaders, had a thought and found his friend Knife. "Maybe a few men can get in closer," he suggested, "say fifteen or twenty."

Knife's eyes glistened. "I think some of us are sneaky enough to do that," he assured Black Horn.

"But wait for us to attack the wagons," Black Horn cautioned, "though you might hang back and see what happens."

Crazy Horse and his decoys had followed the larger force at first but then turned and crossed Buffalo Creek farther to the east and kept to the north of the ridge between them and the log town. Before they came into full view of the log walls and the sentry hill to the south, beyond the fork of Buffalo Creek, they stopped to find cover behind a thick patch of leafless shrubbery. They dismounted and stood with their horses side by side in a double line. Now it was their turn to wait. Big Nose, an imposing presence, stood next to Crazy Horse.

"I have a strange feeling," he said in a low voice, "almost like tomorrow is not coming. I think it means this is a good day to be alive."

Crazy Horse nodded. "Any day we defend the

people is a good day to be alive and a good day to die."

Silence lay over the land, a silence as deep as the pervasive cold. Wisps of glistening mist billowed upward and then vanished as the breath of men and horses crystallized in the air. The ten waited.

———————————

To the north, the ambushers were in position as they had been two days before, many in the same places. The Northern Cheyenne and Blue Clouds were at the northwestern end of the southern side of ambush ridge. Some of the Lakota were on the south side of the ridge as well, but most were on the northern side. Every man had to make sure he could not be seen from Lodge Trail Hill. Once in place, the task was to stay out of the wind. Being warm was impossible, so preventing extremities and exposed skin from freezing was the next best thing. The Mniconju warriors told of the dreamer's vision, and their news spread quickly. A rider galloped from the north side to tell the Northern Cheyenne and the Blue Clouds. From there, it was passed from one man to the next until it reached to the end of the line of ambushers. Encouraged by the prediction of victory, the ambushers encouraged one another.

"Remember," they said, "the signal will be given by the decoys after they cross Prairie Dog Creek. *After they cross!*"

Goings, Taken Alive, Little Bird, Yellow Wolf, and

Rabbit had found a steep bank below the ambush ridge on the west side. They spent the morning piling brush on the lip of the bank. Goings pointed to the ridge. "If it works, we will see Crazy Horse and the others from here, and the Long Knives, too."

"There is one thing that bothers me," Taken Alive worried. "The slope is steep, and going up the snow will make it slippery for the horses. I think it might be better to ride only so far and then go up the rest of the way on foot."

"Yes," Goings agreed, "that might be the thing to do."

"I am worried about the arrows that will be coming up and then over from the other side," Rabbit pointed out.

They all looked at him. No one had thought of that possibility.

"Where are Lone Bear and He Dog?" Goings wondered.

"To the north, I think," Taken Alive replied, "with the Cheyenne."

They all turned and stared silently at the top of the ridge.

———————————

Grey Bull and Hump had ridden east, circled ambush ridge on the north, and returned to the same vantage point they had used the day before, along the lip of the ridge east of Lodge Trail Hill. From there, they had a good view of the broad meadows north of the log town. Like yesterday, they would be able to see the decoys and Long Knives coming. Through the long, shiny glass given to him by Cloud, Hump watched the frozen landscape to the north.

"Nothing yet," he reported to his friend.

At that distance, he could not hear a slight scrape as the west gate of the log town was pushed open. But the decoys were closer, and Big Nose was the first to hear a faint, unusual sound and touched Crazy Horse's arm. Wagons emerged through gate, like a long arm reaching out. The clunk of their wooden wheels on the frozen ground carried through the frigid air.

"Stay still," Crazy Horse whispered to the man behind him, and Cloud passed back the word. "Stay still!" he whispered.

The line of wagons was accompanied by more than two dozen Long Knives and many more men who did not wear the dark uniforms. Motionlessly, the decoys stood and listened to the clunk of wheels, the tromping of hooves, the squeak of leather, and the crack of whips. Soon the noises began to fade as the wagons and men moved farther west along the wood road. In a while, the silence returned.

Crazy Horse turned to look at the men behind him. All were calm, but he did not expect otherwise. He shuddered inwardly. There was deadliness in that icy calmness. "It begins," he said.

On the hill to the north, Hump thought he saw movement. "Something is happening," he said Grey Bull.

Black Horn and the others heard the crack of whips and then the sharp rumble of rolling wagon wheels.

The word was passed: "Get ready!"

―――――――――――

The orderly rushed into the post commander's office. "Sir, there is gunfire, and Pilot Hill is signaling! The wood detail is under attack!"

"Very well. Notify Lieutenant Powell and have the bugler blow assembly!"

In the smithy's shed, Max Hornsby heard the clear notes of the bugle followed by the tramp of running feet and the jingle of bridles. A shiver ran up his back.

Pulling his collar up against the cold, Colonel Henry Carrington found Lieutenant James Powell at the end of the parade ground at the same moment Captain William Fetterman arrived.

"Sir," the captain saluted, "I respectfully request permission to lead this mission!"

Carrington was annoyed. "This is probably no more than a few braves causing a nuisance, like two days ago. The lieutenant followed my orders then, Captain, which is the reason he is leading this mission."

"I understand, sir. However, I base my request on my senior rank."

Lieutenant Powell acquiesced. "I agree with Captain Fetterman, sir."

Carrington turned to Fetterman. "In that case, Captain, these are my orders! The mission is to support the wood train. Relieve it and report to me! Do not engage or pursue Indians at its risk! Under no circumstances pursue over Lodge Trail Ridge!"

"Yes, sir!"

Carrington departed as Fetterman stopped to shake Powell's hand. "Good luck to you, William," said the lieutenant.

"I will not pursue over Lodge Trail Ridge," Fetterman assured him, "but between here and there, I will teach those savages a good lesson!"

He turned and grabbed a sergeant. "Go to the blacksmith shed. Bring the man Hornsby to me. Make sure he is armed and ready to ride."

Hornsby stared at the sergeant standing in the doorway, not believing what he had just heard. He was about to refuse, but then hurried to his room and grabbed his overcoat and rifle.

As he approached the northwest corner of the fort, the gates opened and he watched a troop of infantry march out. Behind them, a formation of cavalry was waiting for the order to mount. He spotted Fetterman just as a young officer ran up to the captain and saluted.

"A reminder from the colonel, sir," he heard the post adjutant say to the captain, "Lodge Trail Ridge and no farther."

Fetterman gave the boy a withering stare and

mounted. Turning to Lieutenant Grummond, who was waiting nearby, he said, "We will do a final inspection of arms, Lieutenant. Let us be certain we are fully prepared."

Hornsby accepted the reins thrust into his hands by a soldier and waited.

"Mr. Hornsby," said the captain after the inspection, "good to see you. Mount up and help me prove a point. We will circle north of Sullivant Hills and outflank the savages."

Captain Frederick Brown rode up, his overcoat still unbuttoned and a pair of gloves in his left hand. "I have acquired permission from the colonel," he told Fetterman triumphantly. "I was hoping for a bit of a lark before I have to leave."

"Welcome!" exclaimed Fetterman. "Now we can put our tactical theories into operation. Glad to have you along."

The order was given, and the column of cavalry moved out through the gate, four abreast. Hornsby felt strangely out of place, not sure where he should be, and stayed to the left of the column. He felt a strange sense of relief and puzzlement at the same time when he spotted two men at end of the column, two other civilians. Out of the corner of his eye, Hornsby saw a soldier approaching. It was Lieutenant Grummond.

"The captain would like you to ride with him," the lieutenant said. His statement was nearly a question, and the look on his face indicated that he did not believe what he had just spoken.

Hornsby did not believe what he heard. He wanted to go back to the fort, but as he glanced back, he saw the gates closing behind them.

———————————

She squeezed the thick chokecherry wands in each hand as the pain hit its peak. To her left, her mother held one wand and Grandmother Willow, who had now taken a seat on the right, held the other. She was surprisingly strong as she clung to the wand. The old midwife was in the middle. Sweetwater Woman clenched her jaw against the pain. The contractions were more frequent. As this one subsided, she released the wands and leaned back against the chair.

"Good," Red Shawl said softly. "It is good that they are getting harder."

Sweetwater nodded as her mother leaned forward and gently wiped her face.

———————————

From the sound of the gunfire, the attack on the wood train was fully engaged. The ten decoys heard the thin blasts of a horn that had to come from inside the log walls. Cloud turned to Little Hawk, whose eyes gleamed with anticipation.

"They are signaling something," he said to the young warrior. "They are coming out to help the wood wagons."

From their vantage point, Grey Bull and Hump heard the faint cracks of steady gunfire to the south.

Waiting behind the thin stalks, the decoys thought they could hear shouting from the general direction of the log town. Crazy Horse listened intently and then turned to motion the others closer.

"My friend Hump said we must pull their beards or poke them in the eyes. That is our task, my friends. There is no way to know how many Long Knives will come out to help the wagons, but they belong to us. This cold will be harder on them, so it is a good thing.

"Do not become too separated from one another, and if one of us goes down, we must rescue him. Two days ago, we were too far ahead of them. Get in close, make them want to chase us, make them angry.

"Only the Earth lives forever, my friends. Whatever we do belongs to the people. Remember that we do this for them, not for ourselves. Get ready! This is a good day to die!"

"Good words! Good words!" Big Nose affirmed. "Make your deeds worthy of the songs they will sing!"

Strangely, it was the earth that told them the Long Knives were coming before their eyes or ears did. The horses sensed it first, as they all looked toward the east. Then the men felt it on the bottoms of their feet, a trembling. Mere heartbeats after that, they heard the thud of hooves, faintly at first, but steady.

Hump saw the thin dark line through his glass. It was moving along the frozen slopes of the hills west of the log town.

To a man, the ten decoys looked in the direction of the growing noise. First, they saw heads bobbing as a narrow front of Long Knives appeared around the hill. As yet, they were still a long arrow-cast away, but they were approaching at a high lope.

CHAPTER TWENTY-THREE

Thumping Death on the Nose

With swift but unhurried motions, they shed their buffalo robes and thick mittens. Beneath the robes, they wore heavy winter shirts, and some had also wrapped blankets around themselves. The buffalo robes were much too bulky to allow free movement of their arms, which they would need in battle.

Each of them carried a six-shooter. Several of them tied their unstrung and encased bow and a quiver of arrows to the front, across their hips. A rifle was either slung across the back in its case or tied to the horse's neck rope. The deadliest weapon they carried, however, could not be seen with the eyes: the heart and the will.

Cloud paused to rearrange his bullet bag and thought of Sweetwater Woman. He refused to think he might not see her again.

Crazy Horse swung up on his horse, flashed a smile at his brother, and called out, "Follow me!"

In the next instant, all the decoys were mounted and riding hard.

Crazy Horse, with the other nine close on his heels, slashed toward the oncoming column of Long Knives. Inside the range of a six-shooter, he opened fire and then angled off to the northeast. As they flashed past the knot of mounted Long Knives, they saw the walking ones far behind, struggling to keep up.

Cloud wheeled his bay around and caught up to Crazy Horse, who had stopped and was calmly watching the Long Knives. Several of the other decoys were feigning a charge at the walking Long Knives. Cloud pointed to Little Hawk, riding closest to the column.

The sudden appearance of the decoys had surprised the Long Knives. The mounted ones had stopped, and then the front of the column turned right, in the direction of the decoys.

Cloud saw the gleam in his friend's eyes, the slight smile on his lips. "Shall we go poke them in the eye?" he asked.

"Before this is over, I want to see how many of them have beards," Crazy Horse replied.

Flashes from rifle muzzles preceded the booms. The walking Long Knives came down an incline, some of them firing as they ran. Left of them, the mounted ones had formed into a narrow column and were coming two by two.

Crazy Horse angled left toward the Long Knives on foot, and Cloud loped toward the right. The ten decoys presented a broad front, forcing the Long Knives to cover a wide area and then choose which target to fire at. Cloud saw Little Hawk suddenly slide his horse to a stop, sending snow flying up, and then spin him into a turn and urge him into a gallop in the opposite direction. The Long Knives were not firing as much as he thought they would, but that did not matter as long as they kept chasing after the decoys.

———————

Max Hornsby remembered the first time he had seen Indians on horseback, when two were coming toward him at a flying gallop. What he saw in front of him now was reminiscent of that recent moment. He tried to count the Indians skittering about on the frozen meadow ahead but couldn't. Still, there were not many. Then he remembered that he had not seen any the day the courier detail had been ambushed on the trail several weeks ago until it was all over. Those unseen Indians had killed four men.

The crisp drumming of hooves on the frozen ground filled his ears. Most of the firing at the Indians came from the infantry to the right, who were quickly falling behind. Ahead, he saw the upraised arm of Captain William Fetterman, waving and urging the column forward.

———————

Black Horn began to think that the Long Knives in the log town would not come to the aid of the wood wagons. No one was coming west on the wood road. Antelope came and said he was out of bullets, and no one had much to speak of. They had been exchanging gunfire with the Long Knives and other whites in the wagons for some time now. *Perhaps something has gone wrong again,* he thought.

"Pass the word," he told Antelope. "We will fall back slowly. I do not think these Long Knives will follow us. We will circle around the hills and see what has happened."

———

Hump knew what was happening. He and Grey Bull could hear the pop of gunfire thinned by the distance. Although he was still too far away to count, he thought there were more Long Knives than there were two days ago. Some of them seemed to be on foot. He passed the glass to Grey Bull.

After a moment, Grey Bull grunted in satisfaction. "This is good! Our young men are like hornets flying in to pester the waddling bear!"

———

They were past Buffalo Creek now. Cloud could see that the walking Long Knives were falling behind. But, walking or riding, all the Long Knives were moving across the frozen meadow. He had fired three shots so far, then decided to save his bullets. Riding away from the column in an undulating line, in the event some Long Knife was aiming at his back, he tucked the six-shooter into his belt and then

321

pulled out and strung his bow. It occurred to him that the task of the decoy warriors was not necessarily to kill Long Knives. In fact, if the warriors' shooting was too accurate, the column might drop back or end the chase altogether. So he decided to use his bow, get in close, and remain a moving target. He galloped toward a Cheyenne lazily loping his horse and recognized him as Wolf Left Hand.

"If they think we are poor shots, they will keep following," he shouted to Wolf Left Hand.

Wolf Left Hand grinned and waved. "You might be right. But you have to admit, the temptation is there, when we can get in close!"

———

Grey Bull was right. The decoys were like hornets buzzing around the sensitive nose of a waddling bear. So far, the Long Knives were just as ineffective at swatting them away.

The decoys knew that they should stay apart from one another to prevent a bullet meant for one of them from hitting anyone else close by. By the very nature of their actions, they were moving in several directions at once.

———

"William!" Captain Brown shouted amidst the crack of occasional gunfire. "Remember what almost happened to you two weeks ago! There might be an ambush ahead!"

"The terrain ahead is open!" Fetterman shouted in reply. "These fellows are unorganized louts, nothing more! We shall dispatch them all, to teach their unedu-cated kind a lesson!"

———————————

Cloud put his bay into a smooth, fast lope and crossed in front of the mounted Long Knives. At the end of six-shooter range, he loosed two arrows then angled away at a flat-out gallop. Looking back over his right shoulder, he saw one of his fellow decoys—a Sicangu with a six-shooter on a fast little buckskin—smoothly slide off on the right side of his horse, keeping his left leg hooked over the horse's back, and snap off two shots from under the neck of the horse. Executing a quick right turn, the Sicangu was again upright, and threw an obscene gesture toward the Long Knives.

Forward came the Long Knives. Those who were mounted began to outdistance those on foot. Gunfire was sporadic from the decoys, but it was not noticeably heavier from the Long Knives, owing to the darting targets and the narrow front of the column. Many of the Long Knives in the rear did not fire because of the risk of hitting those in front. Most of those on foot were running to keep up with their mounted comrades, and thus fired only occasionally.

Through it all, the cold did not relent.

Suddenly, the mounted Long Knives halted. Crazy Horse reined in his horse to a stop, wondering if the Long Knives had already had enough. He was already thinking that he and the others might have to angle southeast to block them from returning to the log town when he realized there would be no need. The mounted Long Knives were waiting for those on foot catch up.

Like him, the other decoys had taken advantage of the lull to rest their horses. He suddenly noticed that his brown-and-white paint was flexing her right ear repeatedly, and then he saw why. There was a hole in the middle of it, with blood already frozen at the edges, a hole big enough to poke a finger through.

He reached forward to stroke her powerful neck. "Do not worry, little sister," he told her soothingly. "I will avenge your injury, and you will wear a red feather in your mane."

Big Nose rode up and gestured toward the Long Knives. "Perhaps the walking ones will cause them all to turn around," he fretted.

"I do not think so," Crazy Horse replied, smiling. "Look!"

Big Nose immediately realized why Crazy Horse was grinning like a wolf that had found a duck frozen in a pond. Some of the walking Long Knives were climbing up to ride double. Many of the others grabbed stirrups.

"This is good," Big Nose said cheerfully. "I think the walkers will not be able to fire, as close in as they are now among the horses. They will all keep coming, not very fast, but I have feeling they will not turn back."

―――――――――

Hornsby did not know if the column was adapting to the situation or if Captain Fetterman was damn determined to kill Indians. Either way, it did not feel good. The infantry were paired with mounted soldiers, and as far as he understood, each man was to hold onto a stirrup so he could be pulled along. *God help anyone who falls*, he thought.

Second Lieutenant George Grummond moved through the lines. "We will move forward at a quick march. You men on the ground, sling arms and hang onto a stirrup! Those of you mounted, it is your responsibility not to lose the man on the ground!"

After Grummond passed by, a sergeant was heard to mumble, "It is beyond me why we don't jus' form two skirmish lines, open fire, and blow them heathens to hell!"

"Officers being what they is," came a low reply, "could be they have a smart way of doin' things."

A low smatter of boyish laughter coursed through the rear ranks.

"Forward!" came the order from up ahead.

―――――――――

Cloud watched the column lurch ahead like a turtle in a hurry. In spite of the illusion of movement, they were not covering swiftly.

Crazy Horse hurried to each of the decoy warriors. "Let us form a long line, face them, and wait," he told them. "Do not move until they raise a rifle or a six-shooter."

They formed a long line, about twenty paces between each man, and waited. Crazy Horse, in the middle of the line, kept a sharp eye on the Long Knives at the front, especially the one riding at the head. He was the head of the snake.

The decoys sat as if watching a dull horse race.

Still, the Long Knives came forward, still in a narrow column, approaching to the outside range of a six-shooter.

Now the warriors could hear the hollow clap of hooves hitting the frozen ground, but still, they stood, and the Long Knives came closer and closer.

A strident voice rang out, and the front ranks brought their rifles to bear. *"Now!"* shouted Crazy Horse.

In almost the same instant, all ten horses spun to the rear and hit full gallop in less than a dozen strides. The clatter of racing hooves rolled like mocking laughter.

High-pitched whines tore through the air above the riders followed by the *boom-boom* of simultaneous rifle fire. Crazy Horse slowed his mount, as did the others, and in a while, they casually turned and reined to a stop, still lined up in a broad front.

Crazy Horse dismounted. "Check your horses over!" he called out.

Cloud dismounted and, with one eye on the approaching column, ran his hands over the bay's legs. The sturdy horse was quickly recovering from the hard gallop. There were no injuries Cloud could see.

Several paces ahead, snow exploded, followed by a sharp whine that was quickly drowned out by the boom of shots from the column. Although the bay flinched, he held his ground. Several of the warriors led their horses farther away from the column, though in no particular hurry.

Wolf Left Hand swung up effortlessly onto his horse and trotted toward the column, pretending to look at tracks on the ground. Near misses splattered the snow all around. Turning his horse, he casually trotted away, unmindful of the two or three rounds erupting near him.

Little Hawk, not to be outdone, led his horse forward, trotting ahead of him for fifty paces, and stopped. When he mounted, he was sitting backward. Kicking the horse into a high lope, he rode in a wide circle in front of the oncoming column. Rifles boomed. Little Hawk stopped the horse, stood on its back, dropped down facing front, and loped away, laughing.

By now, the other decoys had remounted, seeing the necessity again to present moving targets. Some charged toward the column and veered off in one direction or another. Cloud rode in close and loosed a few arrows before he veered off at a sharp angle. As he loped away, he observed the Long Knife column. It was moving steadily. Those on foot were trotting as they hung on to a stirrup, and some to a tail.

Cloud turned to see Little Hawk and two others loping their horses up the slope of Lodge Trail Hill. Then he saw a man and a horse on the meadow perhaps a hundred paces ahead of the Long Knives. It was Crazy Horse, who had not yet remounted.

Cloud saw snow and earth erupting ahead of Crazy Horse, followed by the sharp boom of rifle fire. He could not believe what he saw next.

Crazy Horse was scraping the snow from the bottoms of his horse's feet. When he finished both front feet, he moved to the back, lifting each hind leg. The astonishing thing, Cloud realized, was how calm the horse was. Bullets were impacting closer and closer, and a tight knot began to form in Cloud's stomach. He realized he was holding his breath when he finally let it out, after Crazy Horse casually mounted and loped toward him. Behind him, the column seemed to increase its pace.

Cloud shook his head as Crazy Horse caught up to him. "I know Hump said to thump death on the nose, but that is poking it in the eye as well," he said.

Crazy Horse glanced back over his shoulder at the Long Knives. "I think the head of the snake today is a different man," he told Cloud matter-of-factly. "I think this one wants badly to kill us. If he is angry enough, he will not stop." Then he said, "I do not know about you, but I do not remember a day this cold ever."

Cloud could only chuckle. "If the Long Knives do not kill us, the cold probably will."

Crazy Horse pointed to the lip of the ridge, where several of the other decoys were waiting. "Maybe we can gather up some grass and twigs and build a fire," he suggested and then pointed toward the oncoming column, "while we wait for them."

Cloud saw a different kind of coldness in his friend's eyes. Before he could reply, Crazy Horse spoke again.

"High Eagle and my father told me that white people have strange beliefs about where they go after they die," he said, not taking his eyes from the Long Knives. "Some will go to a good place and some to a terrible place. I think these Long Knives will go to that terrible place. My father said it is a place of ugliness and torment. That is the place for them. All of them."

Cloud rested his bow across his lap and took a moment to blow on his hands to warm them. He watched the column. It was close enough once again for them to see the walking soldiers struggling to keep up with the slowly trotting horses. Then they halted.

"Do not worry," Crazy Horse said confidently. "They are resting. They will keep coming."

From the left side of the column, they saw flashes and then heard the *boom-boom-boom* of several shots. Surprisingly, two bullets tore up the ground only a few paces away. Both men turned their horses for the slope.

———————

On the ridge to the north, Hump and Grey Bull followed the same path they took two days before and hid themselves behind the knob at the northeast rim. The gunfire from the decoys and the Long Knives had not been heavy, and the Long Knives were not moving fast, but they were still coming.

———————

True to his word, Crazy Horse gathered grass and twigs, pulled out a flint and striker, and built a fire. Sitting on the ground to create a windbreak, he managed to build another fire, shielding it from the frigid puffs of wind. His mare stared down inquisitively before she backed away from the flames.

White smoke billowed in the breeze. Even a little warmth was strangely comforting. All the decoys gathered around and stretched their palms over the fire. One of them had managed to find two pieces of dried buffalo dung and laid them in the flames.

"I might ride back through those Long Knives just to find the buffalo robe I left behind," one of them said. His jaw trembled slightly.

Everyone agreed. The wind was cold on the ridge, so bitterly cold.

Crazy Horse nodded in the direction of the Long Knives. "Here is where we lost them two days ago," he reminded everyone. "We cannot let that happen again."

―――――――

Hornsby was changing his opinion about Captain Fetterman. Yesterday morning, in the officers' mess, Fetterman had not shown his true colors. Under the veneer of a uniform was a man hell-bent and driven. The trouble was, Hornsby was being pulled along.

As the column moved out again, he considered what would happen if he simply turned his mount aside and rode away. After all, he was a civilian not bound to the authority of the army. On the other hand, if he was not mistaken, Lodge Trail Ridge was up ahead, and he had heard the order—Lodge Trail Ridge was as far as they could go.

Hornsby wiggled his toes. The shoes he wore were not particularly thick, and his feet were starting to hurt. He looked down at the soldier ahead of him, hanging on grimly to the stirrup, stumbling now and then.

Hornsby tightened the collar around his neck. That damn breeze was cold, and up on that ridge, it would probably blow clean through him. He looked at the soldier again and was glad he wasn't walking.

━━━━━━━━━━━━━

"They are coming!" one of them said. It was not a state-ment of apprehension.

Ten pairs of eyes watched the column start up the incline of the slope, ten pairs of eyes burning with the confidence of a mountain lion circling its prey, certain of its own strength.

Behind them stood their horses, each attached to its rider by the long rein that ran from the war bridle, under the neck rope, and then lay coiled in the man's hand or looped around his waist. Thick winter hair and manes and tails were teased by the cold wind. Incredibly, except for the wound to Crazy Horse's paint mare, all of them had dodged the bullets. Like their riders, the horses watched the Long Knives coming up the slope.

CHAPTER TWENTY-FOUR

Hundred in the Hand

The fire crackled and the flames bent and swayed to the bit of wind not blocked by the windbreak. Two men wrapped in buffalo robes sat by the fire, one old and one young. White smoke billowed from the prairie sage that had been dropped onto the thick bed of coals.

The dreamer looked into the fire, but the images in his eyes were not flames or the coals and the smoke. He saw souls in anguish.

High Eagle pounded softly on his hand drum as he sang a gathering-the-powers song. He could feel them all around and riding the winds.

———————————

Far to the south, Black Horn crossed Buffalo Creek and heard the sporadic firing in the distance off to the east. His trained ear told him that whoever was firing was not shooting in his direction. Low on bullets, he and his men had broken off from the wood wagons, but also because he thought the Long Knives were not coming to help the wagons. The firing in the distance suggested that something had happened, that something was happening. He thought he saw movement to the east, but the uneven intervening landscape was in the way. Suddenly, off to their right, a small group of riders crossed Buffalo Creek. Black Horn recognized Knife. In a moment, they caught up.

"We got in close to the town," Knife reported. "They saw us and fired their wagon gun. Little Dog was knocked from his horse, but he got up again."

"We are almost out of bullets, so we left," Black Horn replied. "I am not sure what is happening. There are gunshots from the east."

"The Long Knives came out of the town and went north behind these hills," Knife said, pointing back over his shoulder. "Crazy Horse and the other decoys, they are leading them away."

Black Horn nodded in relief. "Good! Good! We should go back north, but we cannot be in the way."

———————

Max Hornsby looked up the slope. The Indians were gone, probably scattered into the broken hills to the north. *Why the hell*, he wondered, *doesn't Fetterman turn the column around? It was just a few damn Indians.*

———————

They left the smoky little fire and rode toward the far end of Lodge Trail Hill, the end that overlooked the trail the wagons used—the Bozeman Road. Behind them, the Long Knives were climbing the slope. Halfway across the plateau, the decoys stopped and waited for the Long Knives to reach the top. Spreading out again to form a wide front, three or four of them fired. Little Hawk and Wolf Left Hand faked a charge and got close enough to make obscene gestures before they turned back.

———————

Cloud saw a broad shadow cover the Long Knives and then pass on. They were still coming, but he suddenly felt something different. They were not coming like an unstoppable power. "Something is coming," High Eagle had said. Now Cloud understood: something was coming for the Long Knives.

———————

Crazy Horse picked out the man ahead of the column. He saw the man's light-colored gloves as he gestured. Wherever the head of the snake went, its body followed.

He spun his horse and called out to the other decoys. They rode almost leisurely to the end of the ridge and stopped.

"My friends," he said in a strong voice, "it is time to kill the snake. Go down to the bottom of the slope and wait. Stay close together. I want them to see you and not look elsewhere."

"What will you do?" asked Little Hawk.

"I will bring them down." He pointed north at a gentle slope across a narrow, frozen creek. "We will take them that way to the road, but we cannot get far ahead. Make them think they might catch us."

———————————

Squinting against the bitterly cold wind, Hump and Grey Bull watched the decoy warriors reach the north end of Lodge Trail Hill. Nine of them went down the steep, frozen slope and stopped.

At the lip of the ridge, Crazy Horse stood up from huddling over the small fire and looked south as he blew on his hands. They were coming.

———————————

Sweetwater Woman squeezed her eyes shut against the pain and blew out her breaths as they subsided again. But she knew another was coming, and soon. She hung onto the chokecherry wands and waited.

———————————

From the bottom of the slope, Cloud could only see the head and shoulders of Crazy Horse and the top half of his paint mare.

He checked his six-shooter. It had three shots left.

The rifle slung across his back in its case was loaded. Tied on the bay's neck rope was the other quiver, full of arrows. The one laying across his lap had something less than forty now. His buffalo robe he had managed to roll and then tied across the horse's withers. He was tempted to wrap it around his shoulders because the cold penetrated the thick elk-hide shirt he wore, with a cloth shirt under it. But the robe would be too bulky. A wave of loneliness swept over him suddenly. But he knew Sweetwater Woman and Grandmother Willow were safe from the cold.

He thought of the ambushers hidden in the ridges behind them. How had they kept warm all this time? He crossed his arms over his chest, shivering, and felt the medicine bag against his chest.

———————————

Crazy Horse could see a few bearded faces. The paint flinched as a bullet tore the ground behind her and whined away into the cold air. He had seen a muzzle flash an instant after the bullet hit. Another one hit, closer this time. The boom of the rifle came almost at the same time. They were getting closer. Some of them were charging ahead of the others. Making sure the strap to his rifle case was still tied tightly across his chest, he walked over to the mare.

He patted her neck. "You are brave, little sister," he said to her. "I hope everyone can be as brave as you." More rifles boomed, and several bullets hummed through the air. Another tore up the dirt. He swung up onto the mare's back and looked south.

The man with the light-colored gloves was in front, leading the charge. Crazy Horse turned his horse down the slope and let her pick the way down.

———————

William Fetterman called a halt at the rim of the slope and waited for the column to catch up.

Captain Frederick Brown waved his revolver at the man going down the slope. "You must admit, William," he said, "the man does have a bit of nerve."

Fetterman snorted derisively. "Careful, Frederick, you might talk yourself into thinking they are human."

Lieutenant George Grummond rode up. "There are ten, only ten. What was the point of all this?"

"Must be some kind of manhood ritual common among many Stone Age people," Fetterman postulated. "I have read of such things, about the Zulus in Africa, for example."

"Look at them!" exclaimed Brown. "They are just sitting there watching us!"

"They know we will not chase them farther than this ridge," Grummond said resignedly. "It is all rather like a game, and a pointless game at that."

"Maybe not today," replied Fetterman.

"Sir?" sputtered the lieutenant.

"Do not deign to remind me of the orders!" Fetterman warned. Eyes flashing, he pointed down the slope. "Look at them! Savages, mocking us! Mocking *us*! We cannot let that pass!"

"William!" exclaimed Brown. "It is only a few ne'er-do-wells!"

"Unruly children need discipline!" Fetterman spouted.

Max Hornsby listened half-heartedly to the exchange between the officers until he heard his named called. Fetterman was motioning for him.

"Captain?" Hornsby said as he pushed through to the front.

"Remind us, Mr. Hornsby, how many in your courier detail were killed several weeks ago," the captain insisted.

"Four."

Fetterman pointed down the slope. "There are the murderers, I would wager! It is time for revenge!"

The other officers were bullied into silence by the captain's sudden intensity. Fetterman rose up in the saddle. "Men," he yelled, "the responsibility is mine! The cavalry will follow me! The infantry will bring up the rear!"

Hornsby looked down the slope. All this over a few Indians?

Hump and Grey Bull watched the Long Knives. The column had stopped at almost the same spot as two days ago. Those at the front met in a cluster. In a while, one of them turned his horse and started down the slope!

Cloud watched as the mounted Long Knives came down first. Crazy Horse called out calmly, "Not yet. Not yet."

When all the mounted Long Knives were off the ridge, the walking ones started down as well.

Closer they came, their horses sometimes sliding down the steep incline. At the distance of a lone stone's throw, Crazy Horse called out clearly, "Go! Go!"

The decoys turned and loped toward the gradual slope that was the Bozeman Road, looking back frequently. Crazy Horse was the last to turn and ride away.

They stopped at the top of the slope. After that, it was a gradual downslope toward the narrowest part of the ridge, a corridor no wider than the floor of a lodge.

The Long Knives reached the bottom of the slope, and the mounted ones came at a gallop.

Crazy Horse grabbed his brother's arm. "Do not hurry. Lead the others down to Prairie Dog Creek. I will bring up the rear."

"Be careful," Little Hawk warned. "Even Long Knives get lucky and hit something now and then."

The decoys stretched out in a line, one behind the other. Cloud lingered, staying just ahead of Crazy Horse. The Long Knives reached the top of the rise and began firing again.

Rabbit rose up cautiously from behind a frozen bank. There were gunshots! He had wedged himself into a narrow cut that blocked much of the wind. Goings and the others were farther west along the same bank. Movement on the ridge immediately caught his eye. He recognized the light bay with the black stockings that belonged to Little Hawk. The other decoys were strung out behind him but did not seem to be in any particular hurry. The firing was coming from behind them.

Rabbit's anxious gaze swept along the ridge. Behind the last two riders—Cloud and then Crazy Horse—came the Long Knives, who were riding hard!

"Hey!" he called out. "The Long Knives! Get ready!"

They all heard the firing from the ridge. Rabbit watched the mounted Long Knives. Far behind them, he saw some running and then many of them strung out along the ridge.

Cloud looked over his shoulder past Crazy Horse. The mounted Long Knives were past the narrow point. Ahead, Little Hawk and the others had started down the long slope that led to the meadow and to Prairie Dog Creek. High Eagle was right: something was coming for the Long Knives.

Little Hawk looked back up the slope. Behind Cloud and Crazy Horse, he saw the front of the column coming down. He slowed his horse. The creek was just ahead. Crazy Horse and Cloud caught up but did not slow down. One went left and the other angled right. Four of the decoys followed Crazy Horse and four followed Cloud.

The two lines crossed the creek and loped across the meadow and then veered into each other, one rider crossing in front of another.

Looking back, they saw that the Long Knives were still coming.

Sharp yells erupted into the cold afternoon air, starting from the ambushers in the gullies and washes that had the best view of Prairie Dog Creek at the western end of ambush ridge.

The signal had been given!

The yelling swiftly gained the momentum of a flash flood on either side of the ridge.

"Come on! Come on! They have brought the Long Knives!"

Before the shouts reached the eastern end on either side, fighting men rose out the Earth itself.

———————————————

Hornsby saw the Indians reach the meadow then double back and stop. Then he heard the shouts from the soldiers behind him.

"Down there! Look!"

He looked back to see them pointing left down the slopes, and he saw them. Where there had been barren gullies and hillsides, there were suddenly men on foot and mounted. Dozens and tens of dozens of men! He saw muzzle flashes.

Hornsby's mount collided with the horse in front. He had not noticed that the front of the column had halted. He nearly fell out of the saddle, but managed to pull himself up. Ahead of him, he thought he heard Fetterman's voice amidst the din.

"Wheel about! Wheel about!"

Soldiers yanked on the reins to turn back up the slope, many turning into each other. Hornsby turned his horse around as the horse in front of him jumped sideways and went down, throwing its rider into the legs of another horse. Then he saw the blood spurting from just behind the saddle girth. The unhorsed soldier covered his head and then disappeared beneath the tangle of legs.

Now facing south, Hornsby was certain the whole hillside was moving, and he heard the gunfire. Indians were moving up the ridge, more Indians than he could count.

━━━━━━━━━━

Cloud was next to Crazy Horse. They had a better view of the slopes and hills on the south side of the ambush hill. But on both sides, men were in motion. Some were on horseback, and many were on foot. In the center were the Long Knives, strung out up the slope. Gunfire cracked and boomed on both sides of the ridge. The Long Knives sporadically returned fire.

Ten pairs of eyes watched in near disbelief. They had done what they had been asked to do and watched the consequence of their actions unfolding in front of them. Wolf Left Hand and Big Nose rode up close.

"We want to join our relatives," Big Nose said, pointing to the right. "They are there somewhere."

"I think we did thump death on the nose," Wolf Left Hand said.

"That we did," said Crazy Horse. "But make sure it does not thump you back. It is not over."

"Only the Earth lives forever," Big Nose replied.

"I am grateful for what you did today," Crazy Horse told all the decoy warriors. "I will never forget."

"We had no choice," Wolf Left Hand teased. "We could not let you have all the glory."

Cloud watched the two Cheyenne ride away and turned to his friend. "I think it is time to join this fight," he said calmly. "It is time to send these Long Knives away."

Taking a moment, the eight remaining decoys quickly checked their horses and then their weapons. None of them spoke it, but each of them was astonished that none of them had been killed or wounded in the decoy action. The only one that had been wounded was Crazy Horse's paint mare.

Farther up the slope, the gunfire was now like a continuous beat from an erratic drummer.

Rabbit did not see the signal, but he did see the

Long Knives react to the first wave of the attack from the north end. They turned the column around. The Long Knives on foot had not gone as far along the ridge and were now running back toward Lodge Trail Hill.

Rabbit jumped from his shelter and ran toward the east, staying at the bottom of the incline, glad to see that others had the same thought. They had to get ahead of the Long Knives who were now desperately trying to escape. Where Goings and the others had gone, he did not know.

Rabbit, Goings, and the others were by no means the only men scrambling upslope, or trying to. Even on a dry summer day, the slope was loose and difficult to climb. On this day, with the ground frozen and covered with ice and snow, it was next to impossible. Flat-soled moccasins could not provide traction. Although many of the fighting men improvised and wrapped rawhide strings or braided cords around their feet, it did not solve the problem entirely. Horses did not fare much better. Like many of the men, they slipped frequently. But from both sides of the ridge, they kept coming, slipping, falling, and rising again and again, pausing to take aim and squeeze off a shot or send a few arrows.

The blue-uniformed men on the ridge were franticly trying to find cover. But even so, many of them paused to fire down the ridge before running again.

Knowing that an outright sprint would wear him out too quickly, Rabbit kept a steady pace until he found a narrow gully. It looked like a path to the top of ambush ridge, so he followed it. Halfway up the slope, he had slipped and fallen several times because there was no counterbalance for the rifle in his left hand. Near the top, he stumbled onto a low boulder and took cover behind it. His chest heaving, he covered his mouth against the frigid air. Then he realized he had a perfect field of fire. He was ahead of the narrow part of the ridge, and the first of the running Long Knives had reached it.

Taking deep breaths, he rested his rifle on the top of the boulder and took careful aim. As the weapon recoiled against his left shoulder, he saw a Long Knife jerk sideways and fall. Suddenly, he was aware of gunfire from the slopes of the ridge.

Hump and Grey Bull rode hard to join the charge up the hill from the east side of ambush hill. Many of the warriors were already far up the ridge, some pausing to aim and fire a rifle then ducking down to reload. Those with six-shooters kept going up and kept shooting. Grey Bull noticed, however, that there were just as many warriors using bows, if not more.

Grey Bull decided to ride up the ridge as far as his horse could go on the frozen, slippery slope. Hump had angled off to the left ahead of him and disappeared behind a thicket, but Grey Bull saw a wide depression off to the left. Leaving his horse there, he trotted toward the spine of the ridge.

Long Knives to his left were running south, and

those mounted were coming up behind them. Gunfire was steady now, and he saw several Long Knife horses without a rider.

Goings, Taken Alive, Yellow Wolf, and Little Bird scrambled up the south slope and took cover in a thick patch of soap weeds. They had a clear line of fire at the ridgetop, and there were many Long Knives to shoot at. An arrow hissed out of the sky and embedded itself at the base of a soap weed in front of Goings.

The noise was relentless. Rifles boomed and six-shooters cracked, amplified by the frigid air. Long Knives yelled and screamed as they ran and galloped south. The sound of bullets hitting flesh was not as loud but was now almost constant. A bullet into a man's abdomen or chest struck with a hollow pop. Into a leg, arm, or head, it was a duller thud, though sometimes bones could be heard cracking or shattering. It was difficult to distinguish between horse and human bone, however. And horses screamed in pain with more and more frequency, high-pitched, nerve-racking squeals.

In a camp near Little Goose Creek to the north, the dreamer grabbed his head and let out a strange growling noise. High Eagle kept singing.

Hornsby felt the bullet that killed his horse nick his right calf. How he kicked free, he didn't know. But his knee crashed into the hard ground. Cradling his rifle, he ran, with escape as his only objective. He put his thumb on the lock of the rifle to keep the percussion cap from falling off. Mounted soldiers clattered past him, and he was less and less shocked to see dead soldiers on the ground. He suddenly realized that the almost constant *whoosh* and hissing sounds were arrows.

———————————

Big Nose and Little Wolf worked their way up the south slope of ambush hill with several other Northern Cheyenne warriors. Two of them were Dog Soldiers. Heavy fire came from one particular spot, a group of boulders. Using any cover they could find, they moved up steadily.

One of the Dog Soldiers gasped. "They got me," he winced. "Go! Go!"

Unmindful of near misses, the other Dog Soldier lifted his friend over one shoulder and carried him down the slope. Big Nose and Little Wolf watched anxiously, but not without a large measure of admiration. The gunfire from the boulders was getting too close for comfort.

The Long Knives behind the boulders suddenly concentrated their fire in another direction, giving the Cheyenne an opportunity to move quickly up the slope. They stopped and fired at the men behind the boulders, hitting one, maybe two. But sudden return fire struck Big Nose in the chest. With six-shooters and rifles, the Cheyenne angrily returned fire.

"Carry me up the hill," Big Nose pleaded, "up where the air is good." It was an unusual request, but no matter. Four men carried him while two traded fire with the men behind the boulders, though it was not as heavy from there.

Near the top, where the slope was not as steep, they lowered Big Nose to the ground and formed a guard around him. Little Wolf leaned over his brother and could see that life was leaving him. Then he was gone.

The Cheyenne remained there, as eventually the fighting moved south and away from them. They reloaded, fired, wiped their tears, and kept on. They watched several charges made at the Long Knives hidden in the boulders. Several Lakota and Cheyenne were hit. Crazy Horse charged the hill with his six-shooter, killing two of the Long Knives. After that, the remaining Long Knives were slowly overwhelmed.

Cloud turned his bay loose at the top of the slope, not wanting to risk injury to him. Gunfire had not stopped, but ahead of him, he saw a sight he would never forget. Kneeling behind a low mound to get a sense of the flow of the fighting, he saw flashes in the air just above the ground going in both directions. Then he realized what they were: arrows flying from the north slopes passing arrows flying up from the south slopes. Where those arrows were flying was no place to be. Their effect was clear in the number of

Long Knives' bodies along the ridge.

Cloud turned left and ran down the slope until he was behind the bowmen on the north slopes. The footing was near treacherous. It was difficult to assess where most of the firing was occurring, but it was concentrated on the ridge, where the Long Knives were. He finally reached a depression and stopped to take cover and rest. Some of the gunfire seemed to be moving south toward Lodge Trail Hill. Staying essentially north of the ridge, on the Bozeman Road, he started to the southeast again.

Rabbit had an excellent field of fire. Hidden behind the boulder, he was able to see any target crossing left to right on the ridge above him. He concentrated on the walking Long Knives because they were moving more slowly. At his point of fire on the ridge, several bodies were piled, one on top of another. But several Long Knives had made it past and seemed to have taken a position somewhat behind him, judging from the firing. He decided to abandon his cover and see for himself.

Goings and the others had chosen a bad place. Luckily, none of them had been hit by the arrows that came from the other side of the ridge. For a while, it seemed the air was full of arrows, many now sticking in the ground all around them. But now the fighting was moving south.

Taken Alive looked over at his friends. "We must get up on the ridge," he said. "I do not think we have hit anything from here."

He started crawling up the ridge, and the others followed. Little Bird pulled a few arrows from the ground to put in his quiver.

———————————

Hornsby realized that it didn't take a smart man to figure out that this was not an even fight. The firing had not abated, and he realized that the Indians were picking up guns from dead soldiers. He dropped behind a large rock and stayed belly down as he reloaded his rifle. Amidst the noise, he heard strange voices calling out. It was Indians. In the direction he had just come from, he saw an Indian crunch the base of a soldier's skull with a club.

He was a stranger in a strange land. Nothing in his life and his experiences had remotely prepared him for this moment of sweeping, unfettered violence. His instinct was to get as low as possible or crawl into a hole and cover his head.

He tried getting a glimpse of Lodge Trail Hill to see if anyone had made it that far, but he somehow knew that no one had. The cold seemed unimportant at the moment. Moving to the other side of the rock, he cocked the hammer of his gun and waited.

———————————

Rabbit saw several bare heads among some flat boulders, but they were hiding and not shooting. Behind him on the ridgetop, warriors were wading in among the Long Knives. Anything in the hand was now a thrusting weapon or a club; there was no opportunity to reload six-shooters or rifles. Dead horses were all around.

A shot blasted, and a Long Knife staggered backward and fell. Cloud appeared out of the smoke, six-shooter in hand, knelt, took aim with his rifle, and killed another Long Knife who was running away.

Two more Long Knives appeared. Rabbit watched Cloud meet the first one with a thrust to the belly with the rifle muzzle then a swift uppercut to the face with the stock.

Rabbit calmly shot the second Long Knife and then ducked down to reload. He had two bullets left for his breechloader. Out of the corner of eye, he saw a man rise up from behind a rock, his rifle aimed at Cloud. Rabbit shoved the bullet into the breech, slammed it closed, and stood to take aim.

Hornsby was startled by the sudden motion to his left. An Indian was standing not twenty feet away, his rifle pointed at him. In an instant of sheer incongruity, he recognized the man with one arm and then he saw the muzzle flash.

Something struck him in the chest. There was

only one flashing instant of surprise and then nothing. He would never know that his finger squeezed the trigger of his rifle.

———————————

Cloud heard the blast and spun in time to see Rabbit fall backward, as if kicked by a horse. He ran forward, but even before he bent down, the hole in the young man's chest told the story.

"Cousin!" he rasped past the blood foaming out of his mouth.

Cloud knelt and bent to him.

Rabbit was smiling, and the look in his eyes was like a tranquil pool of water. "Cousin," he said again, the voice weaker this time, "I get to have my arm again." Then his eyes turned glassy and his chest did not rise again.

Stunned, Cloud did not immediately see the movement to his left. After he saw the Long Knife with the rifle, he felt as though he were falling and falling.

———————————

Sweetwater Woman was squatting, gripping the wooden wands held by her mother and Grandmother Willow. She felt the midwife pull the baby out and then heard the soft splash of water.

"Granddaughter, you have a daughter," Red Shawl told her gently. "She is strong, and she will give the people sons to be warriors."

In another moment, Sweetwater heard her baby yell with a clear, strong voice, announcing herself.

———————

First, it was a song like the sound of cooing, like doves, and then laughter, and then giggling. Then the light, the soft, warm light. For some reason, he was drawn to the light. He knew he had to go there.

As he turned toward the light, he heard the giggling again, behind him. When he turned, he saw a little child duck out of sight behind a tree that had suddenly appeared. Then a soft, warm breeze blew across his face.

He went to the tree, though he did not walk. From behind the next tree, he saw the sparkling, dark eyes smiling. She was giggling.

She?

He forgot the light and decided to follow her.

A blast of cold air took his breath away. The pain was tremendous.

CHAPTER TWENTY-FIVE

Song

The orderly carefully handed the list of names to Colonel Henry Carrington and stepped back to await further instructions. Carrington's face was tense, and the haunted look had not gone away even after several days.

"Thank you, Corporal. What—what is the count?" the colonel asked hesitantly.

"Ah, forty-eight from the Eighteenth Infantry, twenty-eight from the Second Cavalry, one unassigned armorer, and three civilians. Eighty, sir, all told."

The colonel nodded absently. "Thank you, Willis. Thank you. I think that is all I need for the moment."

The corporal lingered. "Sir? I was wondering about what the Indians did to the—to the bodies, sir. Why, sir, did they do that?"

Carrington cleared his throat. "They hate us, Willis, with a passion. It is their way of inflicting a grievous insult, to put it mildly."

"It is still not right, sir."

"Yes, I agree. But—but have you ever heard of Colonel Chivington and Sand Creek?"

"No, sir."

Carrington sighed and leaned back in his chair. "Colonel John Chivington and the Colorado Militia attacked a village of Cheyenne and Arapaho in 1864.

They killed women and children, Willis. After that, they mutilated bodies."

The corporal nodded grimly. "I did not know that, sir."

"Was it right, Willis, for Chivington's men to do what they did?"

"But these people here, Colonel, they are savages! The surgeon told me—eyes were pulled out, fingers cut off, and—and brains!—" He could say no more.

The colonel stared pensively at the horrified soldier before him. "What about Sergeant Metzger? Why was he alone not mutilated?"

"I do not know, sir."

"Who is the savage, Corporal? Perhaps we are defined by what we do and not what we are. Something to think about. Meanwhile, we should see to the defenses. We must prepare. We cannot assume they will not attack us here."

"Yes, sir."

As the corporal's footfalls faded, Colonel Carrington glanced at the calendar on the wall. It was Christmas Eve.

———————————

There was light, but it was no longer bright. It had softened to a yellow-orange. Slowly, the soft glow transformed, and a familiar design appeared. Then he realized that he was staring at tiny alternating circles of dyed quills from yellow to red to yellow and then red again— Grandmother Willow's design. A medallion with that design was attached to the top edge of the winter dew cloth and tied at each lodge pole. Turning his head, he saw the circle of medallions. Then he remembered he was home, reclined against a willow chair, his legs covered with an elk robe.

There must be a dove in here, he thought. It was cooing. And then that changed into a lullaby. He recognized the voice, Sweetwater's.

Turning his head toward the song, he saw her and the bundle she held to her breast as she sang. Her eyes lifted to his face.

"See," she said softly to the tiny form with a thick thatch of shiny blue-black hair suckling at her breast. "I told you he would wake. There he is, your father."

The images and feelings and sounds that had been chasing him around somewhere in some strange world began to slip away. Eyes staring sightlessly, bitter cold, screams and blasts of gunfire stopped, chased away by the sight of his wife and child.

The only thing not going away was a pain in his side.

He heard a soft rustling, and Grandmother Willow, wrapped in a buffalo robe with a bundle under one arm, ducked through the door and stopped to quickly secure the inside covering. She saw that her grandson was awake and smiled.

"Meat," she said, holding up the bundle. "They keep giving us meat!"

"They?" he asked hoarsely.

"Taken Alive. He went hunting."

"Taken Alive?" There was an underlying tone of apprehension in his question.

The old woman knew he had questions, many questions, because he had been drifting in and out for several days.

"High Eagle is coming to visit you tomorrow," she told him. "He has medicine for you, and you can talk."

He nodded and turned his gaze to Sweetwater Woman and the baby. He was powerless to stop the smile that came across his face.

He told High Eagle about Rabbit. "He saved my life, I think."

"As you saved his," the medicine man reminded him.

"For what? Only so he could die?"

"No," High Eagle protested. "You gave him the chance to become a man. He saved your life but died a warrior, defending his people."

After a moment, Cloud smiled. "He said something. He said 'I get to have my arm again.' I hope he has found it on the other side."

"I think he has," the medicine man asserted. "Think what a warrior he will be with two arms!"

Another moment of silence passed.

"How many did we lose?" Cloud asked hesitantly.

"Many were wounded," High Eagle replied in a subdued tone. "Many of the wounds were from arrows. Our men wounded each other without intending to. The slopes and the trail were covered with arrows. I have never seen anything like it.

"We carried you and all the wounded to Little Goose Creek. We cleaned your wounds there, all of you. I think the cold stopped the bleeding. We washed off the dead there, too, to clean them before we took them back to their families."

The medicine man smiled. "Little Bird discovered only afterward that he had been shot in the leg," he went on. Then he dropped his gaze to the floor. "Perhaps twenty or so were killed, Crazy Horse's closest friend, Lone Bear, among them. And Big Nose, too."

Cloud could see their faces: the carefree Lone Bear, always quick with a smile, and Big Nose, with the imposing presence of a buffalo bull. "Only the Earth lives forever," he whispered.

High Eagle sighed. "We won this battle, but it will not end there, I am afraid. Hump and Grey Bull are coming to see you this afternoon. Grey Bull was nicked a little, but he dismisses it as nothing." He paused, looking into a memory. "All of the Long Knives were killed, nearly a hundred, I think. It is what the dreamer saw."

Cloud was puzzled. "The dreamer?"

"Yes, the half-man dreamer. He looked into the future; it is his power. He rode out into the hills and came back with Long Knives in his hands. A hundred."

"You dreamt about the winter ahead, as I remember," said Cloud.

"Yes. The winter will be very hard. More cold and snow than we have seen in many years."

Cloud sighed. "I am happy to be alive to face it, Uncle."

"Good," the medicine man exclaimed. "Then it is time for you to return the protection medicine I gave you."

Cloud reached into a case and took out the small bundle. "I am grateful. I know that you had a reason for not revealing everything to me. Maybe someday you will tell me."

For a long moment, High Eagle gazed into the coals in the fire pit. "The spirits do not want to be repaid," he said mysteriously. "Life is a gift, and sometimes we are given life more than once. Do not question why it was given, why you are sitting here alive and—and others had to die. Accept the gift and live well and walk the right path. That much I can tell you."

Cloud placed the bundle in the medicine man's hand and cleared his throat to speak past the hoarseness. "Thank you, Uncle. I will—I will do my best."

High Eagle held the end of a braid of sweetgrass in the coals, and soon a soothing scent permeated the lodge. "The spirits are drawn to the goodness of its scent," he said, looking at Sweetwater Woman resting against a chair on the other side of the room. Beside her was a cradleboard, and wrapped inside was the daughter of Sweetwater and Cloud, asleep.

"We are inviting the spirits into this lodge," High Eagle continued. "I ask for good things for all who live here, especially for the little one."

"Thank you," Cloud said gently.

"What have you named her?" High Eagle said, gazing gently at the sleeping infant.

"Song," replied Sweetwater. "Grandmother Willow picked that childhood name for her two months ago. Her name is Song."

CHAPTER TWENTY-SIX

The Warrior

Fresh snow covered all the scaffolds holding the bodies, though it was not difficult to spot the new ones—they were still well defined, whereas the older burial bundles had collapsed noticeably. Glistening snow seemed to signify a new journey, as far as Cloud saw it, a fitting way to send Rabbit and Lone Bear and the others who had fallen to the spirit world.

Cloud slid gingerly off his horse and, taking up a long cane, picked his way up the slight incline of the burial grounds. Grey Bull followed close behind, ready to help if he should falter. For ten days, Cloud had chafed at the inactivity, anxious to pay respect to his fellow warriors.

Footprints were everywhere, evidence that others had visited already on this day.

"Crazy Horse was here," Grey Bull explained. He pointed to a scaffold to the left. "That is his best friend." He pointed to Lone Bear's scaffold without saying his name. "He and Little Hawk were here very early this morning."

Cloud stopped at a scaffold not far from Lone Bear's. It was Rabbit's. A shield hung from one pole, though he could see only the back of it. He took a deep breath and looked at the long bundle covered with a buffalo robe atop the scaffold. He felt the tears welling up in his eyes and wanted to say something but could not find the right words to express the feelings swirling inside of him.

"Thank you, Cousin. Thank you." After a long moment of silence, it was all he could say.

He lowered his head so Grey Bull would not see his lower lip trembling. Then he realized the tears were freezing on his face.

Grey Bull moved forward, his footsteps squeaking on the new snow. "I lost my brother at the Blue Water," he said. "He was married to a Sicangu woman from Little Thunder's people. He was there when Woman Killer's Long Knives attacked. He fought alongside Iron Shell and Spotted Tail. They say he killed several Long Knives and went down fighting. I still think of him every day. My brother is not in this world anymore, but he has found another place to live."

Cloud heard Grey Bull thumping his chest.

"Now he lives in my heart. In the end, it is the best place to be for any of us."

Cloud nodded. "Yes, you are right. My father and mother are there, in my heart, and my grandfather, too. I know they will make room for one more."

He reached out and turned the shield, to see the front of it. He had to smile, and turned to show Grey Bull.

On the front of the shield, Rabbit had painted a warrior on a horse. A man with two arms outstretched, as though he were flying.

The Monument of the Heart

Katherine Fontonneau and Anne Hail quietly wiped the tears running down their cheeks. Justin Fontonneau looked at the old man's hands and then up into his eyes. The eyes of John Richard Cloud had seen so much.

Anne stepped forward. "Dad, thanks for telling us about that time in your life," she said, reaching to squeeze his hand. "Mom told us the same things in her own way. But now we know the whole story."

"Grandpa," Justin said, "when were you given your other names, your white names?"

The old man chuckled. "It was your grandmother's wish. We were married in the Episcopal Church because a priest kept pestering us. We did it mainly to get him off our backs. So when we filled out papers, your grandmother gave me those names because she liked them. She took the name Agatha Eve because she liked it, too."

"I barely remember her," the young man admitted.

"She died when you were four," Katherine told him.

"So did Grandma never remember who her white mother and father were?"

Cloud shook his head. "No. By blood, she was white; in every way, she was Lakota. Maybe she finally found out when she crossed over to the other side. I hope so."

"She told me one time that her life turned out the way it was meant to," Anne said. "She had no regrets."

"Grandpa, what happened after the Little Bighorn? You did not stay with Crazy Horse?"

The old man stared at the grasses at his feet, waving in the breeze. "We stayed with Crazy Horse until early May of 1877," he told them. "We started south with them, toward Fort Robinson. Your grandma being white, there was no way to tell what the Indian agents and the soldiers would do when we got there. She was afraid they would take her away. So we left. We headed east and found a small group of our people living along the White Earth River, the Big White, as it is called now. The year after—after Crazy Horse was killed—the Sicangu moved north. We were already there."

Cloud touched his grandson's shoulder. "Always remember, your grandmother was a strong woman. Your mother is strong; so is your aunt Anne. Her blood flows in them, along with the Lakota blood. Your blood is strong."

Justin nodded, a light glowing in his eyes. "Someday, when I have children, I will tell them, Grandpa. I will tell them about my family. I will tell them who we are and where we came from."

The old man's eyes misted. "Do that, and your grandpa and Crazy Horse will have their wish: that there will always be Lakota on this Earth."

"There will be, Grandpa, if I have anything to do with it."

"Good!" the old man exclaimed, touching his grandson's chest. "Monuments that are built here, in the heart, will outlive monuments made of stone."

Then he reached down and grabbed a handful of soil and let it slide between his fingers. "The Greasy Grass is north of here. How far is it by the highway?"

"Seventy miles, maybe more," Katherine answered. "Why?"

"Your mother and I were there, too, when our people defeated Long Hair. You were conceived there. Maybe we can go. I have not been there since that time."

Katherine and Anne looked at each other, contemplating. "Well," Anne asserted, "we are this close, we might as well."

"Aunt Anne," Justin said as they turned to walk back toward the car, "I did not know your childhood name was Song. Did you forget?"

"No," she replied wistfully. "No, I guess other things just got in the way."

Justin smiled with anticipation and looked at his mother. "Mom," he said with a boyish gleam in his eyes, "what was your childhood name?"

"Wait!" exclaimed John Richard Cloud. "That is another story. I will tell you when we get to the Greasy Grass. Another story for you and the children you will have."

ACKNOWLEDGMENTS

Sometime in the fourth grade, I realized that Lakota cultural information and stories of the past that I heard from my grandparents and their generation was different from what I began to read in textbooks. Although I respected the teachers who were telling me that the white settlers who "settled" and "tamed" the West had to do that because a new nation was being born, I wondered why their versions of the same story had very little positive to say about the Lakota and other Native peoples. Their perspective was also reflected in novels I read and movies I saw. However, something inside of me silently and stubbornly clung to the stories my grandparents and the other Lakota elders told me about the past. As I now know, theirs is a perspective that adds to the reality of history; and history belongs to all of us.

Writers such as the eminent Dee Brown insisted there was another side to the story, and movies such as *Dances with Wolves* demonstrated that Native cultures and peoples could be portrayed realistically. The next and most logical step is to hear and see those stories from Native peoples themselves. To that end, Fulcrum Publishing has, and is, doing its part to avail the Native perspective to the reading public. This novel is the latest effort of that commitment.

Thank you to Fulcrum's publisher, Sam Scinta, for enabling me to pursue this new venture as a Western novelist. Thank you also to Katie Raymond, an execeptional editor, and to Michelle Baldwin, Erin Palmiter, Shannon Hassan, and everyone at Fulcrum who had a hand in producing this book; dedicated professionals all.

Because of all of their efforts, I find myself in the unique position of having the privilege to write stories from the perspective of my grandparents and their generation, and to portray their humanity and that of the generations that preceded them.

Joseph M. Marshall III is an author, Lakota craftsman, lecturer, actor, primitive archer, and historical consultant. He was born and raised on the Rosebud Sioux Reservation.

He is the author of nine books, including one for children. He has also contributed to several publications and has written several screenplays as well. Several of his books have been published in French, Hebrew, Korean, and, soon, Italian. Two of them (*The Dance House: Stories from Rosebud*, Red Crane Books, and *The Lakota Way: Stories and Lessons for Living*, Viking Penguin) are used as required reading in many Native American literature courses at the high school and college levels.

He has won awards for his writing as well as the for the audio versions of several of his books.

For the past ten years, Marshall has been associated with a management-training firm as a historical consultant and instructor. The seminars he helps to teach use leadership lessons from history as the theme. He has also developed a leadership seminar based on his sixth book, *The Journey of Crazy Horse: A Lakota History*. The course is based on the leadership principles of Crazy Horse.

As a speaker and lecturer, he has traveled to Sweden, Siberia, and France as well as to many venues in the United States. His audiences include elementary, high school, and college students; teachers; historical societies; and professionals from all walks of life. Topics for his presentations include Native culture and history in general, northern Plains and Lakota history and culture, Native storytelling, and portrayal of Natives in literature and film, as well as principles and ethics in leadership.

He has served as cultural and historical consultant to films and television. Joseph's latest work can be seen and heard in Turner Network Television and Dreamworks's epic television miniseries *Into the West*. He was the series Native technical advisor, the Native voice-over narrator, and appeared in episodes five and six as Loved by the Buffalo, a Lakota medicine man.

Joseph's first language is Lakota. He is a specialist in wilderness survival, and handcrafts primitive Lakota bows and arrows.

Hundred in the Hand will be followed by *The Long Knives Are Crying*, the second novel in his Lakota Westerns series, which is based on Lakota history and culture on the northern Plains during the eighteenth and nineteenth centuries.

Donald F. Montileaux

Donald F. Montileaux (Oglala Lakota) is a master ledger artist. Following in the footsteps of his forefathers, he has rekindled ledger art with his collection of striking images that capture the unique Lakota way of life.

Montileaux was born on January 3, 1948, in Pine Ridge, South Dakota, and is an enrolled member of the Oglala Lakota Tribe. He attended college in Spearfish, South Dakota, and received formal art training at the Institute of

American Indian Arts (IAIA), a tribal college in Santa Fe, New Mexico. Upon graduating from IAIA in 1969, he continued to refine his skills and participated in numerous area art shows while pursuing a professional career at the Rushmore Plaza Civic Center for twenty-two years.

Montileaux interned under noted artist Oscar Howe at the University of South Dakota at Vermillion in 1964 and 1965. He also credits his personal friend and mentor the late Herman Red Elk as his primary artistic muse. Montileaux's art is represented in many private and public collections. He has illustrated covers for ten books and has been the featured artist in galleries in New Mexico, Minnesota, Arizona, Colorado, Montana, Illinois, and South Dakota.

In 1994, Montileaux was honored with an invitation from the South Dakota School of Mines and Technology to create a work of art that eventually joined the payload of the space shuttle *Endeavour*. A year later, on March 2, 1995, the *Endeavour* launched from the Kennedy Space Center carrying "Looking Beyond One's Self" around the Earth 262 times at up to 17,500 miles per hour. During the sixteen-day mission, Montileaux's tribute to the American Indian way of life traveled an astonishing 6,892,836 miles—a long way from South Dakota. The original artwork is now a part of the Smithsonian Institution's permanent collection.

Montileaux dedicates himself to further exploring his gift and to introducing ledger art to new generations.

"This book will break every notion you ever had about a cowboy."
—Terri Schlichenmeyer, "Bookwormsez"
Winner: Western Heritage Awards, Spur Awards

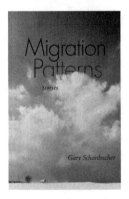

A moving collection of stories featuring characters living in or touched by the American West.

COMING IN 2008 ...

The Long Knives Are Crying

The second novel in Joseph M. Marshall III's riveting new series picks up the story of Cloud and the Lakota ten years later, as the Battle of the Little Bighorn (the Greasy Grass) looms.

800-992-2908

WWW.FULCRUMBOOKS.COM